THE PASSING

A Tale Without Time

Volume One

By Ray Clarke

Thank You,

William.

Ray Clarke

Thank You,
William.

(signature)

Table of Contents

Acknowledgements

I would like to express my most sincere gratitude to MOMS for her tireless contribution in editing this book.

There are many friends and family who have crutched me up in this adventure of writing a book and, though I have voiced my loving appreciation, I'd like to name a few by their first names.

Thank You,

Ron, Andrew, Chris, Ollie, Patrick, Cliff

Chapter 1
"What the Heck"

I woke with a start as I felt a tugging on my sleeve. "What do you think you're doing?" I heard myself ask in a groggy voice. There wasn't much light, but enough to see an old woman, in a hooded coat, jump back as erratically as I did. I repeated my words, but she just turned her wrinkled face towards me, and scurried away into the shadows without a reply.

What on earth was she doing, trying to pull my shirt off? Who was she? How did I get here... wherever "here" is? All I could see were dark shadows on old stone walls surrounding me on three sides. I must have been in some sort of narrow alley. My head was spinning, as if I had over slept with an inner ear infection, and I attempted to sit up too fast. I tried to let my eyes adjust but it was simply too dark for details and this place smells like the men's latrine at a sleezy bar.

I tried to think. What do I remember? Nothing is making sense! Wait. What was I doing the last time I could see something?

Some mumbled words slipped from my lips as I attempted to orient myself. "Volunteer Fireman's Camping trip..." came out of my mouth. The sound of my own voice was comforting until I noticed that my words caused an immediate hush to the subtle din of human voices somewhere nearby. Instinctively, I went silent, hoping for the muttering to begin again, but it didn't. The longer I waited, the more threatening the silence became. I wasn't aware of how long I had held my breath until the voices started once again, and I gasped for more of that foul smelling air.

I kept my questions in my head, this time, because it felt safer. Where the hell *is* this place? Weren't we sitting around a camp fire telling jokes and drinking beer? How did everything change from trees and mountains to this smelly old place?

I always carry an extra flashlight or two in my survival vest but, even in this moonlight, I could tell that my camping vest was gone. My shirt felt thick and heavy, more like a burlap sack, rather than the plaid shirt I had worn on this trip. Absolutely nothing made any sense!

My head soon stopped spinning and I didn't feel as badly. No broken bones or wounds because I didn't hurt anywhere. I am, however, feeling a rapidly growing sense of panic in my gut. The more I discover in this place, the less I understand. This can't be a dream because dreams don't have this much touchy stuff and they definitely don't smell like *this*.

Okay! I thought to myself, back up to first base. 1. Last evening, six of us volunteer firefighters drove into the mountains, west of Denver, for a four-day camping trip. 2. Hot dogs and burgers for dinner that finished before dark. 3. Campfire and a couple beers. 4.? 4. Ah, yes. Jake said he saw something in the night sky.

I'm sure he said something like, "What the hell is that thing blocking out some of the stars?" Yes, we all looked where Jake was pointing, expecting to see something, but then he said, "Don't look for 'something,' look for 'nothing.'" Yeah. That's when we all saw the black spot in the night sky with no stars in it. It took some concentration, at first, because it wasn't very large; but once you found it, the rate that it was growing made it all but impossible to look away. Stars were blinking out, by the second, on all sides of this black dot. That meant it was either growing or approaching.

Jake, the science teacher in our group, muttered, "Something is coming this way and it's moving at an amazing speed!" I hated when Jake made ominous predictions like that! We were all in a fear-trance when he said something just to comfort us. "I don't think it's moving directly towards us. Stars are disappearing on the left and re-appearing on the right."

Some comfort *that* was, since I don't remember much else. Within a couple seconds, over half of the stars were blocked from the night sky and now, I'm in this shit and piss smelling place. Where *is* this place?

2

Once again, the mutterings of human voices captured my focus and I tried to listen for clues. If those were my camping buddies and they pulled a prank on me, then I certainly would want to be a good sport... if they don't go too far.

None of the voices, all male, sounded familiar. Closer listening didn't help much because, even though I was sure they were speaking English, so many of the words were still nonsense to my ears. It must have been the acoustics of the stone walls and the way they are talking in, what I guessed to be, a small group.

What I hoped might happen but feared most, before I was ready for it... happened. I saw a light approaching and it appeared to be the flickering light of a flame, rather than the beam of a flashlight. All I could do is stand completely motionless but ready for the next phase of this prank. As a man came into sight, I realized that he is not one of the firefighters from our camping trip. I didn't know this large man and that really bothered me. He was holding an antique lantern, dressed in very grubby dark pants and a shirt that looked like it had been dragged through muddy streets. And he wore a tri-quarter hat? In all of my 26 years, I had never seen a man wearing a hat like that, except in an old English or Colonial America movie.

The big man jumped back at the sight of me and I braced for his assault, but instead of attacking me, his eyes went soft and his broad shoulders relaxed. He appeared to recognize me! I didn't know what to do. I stood at the ready, as if my slender frame could possibly be ready for this powerfully built man. He must have stood six inches taller than me and outweighed me by nearly a hundred pounds of raw muscle. His shirt sleeves were rolled up above his elbows revealing massive forearms as large as my calves.

His mellow baritone voice whispered, "Raffe? Raffe, lad... ye not be recognizing me?"

There we stood. Me ready to throw as many useless punches as possible at this huge man, and this guy, ready to hug me, as if I was his lost puppy. He lifted his lantern high between us, with no defensive moves at all. He presented his large round face into the light and my punching zone. The glow of his lantern revealed curly auburn hair that continued into his bushy beard as it turned almost raven black around his chin. His bushy eyebrows almost covered his slate-blue eyes which could narrowly be seen between the brim of his hat and his lower eyelids.

"Dunna ye recognize me?" he pleaded once more. "What ye be doing back here in the pissin corner with no light, Lad? I be finishing my business and we be heading back to the pub."

He handed me the lantern and I held it without a thought. I stood spellbound, like a statue, with my hand extended, holding that lantern. I thought to myself, I must look like a lawn jockey with big eyes and quaking knees.

He finished making his contribution to this smelly place and I remained motionless until he threw a thick arm around my shoulders and led me along another alley. I really didn't want to go with him, but with the power of his arm around my shoulders, I knew it would be fruitless to resist. I also knew that it would have been much stranger to insist on staying in the 'pissing corner' all by myself... in the dark.

We approached a narrow wooden door with a sign above the threshold, "Ye Olde Pub." I could hear the voices which had been just murmurs, was now, very clearly English speaking men. Before opening the door, the large friendly man stopped me, held me by my shoulders, and then brought his face directly in front of mine.

Our eyes met, as he said, "We truly be missing thee, Lad. It be wonderful to have ye back."

What, on earth, could that mean? I had never laid eyes on this man before. I certainly would have remembered such a massive hulk of a man!

Without giving me any pause to reply, he opened the pub door, thrust me into what appeared to be a set from an Errol Flynn movie! He loudly announced, "Look who I be finding outside!"

I was bug-eyed as the pub went silent, for only a second or two, then the small cluster of men lifted their mugs in a toast of welcome. Needless to say, everyone was happy except me. I didn't recognize any of them, or this pub, or much of what they were saying.

Silence was my only shield, but I knew I couldn't be silent forever. This just had to be some elaborate joke. I quickly surmised that the guys at the firehouse have somehow put me on a movie set for a picture about Old England. Should I play along or ruin their game? It's obvious that it took a lot of effort to come up with this elaborate set or to time my campsite blackout with the filming of a movie. It certainly looked authentic. It smelled real, but they don't need *that* for a movie.

The big man applied pressure on my back and directed me to a table with benches on either side. I was still in my lawn jockey posture, holding the lantern, when he forced me onto a bench and removed the lantern from my hand. I didn't feel comfortable enough to look anyone in the face, so I swung my gaze from floor to ceiling and all around the room. I made certain that I never allowed eye contact with anyone. Not sensing any hostility, I relaxed my arms on the table before me and remained silent.

Wait a minute! What about that big black thing Jake, and the rest of us, saw blocking out the stars? Was *that* real? Questions were swirling in my mind, as the large guy brought a tankard of something and planted it on the table before me. Without hesitation, I said, "Thanks!"

The pub went so hushed, so fast, that it scared me all over again. The man's big hand wrapped around my mug, like a fist, before I had time to pick it up. He leaned his face so close to mine that our noses almost touched.

With a growling voice, he asked, "What me be 'earring ye spake?"

At this point, I wasn't sure if getting my ass tossed around by an overly large British actor was part of my firefighter friend's plans, but I didn't want to find out through antagonism. I felt a little better when he sat down to wait for my reply. Then he chose to speak further.

"Raffe, lad... ye only be missing for a few hours. We be thinking ye be shanghaied, and now, ye spaking like a foreigner. Did ye hit yer head?" He sounded as if he was genuinely

5

concerned about my health, and my stomach could return to where it belonged.

Playing along, I asked, "What do you mean?"

His eyes got bigger than ever. "There it be again!" he said. "That... that accent! Ye ne'er spake like that since the day ye be born in this village."

How I wanted to bust this game wide open and, in a challenging tone, ask him 'what village' but I resisted the temptation. I took the alternate route of being a bit wacky from some sort of mishap and played along with this prank. All I could say is "I wish I knew why. I wish I knew a lot of things that are strange to me, right now." I was certainly the focus of every man's attention in this pub. The exchange of whispers and sideward glances didn't help my nerves. A couple of them weren't just looking at me, they were *studying* me like I was a strange creature or a ghostly apparition.

The big man sounded sincere enough to believe him, when he asked, "How we be helping ye, Raffe?" If this was a prank, the guys sure were dragging it out. If this is a dream, I want to wake up *right now*. If this isn't a prank or a dream... what the hell is *happening* to me?

The prospects before me were either silly, scary or amazing. I didn't care which. I just knew that I needed a *lot* more information! If I had some people in front of me who were *acting* as my friends, or *really* were my friends, I needed to trust them and see where it leads. I looked into the big man's face and saw only the concern of a friend who could use a wash cloth more often.

I took a large swallow of whatever was in the tankard. Wow! That stuff was not your typical 2% beer. It scrubbed my innards all the way down to my toes and back again. The layers of strange reality were just fortified with whatever brew I was drinking. While the warmth was still boiling in my gut, I began to speak.

"If it won't offend you, too badly," I said politely, "I would like to know where I am and who you good men are?"

"Ye poor lad," were the burly man's first words. "Ye be playing a game with us, or do ye know not ye own name or ye own village?"

"No games, guys," I said, "I'm at a total loss right now. The only thing I could make a guess at is up and down, and I wouldn't place a bet on it either." They stared at me as if I was speaking gibberish. I knew they understood some of the words, so I started again. "I am not playing a game. I am not trying to trick or deceive anyone here. As you look at me, I do not know any of you. You call me, 'Raffe,' but I never heard that name before now. Who is this 'Raffe' you seem to recognize as me? In my mind, I have thoughts and memories, but they don't include any of you... or Raffe."

A question was tossed to me from someone sitting in the shadows, next to the wall, which made me very uncomfortable. "If ye not be *him*, then what ye be doing with our friend, Raffe?"

"I didn't *do* anything with *anyone*," I shot back, a bit defensively, "I don't have any answers right now. I only have my own questions about my being *here*. I don't even know where 'here' *is*."

Their faces were a mixture of deeply suspicious and confusion. Borderline sympathy came from the one man I hoped would be most understanding, the large man. I still didn't know his name, and he didn't know mine. I thought I'd be silent again and let them think and talk among themselves, for a while.

The smart ass next to the wall came forward and, for the first time, I could see his full face. He was as classic an English character as any I have seen. The first notable feature was a very thick walrus mustache that would make a walrus jealous. It wiggled as he spoke, and I caught myself staring at it. His eyes were wide set and black, in this minimal light, and squinting with skepticism. This man was dressed perfectly for a Robin Hood movie. His outfit included dark brown, tight-fitting pants and a light green puffy-sleeved Jacobite shirt. To complete the outfit, he wore a dark green felt cap that was folded to a point between his eyes. He stood about 5'9" and was slightly bowlegged, like a cowboy. The most notable parts of his outfit were the dagger and short sword he wore at his waist.

I had to make myself listen as he came up with a couple questions. "If ye not be Raffe and ye not be from our village, then who ye be and where ye be coming from?"

"Okay," I replied, "I'll play along. You guys can start laughing any time you want." I figured I had nothing to lose. If this was a prank, they'll all start laughing when it's time to end it, or if this is a crazy dream, I'll wake up at some point. The third option, that this is really happening to me, wasn't so easy to consider.   But my belief, that *honesty is the best policy*, prompted me to proceeded, accordingly.

"My name is Broderick, but my friends call me Brody. I'm a firefighter and I live in the burbs of Denver. Yesterday, some friends and I took some four-wheelers into the foothills for a four-day camping trip. The next thing, that I am aware of, is that I woke up in your pissing corner in the dark." Several sets of eyes blinked at me, but no one was laughing, no one is speaking, and it's making me squirm.

Finally, 'smart-ass,' in the Robin Hood outfit, breaks the silence with, "What da 'ell be a 'four-wheeler' and what kind of fool picks a fight with a fire?" This brings a chuckle from all of them and I instantly feel a little better. He adds, "Where be this 'Denver' located? I've ne'er 'eard mention of it, afore."

I answered his last question, first. "Denver is in Colorado." More questions came before I could answer any more. To my comfort, they got better.

The big man asked, "Where ye be thinking all these thoughts be coming from? Did ye say ye name be Brody now?" All I could do was to be completely honest and let events play out.

"Brody is the name my friends gave me in grade school, and I've had it all the way through college, so I guess..." My words were stopped short when the big man grabbed my arm, and grabbed it *firmly*.

"*College?*" he asked, in disbelief. "Ye just be telling us that ye be schooled in *college?*"

I replied proudly. "Yes. Community College of Denver." The room was electrified with their attention on me. These men weren't just curious, they were squint eyed and skeptical.

Smart-ass piped in. "Now ye be going too far, Raffe. For certain, we all be knowing that not a man here hath even one day of schooling under his cap! We all be working on fishing boats from the first day we be out of nappies. Why spake such a *lie* to us, who *grew up* with ye, and be knowing the *truth*?"

This prank was getting crazier than ever. These actors were given the wrong name and the wrong personal history of their intended prank victim... if this was a prank. If it's a dream, it's time to wake up in the Rockies and enjoy some hiking and fishing. But this is feeling less like a dream, every second, and less like a prank, at the same time. I need to get some answers instead of just giving out my information.

I continued, "I really would like to answer every question you ask, but I've already told you that I don't know where I am or who any of you are. And, none of you, other than *this* man..." I gestured toward the big man. "... have offered to help." I wasn't sure if they would respect my request for information, but it was worth a try.

Smart-ass played along. "Well, Raffe, if ye remember not ye own village of Ramsgate, then hearing the name might help." He repeated it slowly, "Rams gate." That was the nicest tone of voice I had heard from Smart-ass since this whole insane adventure began.

"Thanks," I said, "but I've never heard of Ramsgate before you said it." My response prompted several mumbles and a 'humph' or two.

The big man stared into my eyes, with his eyes squinting, as if straining in concentration before asking, "Be ye *serious*?"

Looking directly at the big man, but talking to the whole room, I answered, "I recognize that something is very different here, and maybe very wrong. I can only be honest with you, and share what I know and feel. You call me 'Raffe,' and I get the impression that he is a life-long friend of yours and grew up in this village of 'Ramsgate' but, I don't know where Ramsgate

9

is... or who Raffe is... or who any of you are. Worst of all, I have no idea how I got here from my camping trip. So, yes, I do need your help and patience." This is when I expected the entire prank-team to start laughing and end the joke on me. *That's not what happened.*

The big man began to say, "I be knowing ye yer whole life, Raffe."

I interrupted and corrected him. "My name is *Brody*." His eyes narrowed and I could only see his pupils through his bushy eyebrows. That was not the way I liked to see a big man looking at me.

He growled, "That name be *not* the name be known to us for twenty odd years, Lad, and I be thanking ye to let me spake my piece afore ye so rudely interrupt *again. Understand?*"

I knew this was a very good time for me to be silent and attentive, so I whispered the words, "Yes sir."

He continued. "If it be helpful, me name, as ye must know, be 'Gavan' and me mate with the sharp tongue, is 'Asa.'" It was easy to associate these names. All I had to do with 'Asa's name is think of him as 'Asa-hole' and, as for 'Gavan,' I doubt I'll forget him any time soon.

Gavan went on to name the others in the pub, but I stopped taking mental notes after the primary two. When I heard the tone of a question in his voice, I refocused on what he was saying. For now... this had been a very long day and, in spite of the strangeness of events, I was getting very sleepy.

Gavan's question: "We 'eard ye spake of Dover in ye new way of spaking. How could ye travel all the way from Dover o'er night?"

Gavan said Dover two times, so I replied when certain that he had finished speaking. "I didn't say 'Dover,' I said 'Denver.' It's a city in Colorado? America? *USA?*" The blank expressions on their faces made it obvious that nothing in my words was registering, so I continued. "OK, I'll play along. Who here has a smart phone? Mine is in the vest that someone took off of me! I'll show you on Google Earth." I thought to myself, as I looked around at some very puzzled faces. Damn!

I continued, "I don't know what kind of day you have had, Gavan, but my day has been very strange and I'm ready to crash." The blank stares told me to elaborate. "I'm very tired. Could we please get some sleep and talk about this in the morning?"

Asa (hole) quipped. "I thought ye claimed ye be not from here."

"I'm not." I replied, "I just want to get back to camp and crawl into my sleeping bag and crash!"

"Raffe," Gavan said in a soft voice, "I dunna be knowing about sleeping in a bag or crashing into something, but Lad, ye be living in me home since yer folks died when ye were just a wee one."

WHOA! For a moment, my mind just lost all interest in sleep as I studied the big man's eyes for sincerity. Gavan was not acting, and this wasn't a movie set! They don't need them to smell like this, and these guys would need subtitles for their thick accents.

I had to ask, "Can I ask some really crazy questions and get the answers without being asked why?" I had to try and gather enough information to establish my worst fears.

Asa (hole) immediately snapped back, "Only if we be doing the same with whoe'er ye think ye be this night." Asa may be snippety and brash, I thought, but he was also the most intelligent of these friends, by far.

"That's fair enough for me," I replied, "but I'd like it if you addressed me as Brody, please?"

Gavan said, "Try, I shall, Lad, but I be knowing ye as Raffe these many years. Ye be always Raffe to me."

I nodded. "Who would like to go first?' I was expecting Asa to ask something, but the room was silent for too many seconds, so I broke the ice with a question, to which I thought I already knew the answer. I was very wrong.

"What *year* is this?" I asked the room.
A few glances were exchanged over wrinkled noses because this was certainly an unexpected question.

A new voice was heard. One of the men, whose name I failed to catch, spoke up. He was a squat man with sunburned features and a head void of hair, except for a close cropped bush of curly black ringlets around the sides.

"Me be knowing that one. It be the year of our Lord 1690. I 'erd the town crier just yesterday, me did."

I felt my lips part a little as my lower jaw dropped enough to convince all who witnessed my face, that I was shocked. I repeated the year, "1690?" even though he had so clearly spoken.

He nodded and replied, "As me live and breathe, Raffe. I mean, Brody. Sorry, Lad."

This was Asa's cue and he didn't miss it. "Ye be thinking it be *what year,* Brody?"

I wasn't sure, but Asa's tone of voice implied mockery when he spoke my name. My reply was quick. "Asa, '1690' was not the answer I was expecting... not even *close.* To answer your question, with just the year, will create some confusion. But, I made a promise and I will keep it."

My mind was racing for a way to answer and not be considered crazy... if this wasn't a prank. I still couldn't get that gigantic black thing, passing through the night sky, out of my mind and this weird situation disconnected... if they really were connected. Here goes... the truth at any price.

"The honest answer to your question, Asa," I said, "is 2016, but please allow me to explain before you make any judgments about me."

The reactions varied greatly from face to face. Asa's face remained unchanged and Gavan looked as if he had been slightly offended, but the others appeared dumbfounded and confused. I was mildly surprised when Asa stood and raised his arms to quiet the murmurs among the pub's patrons. He spoke as if he were giving a speech.

"I *understand*, Brody. This is ye reply and ye be honest with us, none here will make judgements on the year ye believe this to be."

This kind of response from Asa really made me think I was in a prank and this would all be over in the morning, so I suggested that we all get some sleep.

"Not so *fast*," was Asa's retort. "I be curious about ye life... the life of Brody. Ye spoke of college, but not ye age... and ye be a fighter of fires but not how many. And why, Lad, wouldst a fighter of fires be having need for a college?"

The desire for sleep was beginning to return so I asked Asa, "Would you mind if I answered your questions after some sleep? I can write down your questions and..."

"Clever try, Brody," snapped, Asa,"but none here, even ye, be having one day of schooling. How ye be writing anything?"

"I'll write down your questions, Asa." I repeated. "Where's a paper and pen?"

"What?" Asa replied, with incredulous doubt in his words.

It only took a nano second to realize that prank or phenomenon, if this was 1690, there wouldn't be paper and pens for many years to come. In an apologetic tone, I said, "I guess that was a silly request, Asa. Can we just start again in the morning? I'm very tired and my head is trying to make sense of several things that don't make sense at all. Is this okay with everyone?"

Gavan put his big hand on my shoulder and spoke for the group. "Everything be waiting 'til the morn. No fish to catch. No fish to sell. Nets be mended. We be having time to talk when rested we be, in the morn. Come on, Raffe, or Brody, let's be getting some sleep in ye."

Questions were scrambling for attention in my mind. 1690? Where is Dover, Colorado? What did Jake and I see last night? Who is this Raffe that these guys think I am? How far is it to Gavan's house because I could sleep right here? And, I *live* with that huge ginger-haired man?

As Gavan escorted me back onto a dirt street, I looked about, as my eyes adjusted to the moonlit night. Wow! This was some movie set. It must have been a whole town built for this movie and it smells of rotting fish, open sewage, and very old buildings. Can't see much without streetlights, but it looked very authentic. 1690?

With Gavan's support, I was plodding along passing hut after hut. Every hut was hardly distinguishable from the next, each was obviously made to look as if they had been constructed by hand, unskilled hands. There were no windows and no hinges on the doors, other than pieces of leather or rope lashed on one side. This must be a movie set because they didn't bother to put any lights inside. They were very authentic looking Medieval peasant home fronts which were perfect for 1690. I assumed Gavan was taking me to a camper trailer at the edge of this movie set.

Ahhh. I get it... we're being filmed from a drone as part of this prank. Without warning Gavan, I stopped and stood perfectly still. I looked up into the cloudless night, listening carefully for the buzz of a drone. No matter how I strained my ears, I couldn't hear any sound above the crashing of waves.

Wait! There was that *black spot,* it was blocking out stars *again.* This time, it was getting *smaller!* "Gavan." I whispered much louder than I intended. "What is *that?*" I pointed towards the black spot.

At first, Gavan said, "I not be seeing anything but stars." But like a true friend, he kept searching the sky where I was pointing. "Aye, Lad, me be seeing an orb in the night canopy with *no stars* in it. What of it?"

"Keep watching that spot, Gavan," I said. "And see if it doesn't get smaller." We stood with our eyes fixed on the sky, for the next few moments, as the black thing got too small to see. "Gavan... *THAT* is what my friend, Jake, and I saw getting bigger, coming *towards* the earth last evening. That black orb we just saw zipping off into space, came *towards* the earth, just as *fast.*" Maybe now, he would have some understanding of why I'm here and what had happened to me. Little did I realize, at that moment, we both had many wonders to learn.

Gavan fixed his face on mine, with a blank yet friendly expression. He softly said, "This mind be understanding none of what ye spoke, and these eyes saw nothing moving 'into space.' It be an opening of the night canopy being pierced by angels to allow light through, and nothing more. Ye *do* need some sleep, Raffe. We be near home."

14

I had to admit, the mention of sleep did sound good. It will be much easier to talk in the morning. My mind was swimming with many positive and negative potentials about the events, of the last couple hours. I didn't even notice that Gavan had stopped walking.

"Where ye be going, Lad?" Gavan called from twenty feet behind me.

I figured we were at the edge of the movie set and there ought to be some kind of fence or security gate with guards for a set this elaborate. Somewhere, in the distance, I could still hear the sound of waves on a beach. But that must be my imagination, or road sounds, because this is Colorado and we don't have any oceans here.

I walked back to where Gavan stood, but couldn't see any camper trailers by the light of his lantern. "Where?" I asked.

Gavan lifted his lantern to light up a narrow door made of narrow vertical sticks lashed to several horizontal sticks, on the front of a thatch-roofed structure that looked much like all of the other huts on the set. He pushed the door open with his foot. My first thought was that's cool... the camper-trailers are concealed behind the false fronts of these village homes. I had to dip my head to enter and, to my surprise, saw a single roomed dwelling and, like the pub, authentic in every detail. I strained to find the doors leading to other rooms, but there weren't any. This was a one room hut with sparse furnishings. 1690, I thought. This was way too detailed for a prop on a movie set, but right now, I needed sleep. "Where's my bed, Gavan?" I felt compelled to ask because I could only see one room with one bed in it.

"Right there, Lad, since ye were a wee one," was Gavan's matter of fact reply.

I've slept in the same bed with this huge man since I 'were a wee one.' *Really*? Try as I might, I don't believe I came across as being casual when I asked, "Where's the bathroom?"

Gavan studied me intensely, as he cleaned the soot from the glass panes of his lantern. After lighting the oil lamp hanging in the center of the room. Gavan tried to sound like he knew what I was asking for.

He replied. "We be having not one of *those* rooms, Lad. We be neither king nor landed gentry, but we be having a tub hanging on the wall for bathing. And a *thunder mug*, under the bed, which has served us well 'til this very evening. Will these suit thy fancy?" Obvious sarcasm.

Okay, I thought. Right now, I don't need to offend one of the biggest men I have ever met, and right before being required to share a bed with him. Maybe the best course, here, is to go with the flow. "Of course, Gavan," I replied. "I'm sorry if I sounded like someone important."

"Lad," Gavan said, with a sleepy voice of his own, "ye be not thyself all night and sleep be fixing that."

The bed smelled of straw, very *old* straw. The sweat-soaked canvas sheet was rough against my skin. The bed's canvas appeared to need that hanging wash tub and soap. Rubbing that bed sheet between my fingers, I recognized the same canvas from which my shirt was made.

My mind began to catalogue the day's events starting with 1690, this movie set was too real, and what was the black spot. I hoped Gavan didn't sleep in the nude. Well, dash that hope, I could see his silhouette against the dim lantern's light, as he stripped. Gavan crawled into the narrow bed and was soon snoring.

Where was I on my list...

Chapter 2

Dreaded morning discoveries

OK, Self, I thought, with my eyes still closed. You're not asleep any longer. The thick musky smell says you are still on the old England movie set. Do you really want to continue this game or just tell these actors that it's time to end the prank? At least you could save the last couple days of the camping trip.

I forced myself to open my eyes in the small one room hut. It was still almost dark inside. Some slivers of light were coming through vertical cracks in the walls. The low-angled sunlight told me that it wasn't very long into the day. The room was dead silent and to support my assumption that Gavan was already out of bed, I slowly reached across the bed to feel for warm flesh. My assumption was correct. I was alone.

The detail of this movie set continues to amaze me, at every turn. The walls, dirt floor, bedposts and door lentils all have what appears to be decades of hand-rubbed smoothness in the right places. Who does that for a movie set? And the smell. Why go to the trouble of making a set smell this old, and *lived in,* for a film? These unanswered questions swirled through my mind.

The now brilliant sunshine was illuminating the hut's interior and morning had awakened the usual *call of nature* that would not be ignored. I needed to find the bathroom and the sooner, the better.

"Gavan?" I called, but got no response. I moved from the niche where the bed was, and into the main area of the hut. I expected to see a doorway leading to other rooms, and found none. I called again, "Gavan?" Still no answer.

The room was about 10 feet wide and possibly 15 feet long, with a ceiling that wasn't more than 7 feet at the most. Every piece of furniture, as well as the bed we slept in, appeared to be hand made by a skilled craftsman but definitely not in a factory. I felt like I was looking at the furniture in the cartoon "Snow White and the Seven Dwarfs." No two legs on the chairs were of the same diameter, and the seats still had the chop marks from the axe that felled the trees. The same could be said of the table. The rough planking that formed its top were crudely cut or split; and, if sanded at all, it was sanded with rocks, a long time ago. My mind was absorbing all of these details as I heard approaching footsteps and turned towards the door, just as Gavan walked in.

"Good Day, Lad!" Gavan said with almost a song in his voice. "I be trusting a night's sleep to bring me ole friend back!"

"Good morning, Gavan," I replied, hoping for the same mental clarity he was expecting. "Can you tell me where the bathroom is?"

The joy slipped from the big man's face as he stood there, completely filling the only portal in this humble cottage. "Ye still be spaking with a crazy tongue."

"I'm sorry, Gavan, I don't mean to be rude or spoil anyone's game here. I just need some help finding the shitter."

"OH!" Gavan exclaimed with a brand new smile, "why didn't ye just spake that? The shitter be where it was always. Lucky ye be, Lad, the tide is out. Ye be needing to gather ye own *woolly mullein* since the last be gone. There be a goodly patch right along the path to the bay."

I certainly didn't want to say anything that would wipe that smile off Gavan's face, so I just said, "Thanks Gavan, you've been very helpful."

Whatever I was going to find outside of this movie set, it wasn't worth delaying my nature call for another second. Gavan stepped inside to make room for me to pass through the narrow doorway and into the bright sunlight.

Everything I could see, in every direction, was made up as authentic Old England. It certainly impressed me. Why so much detail for just a movie set? For only a few minutes, my curiosity over the antiquity postponed my urge for nature's relief. I looked about for a blue plastic Porta Potty. Nothing like that was in sight, but I did notice that the few people I saw were all walking along the same path.

I could hear waves rolling onto a shore and this only added to my confusion. Waves?" I thought to myself. In Colorado? All I could see were two rows of cottages facing each other, across a very narrow dirt street. Gavan had said, 'path to the bay' and mentioned something about gathering 'woolly mullein.' What on earth is *that*? With the growing urge of nature's demands making every step a fight between agony and pride, I walked towards the sound of the waves. As I rounded the corner of the last cottage, I stood in frozen amazement.

"HO-LY SHIT!"

"That's a *bay*." I heard my own voice. "That's a *real* bay, just as Gavan said, but with an *entire ocean* beyond it!" I might have stood frozen in my tracks, blinking, for a much longer time if I wasn't immediately prodded into action by my, now, cramping bowels.

OK, Brody! I screamed in my mind. If this was *not* Colorado, then this was *not* a movie set and you are *not* on a camping trip! Where the hell *are* you? First things first. No matter where I was, I still needed to deal with nature, *first*."

The path, that Gavan spoke of, was easy to find. There were several, but all leading directly to the sandy shore of a narrow bay with jutting rocks on either side. It was obvious that the tide was out. Once again, Gavan was right, but what does the bay have to do with taking a morning constitutional? Not wanting to look foolish, I took a moment to watch the locals.

A young man came from the village and greeted me with a melodious voice, "Top of the Morn, Raffe."

I echoed his words and watched him. He grabbed a few broad-leafed plants, as he walked toward the shore line, and then climbed onto what I thought were fishing piers out over the low-tide mark. I quickly learned that the piers were elevated latrines. The weeds he grabbed, along the way, must be the woolly mullein that Gavan mentioned.

When the young man returned, he stopped this time. "Ye still be waiting for the tide, Raffe? Dunna wait too long, for ye feet be getting wet."

Without thinking, I replied, "I'm cool." He might have walked on, but my words made him freeze and he stared at me.

I knew right away that I was speaking like a crazy man, to his ears. I just walked toward the shore, and grabbed some of the woolly mullein along the way. I was impressed with the plant's leaves. TP substitute! As I climbed onto my throne, I glanced back towards the shore. The young man had watched me a while and was just turning to walk back to the village. That made me very uncomfortable. So, this is what these folks call a toilet... an outhouse on stilts made of fairly thick trees, lashed together with an opening to squat over. Not all that bad an idea for hygiene when you have the tide to do the flushing for you. Now it's time for business as usual. I unbuttoned the front of my pants and let them fall around my ankles.

"WHAT? Who does *that* belong to? *That* is not *mine!*" I had forgotten not to speak aloud. This is just too weird! That is not my dick! *This* one is un-cut. I was shaking like an aspen leaf in the wind and nothing is making any sense! For the first time, I noticed my rough hands. Not mine, either! I quickly took inventory. No scar on my leg... this is *not my body!* I tried to calm myself and took a deep breath. Get a *grip*! Do what you came here for and act normal. Go back to Gavan because he's the closest thing to a friend you have, at the moment. If I woke up this morning with hundreds of questions, on my mind, I had a thousand questions now.

As I made my way back to the shore and the path towards Gavan's cottage, many sets of eyes were fixed upon me and the young man who had greeted me. He was talking with several women and they were all looking at me as if they just discovered a juicy piece of gossip. This was not good. I have never been a man who likes to be the center of attention, and this strange place, and its inhabitants, were making me feel extremely uncomfortable.

I walked a bit faster with hopes that Gavan would be able to answer the tornado of questions, swirling in my mind. My anxiety waned slightly as my eyes fell upon his cottage. Even from the corners of my eyes, I could see every face following my every move.

Gavan was sitting on the largest of the three miss-matched chairs around the table when I walked in. He read my face like a book. "Ye look like ye lost a lot more than shite out there, Lad. What's got ye face so pulled down?"

I hardly knew where to start. If all of this unfamiliar crap I'm feeling, seeing, smelling and hearing was real, then where *was* I? What has happened to me? I've never felt this depth of fear before!

At the sight of Gavan's warm smile, I loosened my emotional fears. I tried to speak calmly, but blurted it out, instead. "I don't know what to say, Gavan, I don't know *who* I am, or *where* I am. Nothing makes any sense to me, and I'm afraid like I have never been afraid *before*. I can only say this to *you* because you have been a friend of Raffe for his whole life... but I'm not Raffe. I'm Brody. When I went to sleep last night, I was sure that you were an actor in an elaborate plot, and this village was a movie set, and I was having a joke played on me by my buddies during a camping trip, and..."

"Stop right there, Lad," Gavan's voice went big and soft at the same time. "I understand we being life-long friends. True, indeed, but ye be spouting words of jibberish. And, to *deny* the name ye departed Mum and Pap gave ye... just ain't *right.*"

Not knowing exactly how to phrase my question, I pulled down my pants and asked, "If my life parents gave me the name, Raffe, did they give me *this, too?*" Gavan seemed confused as to what I wanted him to respond, so he leaned forward and examined me.

"Hmm," remarked Gavan, "Nothin' new here, Raffe. 'Tis the same little fella ye be sportin' ye whole life."

"No, it's not!" I asserted, "As crazy as this sounds, I was circumcised as an infant and this is an un-cut dick."

Gavan mumbled, "A *dick*, it be? He took another look and said calmly, "Aye, that it be, Lad. Might be a wee bit bigger than when ye be a boy but, for certain, it be belonging to ye."

I pulled up my pants and repeated, "I was circumcised. This can't be mine." I displayed my rough hands and raised my pant leg to show him my unscarred leg as I explained, "I had a scar that ran the length of my calf. Gavan, this is *not* my *body!*"

Gavan slowly shook his head, from side to side, as he spoke softly, "To deny ye own body parts be strange and disturbing, Raffe. I be not explaining why ye dunna recognize yerself, but I be sure your body always be the same, Lad." Gavan's warm voice was just too kind and soothing to make any attempt to argue. Logically, I had no alternative except to drop the subject and focus on all of the other new discoveries I was experiencing.

Gavin's tone changed slightly to something more up beat. "I be visiting with Asa, this day. We be liking to visit alone, but t'day be a bit different. He be the smartest amongst our pub mates. He hath not an education more than ye and me, but he be liking to visit with them what does hath book knowledge. Join with me t'day, Lad? I be visiting Asa some other time."

I picked up on Gavan's emphasis on the word, 'visit' but it didn't register as anything peculiar, so I said, "That's fine with me, I need some very strange questions answered and anyone with some answers will be very welcome."

The walk from Gavan's home to Asa's home was about a mile and it eventually took us out of the village. Along the way, it seemed as if everyone took notice of us. I recognized the young man who had passed me to and from the latrine, and he gave me a wave and a nod. I waved back.

Gavan immediately asked in a whisper, "How ye be knowing him?"

I whispered back, "We just passed on the path to the latrine, bay... why do you ask?"

"Did ye spake with him?" He ignored my question.

"Yeah," I replied, "we exchanged a few words. Why?"

Gavan's face broke into a broad smile and then a bit of a chuckle. "That be explaining why the villagers be watching us. He being the busiest gossip in this village, maybe the whole of England, and he be spreading the news of yer strangeness."

In my mind, I played back Gavan's words, 'maybe the whole of England.' England? We continued to walk but my knees were feeling weak. My eyes lost focus, for a second, as my mind attempted to process the word 'England.' I was hearing a buzz in my head that was louder than anything Gavan said. England? Every time I repeated the word, 'England,' in my mind, I sensed a growing awareness of something approaching my psyche like an F5 tornado. The realities of the visual, olfactory and irrefutable world around me was invading my mind and I was powerless to stop it. I wanted to believe what

23

my senses were telling me but the transition from 2016 Colorado to 1690 England was becoming an undeniable truth. I felt weak all over, inside and out.

I asked, "How much farther is it to Asa's place?" I feared my legs might fail me.

Gavan replied with a gesture of his big hand, "This be it."

OH, great, another big surprise. Asa's cottage wasn't anything like the other cottages. It was taller and certainly wider, and it had shake-shingle siding and a slate roof. A five foot tall stonewall fence clearly defined his property line from the adjacent open pastures. The elevated view gave a vista that anyone would have envied. It made me wonder how Asa came to own such a prime piece of real estate.

Gavan stopped at the gate and called out, "Asa, ye be alone? This be Gavan. Raffe be with me."

The front door opened almost instantly, and Asa stepped out with a cloud of pipe smoke filtering through his massive mustache and encircling his bare head. He was bald and shiny on top, except for a halo of thick brown hair. "T'was hoping for a visit from thee, Gavan, but ne'er be expecting ye to bring Raffe along." Asa was all smiles and sincerely warm in his greeting, nothing at all like the cynical and challenging man sitting in the shadows of the pub last night. Maybe the domain of his own home, and master thereof, brought out the kinder Asa and possibly the intelligent helpful man I needed right now.

We passed by Asa to enter his home, but he gave us only enough room to pass if we brushed against him. Gavan entered first and he was met with an embracing hug which included cheek to cheek contact. I thought that this was a lot more contact than I wanted from Asa, but I was offered a rather formal handshake, instead.

The inside of Asa's home impressed me much more than the finely finished exterior, since every piece of furniture appeared factory made and of the very finest quality. He had wood floors, padded chairs, and a large window on the wall facing the grand vista with the small village of Ramsgate almost centered in the view. Away from the main entrance and street view, Asa's home might have been very comfortable, except for the lack of electricity, in 2016.

Oil lamps, on several walls, were lit and made the room quite bright. We could clearly see that there were several rooms leading off from the great room at the front door. Asa had a very nice home! Asa led us through the large central room to what was obviously a dining room. Until I smelled the bread and cheese on the table before us, I hadn't given much thought to food. I did notice that only two places had been set and instantly realized that Asa wasn't expecting me. I turned to leave and began to apologize for my presence when Asa, genuinely surprised by my sudden wish to leave, put an arm around my shoulders.

"Raffe," Asa spoke with a warm voice, "Ye be welcome always in my home. It be obvious that ye not be expected this morn, but there be more than plenty for all, and I be most pleased that ye be here."

Asa broke my awkward silence. "May I be getting ye men something to drink? Please be sitting about my table and I will fetch another plate for meself. And, Gavan, if ye not be here to visit, then what be bringing the two of ye to my home?"

As we sat down, Gavan spoke first, "The Lad be as batty this morn as in the pub. I be not having any answers for him, but the moment he said that his dick... his *body* be someone *else's*, I be thinking ye might help the Lad."

"Hmmm..." Asa sounded, as if he was thinking out loud as he retreated from sight and instantly reappeared with another place setting and took his place to join us. "I may be the local authority on human anatomy and some other things, Gavan, but from what me witnessed last night, this not be the issue...

wouldst ye agree, Raffe? Or whatever name ye be giving us last. 'Brody,' be it not?"

Setting the example, Asa took up the loaf of bread and tore about a third from one end. He handed the loaf to Gavan, who ripped the loaf in half and handed me the remaining third. It was still warm from the oven and smelled wonderful. To make me more comfortable, Asa cut the wedge of cheese into approximate thirds and handed each of his guests a portion. I was so impressed with how different Asa and his home were, I sat quietly and soaked it in. I realized that I hadn't answered Asa's question about my name being Brody and chewed quicker to swallow and reply.

Asa didn't wait for me to answer. He had more to say. "Ye be getting me thinking last night, 'Brody.' T'was remembering some conversations I had with a dear monk friend, o'er the years. He spoke of ancient manuscripts, kept within the monastery, recording a 'Passing' what occurs every several hundred years. The stories he shared be amazing but ne'er believed him enough to remember details. I *do* remember of people 'burned at the stake' or 'drawn asunder' for heresy because they spake things that be not in scriptures or made claims what couldst not be proved in a court."

"Oh shit," was all I could say at this moment. I began to wonder if Asa was baiting me. Or perhaps he was letting me know that he understood me, in a limited way, and wanted to get me some help.

Gavan, who seemed more of the protector type, looked across the table and read my face. He spoke first. "What be all that to do with the Lad thinking he be in someone else's body? He's just confused, and ye start off spaking about some ancient records in a monastery and be getting 'pulled asunder?' I be seeing not much comfort in ye words, Asa. Most certainly not good words for sitting over food."

"Gavan," Asa began, "Please be so kind as to understand that *ye* not be seeing any comfort, but me wonders if the *Lad* here feels the same." Asa looked at me and asked, "Did the words 'ancient Passing' sound familiar to ye? I want ye to know, Brody, ye be with friends here; and, your companion,

26

Gavan, be the truest of them *all*. As for me, I be doubtful of what I heard last night... but if there be another 'Passing' and ye be one of the souls affected by it, then ye be needing to spake with this monk, and *soon*. *Things* be getting real nasty 'round here."

Gavan's face went pale and his eyes glazed as if the big man were about to cry. His voice was so weak. "Did me see it?" he started in a rasp whisper. "Lad, that be what ye pointed at, in the night sky last night? The black spot that be smaller and smaller, Raffe... did we see the 'Passing' as it went away?"

This caught Asa completely off guard and he leaned back in his chair, as his mustache twitched from side to side. "Hope, me hath, that one of ye be coming up with some *answers as to what ye saw in the sky last night.*"

I attempted to explain, "I have no idea what the thing was, Asa, but I can tell you that I watched that thing coming *towards us* the evening before, and in a very different location and situation than *this place* we're in right *now*." These were the only honest words I could find.

Asa asked the big question: "Just how *different* be ye spaking about, Raffe? I be sorry, Brody?"

Gavan was trying to wipe the tears of denial from his eyes, as he mumbled, "I sure be not wanting to hear the answer to your question, Asa."

Asa insisted, "If what Brody spoke to us, thus far, be true, Gavan, he may be in danger from ignorant people and maybe even the church. It thought to be evil or demonic by the same group of people. We hath ne'er seen this because it all happened over 300 years ago. The monk's stories sounded so gruesome, I not be wanting to learn the stories, and the 'Passing' can harm a close friend's life. What be yer opinion, Gavan?"

"Drop anchor a moment!" snapped Gavan. "Ye spoke of church people to be the same as dangerous ignorant people, so why be ye so friendly with a *monk* on this subject of a 'Passing' and spake ye of *him*, as an *authority*?"

Asa snapped back, his eyes locked on Gavan's. "Because *THIS* monk *IS* an authority on this subject! *This* monk hath access to the old manuscripts, and he be *not* one of those clerics who be doing all he's told, without thinking!" After a few seconds of thoughtful silence, Gavan's face lit up as he recognized the meaning of Asa's words. Asa emphasized his words further. "I be *certain* you would like *this* monk and *trust* him."

Gavan smiled as he replied, "I be knowing only *one* monk I trust *completely*." He smirked, as he continued. "Ye consider this monk to be a friend, Asa? Then, he be a thinker, and open minded to be making his own opinions."

For reasons unknown to me, both men thought this was funny enough to chuckle. I still hadn't answered Asa's big question about how differently last night ended from how it began. I'm really not sure if I know how to answer his question. I *now* know that I can't explain it as if I'm speaking to typical Americans in 2016.

"Brody!" Asa's voice really owned my attention right now. "Has it occurred to ye that we be seeing ye as Raffe? Does that not strike ye as *odd*?"

That was the kind of question that makes you feel more than a bit stupid, but then, who has ever expected to look like anyone but themselves? I muttered, "I haven't thought about that until you asked, Asa. And now that you have posed this question, I'm reasonably certain that the answer is the exact reason for Gavan and me to be here."

Gavan had stood and walked around the table until he was standing close by me, like a sentry, soaking in every word Asa spoke. He kept looking at me like a troubled father might view his child upon receiving bad news. Having eaten, I initially thought Gavan was about to leave the room, but he just stood over me until Asa began speak again.

"If ye and Gavan mind not, I want to try something. Ye may be wanting to finish yer tea, Lad, I'll be right back." At these words, Gavan moved to stand directly behind me and placed his powerful hands on my shoulders. I felt no threat from his thick fingers, as he gently squeezed and massaged my back with his thumbs, but I did feel that he and Asa were aware of something that I wasn't.

Asa returned carrying a mirror. He placed it directly in front of my face and held it motionless for me to see myself. I could easily see a face of a young man looking back at me, but I didn't recognize him. For a few seconds, I examined the reflected face until the reality began to sink in. That's my face? My fingertips roamed the contours of this new face. That's my *new* face. Initially I rejected the image by saying, "that face belongs to Raffe." Unable to deny the truth before me, I relented, relaxed into Gavan's hands and mumbled. "no, that face belongs to me, now." The eyes were not as sharp and intelligent looking as I believed my eyes to be. The ears stuck out a little, the... *my* mouth is now smaller, and I have a weak chin. I hadn't given any thought to it, but I hardly have any beard growth and a very spindly mustache. I wouldn't call this Raffe face "ugly," but he certainly isn't as bright-eyed and handsome as my Brody face.

I was neither pleased nor disappointed, but I was certainly surprised by my own reaction. I have always thought more of character than beautiful or handsome features when evaluating my friends. I had to laugh at myself when the thought entertained me. I'm not as handsome as Gavan, but I'm not as bland as Asa, so I guess I'll be just fine. Although, I wouldn't mind having a big mustache, like Asa's, some day. While trying to remember my 'Brody face', I began to remember other things to help me gain the self-awareness I once enjoyed. I became a fireman because I wanted to help people, not just to recover from a fire but to reclaim their lives after a fire. I needed to put my desire to help others into helping myself, like a man who lost everything in a fire, I had to accept the reality of where I am, what I have to work with and who I wanted to be known as, as I recover.

I looked again at that face in the mirror and found my thoughts not very concerned with how I looked. That's not me, but it going to be my face, for the time being. I felt Gavan's hands tighten about my shoulders as he gave me the moral support, he expected I would need.

I could hear Gavan's deep voice. "Steady, Lad. I have ye. I be ne'er letting ye fall. I be ne'er letting ye down."

I placed my hands on Gavan's hands and said, "I'll be okay. Thank you both for being the good friends any man would like to have." Referring to the mirror, I said, "At first glance, Asa? I thought you played some sort of trick on me."

Asa quickly said, "No trickery here, Raffe or Brody. I may suggest 'Raffe' for ye own safety!" He held the mirror up, once again; but this time, Gavan bent down and placed his big whiskered face next to mine, so I could see a face I recognized in the reflection. The Raffe face was still new, but Gavan's face was unmistakable. That big galoot was easily recognizable, and now I know what these friends see when they look at me.

I replied, "This is a bit of a surprise, but nothing too shocking." I started to make some sort of teasing remark about Asa's gigantic mustache, but changed my mind.

Asa warned, "If ye know what be good for ye, Raffe, ye will learn to spake and act as we be doing, for yer own safety." Asa went on with genuine concern in his voice. "This village, like e'ery other village in England, hath superstitious people what hath no will to learn 'bout things they understand not. They accuse those who be different of being demon possessed and kill them; some, for just spaking words like ye spake. Words like 'guys' and 'OK' will draw much attention to ye... and ye *friends*."

I could see why Gavan thought of Asa as the smartest member of their group. "Thank you, Asa... Is there any way I might be able to have a meeting with your monk friend?"

"Yes." Asa said bluntly, "I be making plans for the two of ye to meet." Gavan and Asa thought this was terribly funny, because they both laughed out loud.

It's obvious that I'm not in Colorado anymore, and these guys... no, 'me mates,' say that this is England, the village of Ramsgate in England, and the year is 1690. And... OH Yeah, I'm *un-cut* now! WTF?

So much information to process, and now I'm hearing Asa tell me that I'm in danger, simply for being myself. I recognized that Asa and Gavan had some inside humor, but it felt to me that it was just the banter of good friends. I felt safe around them.

I heard Gavan say, "It be time we returned, Asa."

As we left, Asa assured us that he would only need a few days to make the arrangements for Gavan and me to meet his monk friend at some monastery. Our departure was quite different from our arrival, this time, I was embraced by Asa, and it felt very warm and natural. The walk back to Gavan's cottage was filled with whispered questions between us about Ramsgate and what to expect from neighbors.

Before entering his, um, *our* home, I stopped to tell Gavan how much I appreciated his friendship. I knew he still saw Raffe when he looked at me, but he made every effort to encourage and tutor me in local speech and mannerisms. This was a challenge because the only Old England English I could remember, was from movies and TV.

Chapter 3

The Dangers are Real

After a couple weeks of adjustments to daily life which included daily lessons to learn how to speak 1690 English, my life had settled into a routine. I had all but forgotten about Asa's 'few days' to prepare for our journey to a monastery and invested my energies into learning everything I could about my new life as Raffe.

It startled me when Gavan burst through the cottage door at almost a run. "Keep ye yap shut! Dunna answer any questions! Let *me* be doing the spaking, if ye be knowing what's *good* for ye!" With these simple commands, Gavan told me, "Sit at the table and look busy." I immediately complied and sat at the table. I knew there was always something to do so I picked up a lantern and began to wipe it down with one of the many dirty rags lying about. Gavan stood just inside the door, as if he was waiting for someone.

The young man that I had met my first morning here, threw the door open without knocking... apparently not yet invented in 1690. He jumped back because he found himself almost nose-to-nipple with the biggest man of the village, but he still managed to mutter his message, "Soldiers be coming." He glanced at me and then ducked out as quickly as he had come in.

Gavan's answer to the already closed door, was, "Me knows."

"What's going" on?" I asked Gavan, in almost a whisper.

Gavan assured me, "Ye canst be found outside with everyone else, Raffe. The rumors be going round that the King's soldiers be visiting every village on the coast, but we dunna be knowing why. I be at Asa's cottage this morn and saw the soldiers coming from afar, and thought to make sure ye be inside when they get here."

"Why should the soldiers care about me?" I asked.

Gavan warned, "Do ye really want to know if it's *ye* they be seeking?"

I whispered. "No. Thank you for coming back, Gavan." i was learning that Asa was right. Gavan really was the best of men to have for a friend.

The soldiers walked down the center of the village street; making much more noise than the locals, with their clanking armor and heavy boots. There couldn't have been more than twelve or fifteen men, but it was enough to level this little fishing village, if they wanted to. Their obvious leader walked front and center. I was very curious to continue watching through the cracks around the door, but Gavan said that I should be sitting at the table when they got to his cottage. I didn't argue.

One of the soldiers was directed to come to Gavan's cottage. This soldier looked like he was only in his teens and very skinny, like a 16 year old Ichabod Crane. When he knocked on Gavan's door, a harsh voice bellowed from the troop commander.

"Lad! Ye be the King's soldier! Ye dunna *knock* on doors — ye *bash them in,* and in the name of the *King!*"

The rattled young soldier was about to use his foot on the door when Gavan jerked the door wide open. The soldier stumbled into the cottage landing on his knees... right against the table in front of me. Gavan bent down until his mouth was almost touching the disoriented soldier's ear, when he growled, "What do ye *want?*"

The soldier whimpered, "Forgive the rude entrance." He became more confident. "King's Orders, ye know, we be having to search every home for crazy people. Do ye be having any in this house?" He looked as if he were about to cry.

Gavan leaned his massive frame over the young soldier and growled again, "I be the head of this house, and there be *none here.*"

Fearfully satisfied, the soldier scurried out to join the rest of his troop who had passed by towards the bay. We knew they would be back, because there was no other way out of the village, except to pass through again.

Gavan sat down at the table across from me and his face was grim. "If they be back demanding ye to spake, I fear they be taking ye away... may be worse... kill ye right here."

"*Why?*" I asked, "I haven't done anything *wrong*. I'm not a criminal or fugitive."

"It be the way ye spake, Lad." Gavan tried to explain, in a very low tone. "Folks here be well aware of the *new* Raffe, and how ye dunna spake the way of the *old* Raffe. And, I dunna be having a plan to help ye."

There was a light rap at the door and we both jumped. It was Asa. He opened the door just enough to let his voice in. "I be thinking this be a good time for ye to meet my monk friend, Raffe, and me thinks we should be leaving now!"

Gavan patted me on the back and spoke softly, as I moved quickly passed him, on my way out the door. "Take care, Lad, I be hoping to see ye again and *soon*. Asa be taking good care of ye. Be careful. God's speed." The welling in his tender eyes brought tears to mine, as well.

As we walked, Asa was silent and he motioned for me to be silent, too. He didn't walk in the center of the narrow street. He chose a path where our steps were almost under the thatched eves of each cottage until we came to the first lane leading towards his own cottage. Once we were out of direct sight of the center of the village and the soldiers, we walked cross-country to his cottage to make better time. From a ridge, we concealed ourselves near a pile of boulders, and looked back to see the young male gossip talking to the leader of the soldiers and he was pointing at Gavan's cottage. What followed made my heart sink.

The entire troop followed the young man directly to Gavan's home. Asa nudged me as he whispered, "Gavan be not wanting us to wait here to learn what happens next. Let's be moving."

Asa had two travel sacks already packed, sitting by his back door. We grabbed them and never stopped walking until the sun was almost set. We didn't use a public highway for two days, as we made our way North, then West. I was amazed at how well he knew his way around when there were no road signs to follow. He said that it was best if we didn't ask for directions or help. Our bread rations ran out on the third day and I was beginning to feel like a 'mooch' (another word to forget) because I was penniless, and had been, since arriving in 1690. I felt somewhat useful when I could help Gavan on his fishing boat but traveling with Asa, I was just a beggar. I hated feeling like this.

Asa was good at reading people, almost like he did it for a living. He knew that this was a strange world for me, and he understood my situation in ways that I did not. To some degree, that contributed to my discomfort.

"We should be reaching the Monastery before nightfall, if we be keeping a steady walking pace," Asa announced, with confidence.

"Have you been here often?" I asked, "You seem to know your way around."

"Oh yes, Lad" Asa gladly admitted, "Been here many a time, o'er the years. I spoke to ye, the night we met, that none of us be having a day of schooling and that were the truth. But I got my schooling inside the walls of the monastery, and I got a very *good* education, to boot! I dunna spake about it, for most people in the village resent those who can read, write and work with numbers. They be fearing them, and those they fear, they hate. Be soundin' familiar?"

"*Yes*. Yes, it *does*." I had to ask, "Then you believe I have a college degree?"

"Believe it, I did," Asa confessed. "I be believing afore ye proclaimed it, and so did Gavan! But, we knew not how to shut ye up in that pub, so we let ye spake what ye be wanting to amongst men we could trust."

"Asa," I pleaded, "How could you believe me, before you met me?"

"Well," he explained, "The first night we met... in the hours *before* we met, ye... Raffe, Gavan and me be the only mates in the pub. Suddenly, ye... Raffe, dropped dead. Right in front of us. No warning, no cries of pain, no bleeding and no breathing. Gavan and I carried ye... Raffe, out to the pissing corner because we be fearing we be accused of killing ye with too many tankards of grog. Gavan's heart be breaking and feeling terrible 'bout where we left ye. He went out to move ye... yer body to a place of respect til the morn. That's when the two of ye met. Ye be knowing all, since then."

"You dumped me in the pissing corner?" My question came with a big smile and it put Asa at ease. He needed the laugh, as much as I did.

Asa came back with a little humor of his own. "How you be getting on with ye new un-cut *tallywacker*?"

I sheepishly chuckled. "I'm doing just fine with it. I believe it's a little bigger, so there are no complaints from me." I tried to mimic Asa, "Tally*wacker*."

Perceptively, Asa used the casual questions to introduce the question he really wanted to ask. "How have ye been feeling about this new life and the family ye left behind?"

It was impossible for me to verbalize how grateful I was for his question, because I wanted to share my feelings for some time. "I'm beginning to feel as if I'm going to be here, in 1690, for a very long time... maybe the rest of my life, Asa. You are the first friend to ask me about my family in 2016 and the simple answer is; there isn't any family back there, that I know of. I was orphaned when I was too young to remember and I don't have any brothers or sisters. I was put into an orphanage, that's a fondling home here, and lived there until I was old enough to be on my own."

"Tell me 'bout ye college education?" Asa asked, "This be the most interesting thing for me to be hearing."

"College, for me was almost as new and strange as waking up in the piss corner. I smiled to assure Asa that my reference to the piss corner was intended to be humorous. He smiled back.

"For truth?" Asa asked, "Was it such a terribly smelly place?" We both smiled at this.

"No, Asa." I replied, "It was an amazingly large campus with hundreds of students. Each wanting to earn a degree and get on with their lives."

"How many years of study were required to get this 'degree'?" Asa asked.

"The average time to earn a degree is four years for a Bachelor's Degree. That's what I earned, Asa." I went on to share that my degree was in a subject called Social Studies.

"Social Studies?" Asa asked, "What kind of education is that? Is it dedicated to a particular religion, or type of science?"

I really wished he hadn't asked that last question because it was going to be a challenge to describe 2016 Social Studies to a self-educated 1690 man. I began by telling Asa that my education was about the study of people and how different their lives can be. There was no shortage of conversation for the rest of the day. Asa's curious mind absorbed all I could tell him and wanted more.

Later in the afternoon Asa asked, "Would ye like to return to 2016?"

This question truly stumped me and I shared my emotional as well as my intellectual response as we walked. "That's another good question. Only you have asked me, Asa. I've only been here, in 1690, for a few weeks, but in that time, I have been befriended by Gavan and you, and the two of you are as close to me as any brother, which I never had. My guess is that I'm here to stay, if that 'Passing' you spoke of only happens ever 300 years. I have no idea how I got here and I haven't given any thought to trying to return."

Asa, pleased with my sincere response, smiled as we walked on.

Just as Asa predicted, we came in sight of what had to be the Monastery. It was the biggest stone structure that I had laid my eyes on in weeks. It was late afternoon and I was more than ready for a hot meal and a soft bed under a roof. Asa thought it would be best if he went the last quarter mile alone, to be sure his friend was still there. He gave me strict instructions to not talk with anyone. If they insisted, I was to pretend I couldn't speak. I was hoping that Asa would return before I needed to play any charades.

Asa was back in less than half an hour and I couldn't have been more pleased. The sun was already sinking into the western trees by the time we got to the Monastery.

It had a magnificently carved front door and gate, but we didn't use them or go anywhere near them. Asa led me along a shoulder-high stone wall, that surrounded the ancient building, until we were behind it, and a large cemetery. There we entered through a very small and narrow gate which required us to bend over to pass through. Once inside the wall, we could hear monks chanting but saw no other residents. Asa walked as though we had nothing to fear and that made *me* feel safe.

We walked directly to an annex at the back of the main Monastery which was obviously built long after the original cathedral. The annex was constructed of uniform bricks and the main building was made of hand-cut stone. The annex looked like a military barracks. It was long and only one-story high with several doors at uniform intervals and a few narrow openings near the top of the walls, which I assume to be air vents.

We stood before the annex door closest to the chapel and Asa said, "We be needing to wait here."

I could hear the chants very clearly through open vents, atop the large stained-glass windows above us. It occurred to me that this was the very first music I had heard since I found myself in England. The harmony of their voices were very comforting. Although Asa didn't say a word, I could read his face, as he closed his eyes, and bathed in his own sweet memories of this place. The smile that grew across his face was contagious. When he opened his eyes, he caught me staring at him, with a smile reflecting his. This was the first time I had seen this man blush.

Asa gave me a friendly frown. I don't believe he minded sharing his love for this place with me. The chanting stopped and Asa said, "Our host be here soon, and I be thinking you will be pleasantly surprised."

Asa is really someone special, I told myself, as I heard the shuffle of many feet along the corridor just behind the door. He tapped lightly on the door which immediately swung open.

"Gavan?" I asked, "Is that you, Gavan?" There stood Gavan, minus his bushy beard, in the small doorway and all I

38

could hear was Asa's roaring laughter. I could barely hear the monk's response over Asa's uncensored laughter.

"No, Lad, I'm Brother Gabriel. Gavan be me twin brother." Asa continued laughing.

He was having the time of his life reading the expressions on my face. He must have been looking forward to this moment for days. Who would have thought there would be a monk who was as huge a man as Gavan? I thought I was beginning to see Asa's connection to this Monastery, but it was just the tip of the iceberg. Brother Gabriel looked passed us to see if there was anyone else around.

Asa said, "No one be following us, dear Gabriel. I assure thee."

Still looking about, the big monk pulled us inside, closed and locked the door. Once inside, we each were wrapped in one of his huge arms, just like Gavan might do when we get back home. Home. Strange to hear my own thoughts of a cottage in Ramsgate, England in 1690 as someplace to get back home to. My experiences here were just too weird for words anymore. My pondering thoughts were interrupted.

"Ye be hungry, Lad?" asked Asa.

"I could eat a *horse*!" I eagerly replied.

"Good, for me thinking that's what we be having." Asa quipped back. Once again, he was teasing. In this place in which he felt so safe and comfortable, Asa was revealing a new side of himself. "Funning ye, Lad, the horse be needed for pulling carts, so we'll be having some vegetables and the finest bread, made from white wheat from southern France. Be that good enough for ye?"

"Sounds wonderful, Asa." I replied, "I'm learning your jokes, so one of these days, you won't be able to trick me."

"You'll never be learning them all, my Lad," chided Asa.

Interesting... that was the first time Asa addressed me as 'my' Lad. He's as good a man as Gavan to have for a friend and I kind of like being around him. The food was simple but delicious. Imported wheat from France? After dinner, Gabriel invited Asa and me to enjoy a glass of wine and listen to the evening vespers. The atmosphere of this monastery was almost like an emotional medicine. Whether we talked, or listened in silence, to the chanting, everything was peaceful and comforting.

The long brick structures behind the main chapel were divided into cubicles. A monk, sworn to silence, escorted us to our individual sleeping chambers. They were simple but very comfortable. I noticed that only the exterior doors had inside bolts for locking; but none, of the interior doors leading to the many sleeping chambers, had locks. I took this to be a sign of trust among all who slept here. The young monk stopped before a chamber door near the end of the brick structure and with a hand gesture indicated which room was to be my sleeping chamber. I was about to ask when breakfast would be served, but remembered the oath of silence. I expected the smell of cooking or morning chants would wake me. As for myself, sleep came so quickly after I laid down, I had no time to think of anything before the sweet oblivion of nothingness engulfed me.

Chapter 4
The Grand Table of Consciousness

Morning came with a light mist and the beautiful sound of sacred chanting in their chapel. Breakfast was meager fare of some kind of lentil soup, bread and ale that Gabriel said he made with his own recipe. Everyone, guests included, was assigned simple cleaning chores which didn't last very long. My assignment was pulling weeds around the front entrance to the Monastery. It gave me the feeling of being a contributor, rather than a leech.

Just as I was pulling the last of the few weeds around the chapel steps, a young novice approached me. He was carrying what appeared to be a burlap garment, very similar to the one he was wearing. When he stopped, he extended both of his hands toward me, with the garment, in an offering gesture. "Is this for me?" I asked. He nodded his head and smiled, but didn't speak. "Am I supposed to wear it?" I must have sounded silly with that question. I accepted the robe and the young novice left without having uttered a single word. My assigned work was finished so I carried the robe to my sleeping chamber and changed into it. The first thing I noticed, beyond the itchy sensation of the material against my skin, was that it was not a new robe. I immediately liked the idea of a slightly used robe because I looked as if I had been here for quite some time.

I found Asa and Gabriel walking through the cemetery. When I approached them, Gabriel told me that Asa had filled him in on the last few weeks of events in Ramsgate. I had no idea how much Asa knew but I did know that I could trust him to be thorough and truthful.

Gabriel asked, "Asa informed me that ye be having a college degree. What was the discipline of your degree?"

I speculated that he meant major and replied, "I have a BS Degree in Sociology, from a community college." I could immediately see that very little of what I said made much sense to my listeners, so I elaborated. "I have a Bachelor of Science

Degree in Sociology, the study of human relationships. The college I attended was a small community college in Denver, Colorado." Probably, just to be polite, Gabriel didn't ask me to clarify anything he didn't understand. He did ask if I was versed in classic or vernacular Latin and I told them that Latin wasn't required to earn a degree. This put a frown of disappointment on Brother Gabriel's face and I wasn't surprised to see it.

Brother Gabriel offered, "Would ye be liking to see the ancient charts and documents we be storing here? I be suspecting ye to find them extremely interesting."

"Yes, Sir," I replied, even though I only knew from Asa that the old documents might help me. I just wanted to be involved.

Gabriel put his big hand on my arm and leaned very close to my face, *just* like Gavan did when he wanted my full attention. "I *strongly* suggest ye ne'er again address me as 'Sir.' You are a friend of my brother, Gavan, and as such, a friend of mine. Should ye be using 'Sir' in public, *both* of us be losing our *heads*. I am 'Brother' or 'Brother Gabriel,' for reasons being of *life and death.* Are we *clear?*"

I knew his warning was both friendly and deadly serious. "I'm sorry. It will never happen again, Brother Gabriel. "The formality put a little smile on his big face.

"Now." Brother Gabriel said, with the levity back in his voice, "I be having some very old manuscripts to show ye. They be not the originals, mind ye. Originals were carved into the stone walls of caves and on stone monoliths. These be carbon stroke likenesses of those original Rune inscriptions and I be believing ye will find them illuminating." I had to notice that Gabriel, Brother Gabriel, has a sophisticated vocabulary.

"Has anyone been able to *translate* the Rune inscriptions?" I asked Gabriel. "As much as I wish to see them, they won't mean much to me."

"Then ye be in double fortune this day, Raffe," the large monk boasted. "for I am the monk assigned to be keeping the texts safe, *and* it be me, among the monks, who be most proficient in the reading of complex syllables of this long-lost language. I be literate in Latin, too."

42

I could see how Asa received his secret education through Brother Gabriel and the other monks in this monastery. They were all scholars, and each had their field of academic specialty.

To familiarize me with the monastery, Gabriel gestured with both arms to imply the inclusion of the building in which we stood as he said, "This great stone structure was built over a labyrinth of rooms which each of the monks has dedicated to their discipline of academics, according to their desire to serve their faith. Because I be chosen to preserve the 'history of humanity,' it was considered vital that my chambers be those which were the driest, and with the strongest walls and thickest door."

As expected, the sub-chamber, into which Gabriel led us, smelled of very old parchment and mold, lots of mold, which was the kind that makes you try not to breathe. Along every wall of the dark room were shelves from floor to a high ceiling and every nook and cranny filled. Every shelf was stuffed with a few laid out sheets but many, many rolled parchments in bundles and a few wooden tablets. The walls looked like the honey comb of bees with all of visible ends of the rolls stacked to fill every shelf.

Gabriel and Asa lit a dozen or more candles, with their torches, to provide some even light to the room and with each candle, the room became more interesting. The last candles lit were directly over a large, banquet-sized table in the center of the room. This table was much too large to have been carried through the only door into the room. It must have been built in there with its tree-trunk legs and cross grain single tree-trunk top that looked to be about 15' long and 8' wide. The tree from which this table top was cut must have been massive. It was finely carved around the edges and almost as smooth as glass across the top. Every growth ring was clearly defined and there appeared to be thousands of rings. It was long enough that a man as tall as Bother Gabriel could lie on it with both arms extended and not reach the edges by a foot or more, in every direction.

My first thought was who would have commissioned such a royal table as this to be built for a dark cellar room? The splendor of this table almost made me forget what we were there to see.

"That be an amazing table, be it not?" Asa saw me gawking at it.

"Yes, Asa," I said, never lifting my eyes from the table. "I've never seen anything like it."

Brother Gabriel took over, "That table hath a history as rich and interesting as the building in which it be housed, Raffe, but we should be leaving that historical discussion for another day. What we be having here," he continued, as he laid a stack of large old parchments on the massive table, "are the original manuscripts, made by monks, of the Rune inscriptions from hundreds of years ago; and, some are believed to be from thousands of years ago."

I remember thinking, WOW, very old can still be old, even in 1690.

I initially hesitated to touch the documents because I knew that the oils on our hands would eventually cause harm to them, but I also knew that neither of these men has any such knowledge, and this was not the time to educate them about bacteria.

The entire stack of documents looked the same to me with short vertical lines on them. Most of the documents had writing around the edges which Gabriel said was Latin. I was glad to hear him say he could read both.

Brother Gabriel explained to both of us, "These records spake of everyday life and record major events to identify when the inscriptions be originally made; however, the documents which may be of greatest interest to Raffe, are those which refer to 'The Passing.'"

"The *Passing*? What's The Passing?" I asked both men.

Without speaking, Asa walked over to the only door in the room, pressed his ear against the old oak surface and listened for a few seconds. He then braced one of the heavy oak chairs against the inside of the door. He returned to the edge of the table to give Gabriel a little nod indicating that we were alone.

Gabriel continued in whisper tones. "'The Passing' be a myth, supposedly, of legendary proportions. A legend what some strongly be believing, some deny, and some be having ye killed for spaking about."

As if I needed to be convinced of anything *strange* happening recently, I asked the dumbest question I could think of. "What do you mean by '*Passing*'?"

"That be the mystery, Raffe," Asa answered. "These documents record many Passing's and the names of those who be impacted by those events. We still be having a lot of missing pieces to the mystery."

Gabriel smacked his big hand down on the stack of old documents and I noticed that there wasn't any dust on them. I asked him, "Do you read these papers every day?"

"What be 'papers?'" Gabriel asked. He could see that I was focusing on the old documents and concluded, "Oh, ye must be meaning these old parchments. Ye be having to learn to spake like us if ye be wishing to keep that young head on yer shoulders, Lad. These be parchments, made from animal skins. Why do you ask?"

I casually explained, "I noticed that they don't have any dust on them like everything else in this room."

This brought some raised eyebrows from both men. "That be a very good observation, Lad," Asa remarked, "and I'd be hating for someone else to be making the same observation. Wouldn't ye agree, Gabriel?"

Gabriel nodded in agreement as he said, "I guess we be of help to each *other*, Raffe. Thanks to ye for being so observant. To answer yer question: yes. I be reading these parchments just about every day and I be finding this one most mysterious and disturbing."

Gabriel pulled the third parchment from the top of the stack and shoved the rest towards the center of the table. He drew three candles closer and placed his selected document on the table before him. Asa was on one side of him; and me, on the other. Using his thick index finger as a pointer, he studied a line or two of the Rune lines of text.

I impetuously asked, "What does it *say*?" was met with a quick turn of Gabriel's huge head and a nose-to-nose response which needed no words. The strong message: 'I'll read it when I'm damned good and ready and not a second before!' I smiled, a bit sheepishly, and looked back at the document.

After a few seconds of concentration, on Gabriel's part, and a glance at me, he began. The monk read each phonetic syllable by itself as if they were single words. "In the... 'time' of... '36', the people be traveling on the...   'Je-Tar Plaines' and spake round the earth with the... 'Light of the Saints' or 'Saint of Lights.'"

As I listened to Gabriel read, my ears put individual sounds into groups which implied words that were familiar to me. "Could "Saint of Lights" be read as, "Sat 'a' Lights?", I asked the Monk.

"Yes. On 'Foe-nez,'" he added.

I could hardly believe what I thought I heard Gabriel reading and asked him to read it again but faster, if possible. My request was initially met with Gabriel's scowl that melted into a curiosity of his own, and he complied.

Gabriel read, "In the time of 36, the people will journey on the 'Je-Tar Plaines' and spake around the earth with the 'Saint of Lights' on 'Fo-nez.'"

I remarked, "I believe those last marks are pronounced 'Phones,' Gabriel, uh Brother Gabriel, but the 'time of 36' doesn't make any sense to me. Would you read it again, and this time, read it exactly as the runes sound it out?"

The monk studied the series of marks and read, "In the... 'time', or 'year'... of 'twenty'... plus 'sixteen', or '36', the people..."

"THAT'S IT!" I shouted, loud enough to scare both of them. "In the year '2016'... 2016 is *my current year!*... or at least it *was* up until a few weeks ago. And I believe the rest of those Runes read as: 'The people will travel on 'jet planes' and talk around the earth with 'satellites' on their 'phones.'"

I was feeling pretty smart about myself, at that moment, but Asa and Gabriel were just staring at me! And they were not happy. "Of *course*, you don't understand. How *could* you know that there's a great difference between a place called 'Je-Tar Plaines,' which isn't a plain named Je-Tar but a 'flying machine'... a 'jet airplane?' or 'Saint of Lights' means 'satellites?' And 'Foe-nez' makes as much sense to you as 'phones' in this point of history."

Brother Gabriel looked at me intently and asked me a question which sounded very accusatory. "Might ye be playing with the way these words be *spaking* as if *changing* them will be making them hath more *meaning?*"

"NO. Because these words only mean something to *me* when they are spoken the way of the year 2016," I answered as sincerely as he asked.

"Be these some sort of magic words that must be spoke in a special way to be working their evil?" Asa asked.

I could see that they were expecting the worst from these ancient Druid writings and I had to find a way of communicating their benign nature as mechanical and electronic inventions.

"No, Asa," I began to explain. "These words are only words to describe objects and machines in the time when I used to live." Maybe that wasn't the best way to start this explanation. I could imagine the gears in their heads grinding to a burning halt when I mentioned, "the time when I used to live".

Just like his twin, Gabriel gave the order, "Drop anchor, Lad! Do ye be knowing *where* these parchments be coming from?

I shook my head, 'no.'

"Ye be knowing how *old* these parchments be? Or, how old the *Runes* from which they be copied might be, afore ye be making remarks ye just spoke?"

I never stopped shaking my head. "No," was all I could say to the obvious ire I saw in Gabriel's face.

"Allow me to be giving ye some history afore ye attempt to spew so much knowledge from yer young mind," was Gabriel's next counsel.

I realized that I was overly excited at what I just heard, and I expected too much of these men. Listening, instead of speaking, would be the best policy here because Gabriel was the key to what's contained in these amazing documents.

"I'm *very* sorry, Brother Gabriel," I said, and I meant it. "I thought I heard something that sounded so *familiar* to me and I spoke too soon. *Please* keep on reading."

Gabriel re-focused on the parchment, with a hint of a smile. "According to Latin notes what be in the margins, these Runes be discovered on the wall of a cave on the Island of Anglesey. It be believed to be a record left by a Druid priest who witnessed the Roman slaughter of nearly all of his kinsman. The text be describing many things but be making no sense, but the historical years and events be verified as accurate." Gabriel slowly turned his head toward me and gently held an eye-lock with me.

I assured him, "I'm not going to say anything until you ask."

He smiled and spoke to the parchment, "That wouldst be nice; if it happens."

Asa was smiling from ear to ear with impish delight at my learning to respect a man he has respected and admired for many years.

"This inscription be very interesting because it refers to the author's birth location." Gabriel searched the parchment for the Rune marks which he had studied many times before. When his finger stopped, I could see that the parchment was smudged, no doubt, with the oil from many fingers.

"Here it be," Gabriel remarked, as he brought a fourth candle closer with his left hand. "I, 'Amergus,' be born 'Lynn-Wayne' in the time of... 123, be an 'Elder' of the priesthood of the Druid people... 'taken-in' by the Druids for I be not Druid in me youth." He looked up at me. "Do any of these words sound 'familiar' to ye, Raffe?" Gabriel asked.

I answered, "Could you read the, 'in the time of' and the numbers, again, for me? ... and sound out the numbers *exactly* as the original text recorded them, please? It may mean something that way." Gabriel wasn't the least bit bothered to

48

repeat the words. "I, 'Amergus,' be born 'Lynn-Wayne' in the time... "

Gabriel was interrupted by an intrusive knocking on the chamber's door. Three knocks... one knock... three knocks, on the door, and the three of us stood in silence as Asa and Gabriel exchanged concerned looks.

Gabriel whispered, "There be soldiers at the outer gate, Asa. I thought ye spoke that no one knew ye be here?"

That's interesting, I thought, these monks have an internal warning system. Nice to know.

Asa looked as puzzled as Gabriel and me, when he responded, "I be certain we be noticed *not* as we be traveling here. They may be here for any number of reasons. Don't be jumping to conclusions or act suspicious, without good cause."

"Raffe," said Gabriel, "ye be seeing where I found these parchments, please return them to that shelf... not be disturbing anything 'round them."

I carried the stack and placed them back on the shelf, but immediately noticed the distinct difference between the parchment Gabriel had just read and the stacks on either side. The other stacks were dulled with years of undisturbed dust and the 'Druid texts' we were reading, were smooth and dust free.

We stood in silence as we listened to the pounding on the monastery's front door, over our heads. Asa extinguished more than half of the candles. We could hear the hinges groan with the weight of the massive oak doors, as they were swung open. This was followed by the thumps of several sets of heavy boots as they made their way across the cathedral floor above us.

I very carefully took the top parchment from the fourth stack to my left, and placed it on top of the stack of Druid parchments, and quickly re-joined my friends.

The instant I was at Gabriel's side, he leaned close to my ear and whispered, "Do ye solemnly swear to spake not another *word* until I be giving ye permission, so help ye *God*? Answer me 'yes,' right now."

I was staring at the door because I could hear the approach of many feet, but I still managed to whisper, "yes."

Asa was fussing with something around his neck. He produced a bright colored scarf which he flipped to the outside of his shirt and spread it out so all of its colors and the embroidered crest could be clearly seen. Asa was just full of surprises.

I was very glad to be standing in the middle of my two new friends, with the large table between us and the door. When the soldiers pushed their way in, their leader stood front and center, and his four lackies spread out, two on either side, in front of the shelves of parchments.

Gabriel didn't wait for the soldier to speak. "Who be *ye* and what be bringing ye *here*?"

The lean soldier appeared to resent losing his edge by not speaking first, and looked around the room as if he were considering not answering at all.

Asa spoke up and addressed him as his lessor. The tone was the unmistakable voice of the 'Asa (hole)' from my miserable first night in the pub. "The monk asked ye a *question, stranger.* Do ye intend to be making the monk wait all day for the *answer*?"

The soldier was bitten by the words and snapped his focus onto Asa, and then to his bright red scarf, just in time to silence him. It was then that I noticed the crest on Asa's scarf, which was the same crest emblazoned on the breastplate of this soldier. His entire demeanor changed, and his head tipped slightly forward.

The soldier mumbled, "I be begging yer humble pardon, me Lord."

Asa ignored the soldier's request and replied, "Ye be having *yet* to reply to my friend's *question*."

The soldier nodded towards Asa and addressed his reply to Gabriel. "I be the King's servant and we be seeking those be going mad within the last month."

The soldier didn't wait for any reply. He turned directly toward me and demanded, "Who *ye be* and what be yer *business* here?" I froze in my tracks.

"He be having no answer for ye," I heard Gabriel say in an authoritative voice.

"He WILL answer me," the soldier retorted, "or there be trouble, I *assure* ye."

The monk was unruffled by the soldiers or their weapons. "As a novice, he be taking a sacred oath of silence this day, before God. He be spaking *not* to *any* man, for any .reason."

"He will spake to my *blade* or he will spake to yer God *face-to-face,* monk," was the soldier's taunting reply.

Asa stepped in front of Gabriel and me, before he spoke directly into the soldier's face, "I be forced to address ye *once* this day, and it displeased me terribly. I be seeing that I be *again* required to utter words in your direction, soldier of the King, but *only* for the sake of a young man who is my *charge* and under my *protection!* Have ye any idea how swiftly yer head can be placed on the end of a *pike* should I desire to be *seeing* it there? Force me to speak to ye *once more* this day, and I assure *thee* of this: you will not be seeing the sun set today. *ARE WE CLEAR?*"

The color left the soldier's face almost as quickly as the five soldiers left the room. We listened to their footsteps retreat across the cathedral floor and out through the great doors where they had entered. We all stood motionless until...

One knock... three knocks... one knock... three knocks... was sounded through the chapel floor.

"They may be gone," said Gabriel, "but they not be gone for long. Their leader was suspicious and too ready to shed blood for answers. Raffe, I release ye from yer vow of silence. Ye can spake now, if ye wish."

I reported, "I saw the others looking around while their leader was talking. They appeared to know what they were looking for, but I didn't see them touch anything."

Gabriel walked immediately to the stack of parchments he had selected before the soldiers arrived. He thumbed through the top few and said, "My parchment be missing!" I assured him that it was safe and showed him where I hid it as the soldiers were getting closer.

"Very clever thinking, Lad," Gabriel said, "but hath the soldiers taken ye, we might have ne'er be knowing where to *look.*"

"The Lad be using some fast thinking, Gabriel, and he deserves credit for it," praised Asa.

I asked, respectfully, "Brother Gabriel, can we get back to reading the parchment? You read some words that maybe made sense to me."

I retrieved the single parchment that Gabriel had read from. I could see that there were hundreds, perhaps thousands, of parchments of Rune writing filling the shelves. Asa was re-lighting the candles. I wanted to ask him about his scarf and the way he could order the soldiers around, but that would have to wait for some other time.

I placed the parchment at the edge of the table, surrounded on three sides by candles. Gabriel searched for the portion of the Runes where he had been reading.

"Here it be," said Gabriel and he began to read again. "I, 'Amergus,' be born 'Lynn-Wayne' in the time of... 123, be an 'Elder' of the priesthood of the Druid people. I be 'taken-in' by the Druids for I be not Druid in me youth."

"Why do you pause before you read the 'time of' number?" I asked.

"Because the numbers be written as two double numbers which I be having to add together before I spake the time it be," replied Gabriel.

"You read this way earlier, when you identified '20' and '16' as the number '36,' Brother Gabriel, what are the two numbers here? And could the word for 'time of' be read as 'the year of?'"

"Yes, the two be interchangeable according to the subject," Gabriel answered. "The two double-numbers be, 'in the year 29 and 94'. Does that help?"

"They don't mean anything to me," I said, and it was a disappointment because the '20' and '16' were so familiar.

Gabriel added, "The two double numbers are repeated several times, and always in the same order."

"Ah," I said with renewed vigor. "You said there were accurate events recorded in this parchment?"

"I be believing there are statements recorded here," Gabriel replied, "which be as accurate as anything I found, for they agree with the Jewish Roman historian, Joseph ben Matityahu."

"That is impressive because I recognize that name from high school and college." I responded.

"There you go again, Raffe," countered Asa, "making claims of Biblical knowledge. Didn't ye tell me that ye studied 'Sociology' in that Dover college?"

"Asa, I owe you too many kindnesses and the last few weeks have been far too confusing for me to understand what has happened to me, but, as I shared with you, I attended a 'Denver' community college and , yes, I majored in Sociology, but I also learned many things in other academic fields. I'm asking both of you to be patient and understanding right now. I'm not lying to you, Asa, and I don't have any answers beyond the few things I happen to recognize as Gabriel reads these documents."

Looking back at the document before us, I felt free to speak my thoughts. "I get the feeling that this 'Amergus' or 'Linwane' and I have a connection."

Gabriel corrected me, "The second name is 'Lynn' and 'Wayne'— it be two words."

"Well," I said, "that does sound more like a name to me. 'Lynn Wayne' may not be a common name, but it definitely sounds more like the kind of names I heard back in 2016." I had to smile at my own words... back in 2016. "Could we read something more about this 'Lynn Wayne?" I asked.

Gabriel turned his focus to the parchment once again. "I, Àmergus, born 'Lynn Wayne' in the year 29-94, be an 'Elder' of the priesthood of the Druid people. I am 'taken-in' by the Druids for I be not Druid in me youth."

"I'm trying to read this in the manner ye be describing to us as being familiar with yer way of spaking, Raffe," Gabriel explained. "How be it sounding?"

"You're doing just fine, and I'd like to hear more, please."

Gabriel read on, "My years, or age, at my Passing was 19. There were many who passed with me. Those who passed with me be dead. The time of this record be the year of the great Roman invasion."

Asa added the comment, "There be many references on this and *other* parchments about 'passings,' Raffe, but only *this* parchment contains multiples of numbers which may be significant."

"It would be helpful," I said, "if I had something to write on and we could take notes to compare dates, names and events."

Asa looked at me with a combination of challenge and amazement and asked, "Ye can write?"

"Of course, I can, Asa." I laughed. It was obvious to me tnat Asa was having trouble accepting my academic abilities. I began to wonder a little about the original Raffe and what sort of man he was. It was only then that the fleeting thought came to me: 'If I'm here in Raffe's body, what became of the original Raffe?' I had to push this thought aside for later, and focus on the immediate situation.

Gabriel walked to a cabinet at the back of the room, and pulled out a ring of old odd sized keys from a pocket in his robe. He unlocked one of the drawers, and pulled out a rolled sheet of parchment and sticks of dried clay. After spreading out the parchment and weighting down the corners with candles, he handed me the sticks of clay. I didn't recognize the four sticks until I noticed they had a black core. These were writing instruments... crude pencils.

"Raffe, Lad, choose ye weapon," Gabriel said with a smile.

I examined the clay pencils. I could see that this was going to be a bit of a challenge. Interesting that the clay pencils were actually well made. I chose the one most similar in diameter to a wooden pencil because it would feel familiar. "I'm sure I can manage with a little practice. Let's start with the times we know for a certainty." In my mind, I wanted to ask Gabriel if he had an iPad but kept that not-so-funny joke to myself.

I continued, "How about we call this Druid, Lynn, and start with a date we can identify in these records. You mentioned 'the great Roman invasion. Was this the invasion of Gnaeus Julius Agricola in 60 AD?" I asked, "Is there any mention of Hadrian's Wall? It is historically believed that the wall was completed in 122 AD."

"Clever, Lad!" Asa exclaimed. "That most certainly be the great Roman Wall built in 122 AD."

Excitedly, I remarked, "I'm glad *you* knew that, Asa. Because we now know the exact year in which these Runes were inscribed on the wall of that cave, but we need to read more information from this parchment."

Every time I heard Gabriel read the word 'Passing' I got this knot in my stomach as if my name was being called and I was the only one who could hear it. From the way the Runes spoke of 'The Passing,' I was certain that it was a major event, but I couldn't comprehend what kind of an event. My mind kept having flash-back images of Jake, a *black ball* growing in the sky and me waking up in the piss corner."

I gripped the clay pencil and wrote down "Lynn"... "Passed in 2994 at age 19"... "Runes made in 122 AD."

Asa was watching me and mumbled, "I be bloodied, he be *writing*."

Feeling validated, somewhat, I asked Gabriel, "Let's see what other times, places and pieces of information we can find in this parchment."

Gabriel asked, "What do you think Lynn meant by 'many passed with me?'"

"I'm not certain, but I'm beginning to have some thoughts that this 'Lynn Wayne' had an experience similar to mine... the night Gavan and Asa carried my body, Raffe's body, out of the pub."

"What do you mean?" Asa asked. "Ye be not making any sense to me."

I confessed, "I'm not making a lot of sense to myself, either, Asa, but I'm the one with a weird experience and can't be put into natural words. I have been completely honest with you and Gavan, even when it sounded like a lie. Maybe, just maybe this parchment, or others in this room, has the information we need to answer our questions."

Gabriel stood by quietly listening to every word before he spoke. "There be more information in this parchment, Raffe, and I be waiting for many years to find someone with the knowledge to be explaining some of the mysteries. Maybe that person be thee. This 'Lynn' has listed quite a few 'times' or 'years' that may hold the key to why the King's soldiers be here today, and in Ramsgate a few days ago, searching for people thought to be crazy. It may also explain why spaking about 'a Passing' outside of this room could get you killed."

Gabriel continued, "Let me find the place on this parchment where the times be listed, and we be seeing if they be meaning anything."

I spoke my thoughts. "Maybe we already know of two: 2994 and 2016."

Gabriel studied the parchment filled with small lines of black ink marks. They all made perfect sense to him, but it was a page of tick-marks to me.

"I believe I have found them." Gabriel began to read, "Knowledge of the Passing was known to all in my first time. The Passing event took souls in old, or ancient, times. Times of Passing 60, 386, 712, 10 and 38, 13 and 64, 16 and 90, 20 and 16, 23 and 42, 26 and 68, 29 and 94. There be more," Gabriel said, "... but no more numbers."

"I wrote those numbers down without the 'and' in them, like we did the '2016' and '2994'. The sequence of numbers had exactly *326 years* between each 'time' identified, and one of them is the year 1690! *THIS YEAR.*"

"If I be understanding ye correctly," Gabriel observed, "ye be saying that this Druid priest, who was a lad of 19 years, in the year 2994, scratched a prediction into a stone wall of a cave in the year 122. A prediction that there be a 'Passing' this year, 1690."

I was amazed that this monk grasped the concept of time both future and past.

Asa just said, "What the 'ell the two of ye be spaking about?"

Gabriel didn't explain anything to Asa, he just said, "let me translate a few more texts which may mean something to ye,

56

Raffe, before I attempt to give you the answers you may not be wanting to hear, Asa." I could hear the excitement in Gabriel's voice. He recognized the threshold of discovery and he was obviously excited.

It was clear to me that this monk had been studying these parchments for many years. My reactions to the things, which made perfect sense to my 2016 mind, were like light bulbs being turned on for him. (Mental note: light bulb, more words *not* to use in 1690.)

Once again, Gabriel turned his focus to the parchment laid on the massive table, "In the time of me youth, the knowledge of the Passings be known by everyone. In my time as a Druid, the knowledge of the Passings be known by only a few. With the moving of the soul was also the moving of knowledge."

Gabriel stopped reading and looked at me for a second as if I was supposed to say something, so I did.

The only thing I could think to say, "What?"

Gabriel repeated the last text with the question, "Does this mean anything to ye, Raffe? ... With the moving of the soul be also the moving of knowledge."

For some reason, I knew Gabriel was asking a question that had an answer he was almost afraid of. He and Asa stared at me in silence until I felt compelled to say something.

I asked, "Have you used every word in the only possible way that it can be interpreted?"

" Of course not," Gabriel responded. "I'm translating as close as I can, but there almost always be room for other word choices. The word 'soul' used by this Druid could mean several things: knowledge, personality, character, or belief. I be just using a word that be easiest to understand. Another difficult word to translate is the word he used for 'moving.' It be not like the word for hauling a cart or carrying a log... this word be more like smoke in the wind or a mist caught in the first rays of sunlight."

I was very impressed with the intellectual depth of the Druids and this monk but, I still didn't find any identity with the text Gabriel just read. I suggested that he read it once more and translate the Druid words with those he personally felt might be the most appropriate. I wasn't expecting *this*.

Gabriel wasn't even looking at the parchment when he spoke these words, "With the transferring of our consciousness be also the transferring of our knowledge."

"What did you just say?" I had to hear it again.

Gabriel repeated the words as if he had rehearsed them in his mind a million times. "With the transferring of our consciousness be also the transferring of our knowledge."

"OK, Gabriel, Asa, how much do the two of you know about me that I do not know about myself? I have a feeling that I'm not in this monastery by accident and I'm being introduced to something really weird but important."

"Ye be quite correct on all counts, Brody," said Gabriel.

That was a shock in of itself. Gabriel addressed me as Brody, so it was obvious to me that Asa had told him about my 2016 name. What else am I about to hear that will either comfort or disturb me, for the rest of my life?

Gabriel interrupted my self-pity thoughts by saying, "I be noticing how ye be admiring this great table before us. Would you like to know its name and history?"

"Yes, I would," was the only answer. A table with it's own name?

Gabriel and Asa stood side by side as if they were preforming a ceremony of some sort. Asa suggested that we each have a seat.

"This may be taking a while to be explaining the 'what, where and how' this table came into existence."

Gabriel asked me to close the door, left open by the hasty exit of the soldiers, before I took my seat.

As I turned back from the door, I could see the reflections of both Gabriel and Asa in the mirror smooth surface of the great table. It appeared as if there were four men instead of two, in this darkened room, two being perfect opposites to the others. I sat across from my friends with what I thought was some inkling of what I was about to hear but actually, I didn't have the first clue.

"First," Gabriel said, "allow me to introduce you to the 'Grand Table of Consciousness.'"

I instinctively ran my hands across the amazingly soft and smooth surface of this large and beautifully crafted table. It was far more than a banquette table or a conference table and much too thick in the legs to be a kitchen or domestic table of any kind. This table had a way of making you feel important and needed. It's intricate lines of ancient rings of life told that it had been here from the beginning of life on this planet. This all seemed a bit out of place for a Monastery but right now, I'm just here to learn.

"'SPLENDUS MENSA de CONSCIENTIA' was crafted in the year 392, and we've already done the cyphering for ye, Lad," said Gabriel, "that's just six years after the '386 Passing.'"

I didn't want to speak at this moment. I just wanted to hear what this monk had to say. I could see that Gabriel was reading my hunger, and my fear, revealing too much about the thoughts in my mind. I found myself identifying with the Druid priest who wisely chose to leave his message in stone on the cave wall instead of out in the open for anyone to find.

I remember seeing something carved into the edges of this great table, so I got up from my chair and took one of the candles to illuminate the table's edge. There in deep relief were the Latin inscriptions centered on each side, 'SPLENDUS MENSA de CONSCIENTIA - CCCXCII' The Grand Table of Consciousness - 392. Of course, I couldn't read the Latin words, but I could read the Roman numerals.

"This is a really impressive name for a very beautiful table, Brother Gabriel, but who named it and why?" Gabriel and Asa both smiled at me in unison as if they were about to play a trick on me and I was helpless to prevent it.

"That, Brody," Gabriel began, "be why ye be sitting in that chair, at this table, in this room, this monastery, in England and breathing the air of 1690, instead of 2016."

Chapter 5
The Link Between 2994 AD and 60 AD

I don't know how long the three of us sat staring across the table at one another, but it didn't feel as if it was minutes and seconds which passed as much as ages measured in centuries. How much do these guys know? What are they not telling me? Should I be weary of them? What choice do I have? These two men, and Gavan, are the only friends I have in *this* world.

"Where do we go from here," I asked staring at the space between my friends. Gabriel was the obvious scholarly leader of the two, but Asa was every bit his equal in intelligence.

"Around the 'Grand Table of Consciousness' be the one place where we can share any and all knowledge," Gabriel began. "It be for this purpose the table be made, and every 326 years, new members be found and brought here to share their personal 'consciousness' with the remaining members from the last Passing."

"OK," I interrupted, "am I hearing you say people live long enough to be here from one of these Passings until the *next* one, 326 years later?"

"No, that be absurd!" snapped Asa, always ready with his sharp tongue. "What we be saying, be that to be identified as someone with a 'transferred consciousness' in the year of a Passing, or the years following a Passing, be having a death warrant with ye name on it."

"WHAT? I haven't done anything *wrong*. Those soldiers were looking for crazy people and I'm not crazy... a bit confused, maybe, but I'm not crazy, so they weren't looking for me."

"Just the way ye *spake* be cause for them to arrest ye and place ye in their dungeon, Lad," quipped Asa. "I be after ye to mind the way ye spoke from the first time we met."

"I have been accumulating a lot of questions," I pleaded, "and I'm about to burst if I can't get some answers. My first question is: if my 'consciousness' has 'transferred' into this person, Raffe, where's Raffe?" I just kept looking back and forth between them until Gabriel responded.

"Exactly where or when Raffe be, we not be knowing. But from what I understand from the Runes inscribed by Amergus or Lynn Wayne of 2994, Raffe be in any one of the other years of Passing... past or future... and we be having no way of knowing which one... unless it be one in the past, and he be writing a message which survived for us to read. The 'where' be e'en more difficult to be knowing because the transfer of souls be always in a very narrow location which be the closest to the Passing — at that moment when it passes the earth. Iffen that location be over the ocean, there be no transfers. If that location is over a city, there could be hundreds, or e'en thousands, of transfers. When someone with an *education* is transferred, like Lynn Wayne/Amergus, they be having the ability to *leave a record* of their existence in their new time. Because Raffe had no education, he be having no way of leaving a record, unless he received an education after his transfer."

I'm sure my eyes were blinking much more rapidly than usual because my brain was being fried with the information Gabriel was giving me. I *had* to ask, "Then how would I *return to my own time? Or is it even POSSIBLE?"*

Both men slowly shook their heads, 'no,' as Gabriel explained, "There ne'er be found any writing which describes a 'return'. With 326 years between Passings, them which be transferred must stay where they find themselves. For you, dear Lad, that be 1690."

I looked down at the parchment on which I had written the list of dates, as Gabriel had translated, to give myself some sort of time perspective. I *had* to concentrate on the academics before us, to drive out the natural impulse for *panic*. It was much easier to intellectually realize that I was stuck in 1690, and might never return to *my* time, than to feel like I belonged here.

To control my urge to panic, I focused on the factual evidence before us. The earliest date listed by this Amergus was

266 BC, followed by 60 AD, 386 AD, 712 AD, 1038 AD, 1364 AD, 1690 AD, 2016 AD, 2342 AD, 2668 AD and 2994 AD. I found myself wondering if there were more to add to either end, and how many? I also couldn't avoid thinking about the Consciousness of the Raffe who once occupied this body. In which of the Passing years is he now struggling to exist or survive?

I heard a friendly voice say, "If ye not careful, Lad, ye *really be* going crazy." It was Asa, and there was no sharpness in his voice. He was speaking with warmth and tenderness as if he were helping me take my first intellectual baby steps in a new and frightening world.

I challenged them, "How can you know all of this in 1690, and I've never heard of any such theories or 'The Passing' events in 2016? This kind of knowledge would be spread all over the world. You can't *hide* something like this!"

"*YES*," Gabriel explained in a sinister tone, "There be ways; IF ye be killing everyone with the *knowledge* of the Passings."

"How can that many people be found and killed over intervals of 326 years?" I skeptically asked.

"By dynasties, monarchies and empires manipulated by controlling families, Raffe," Gabriel explained. "Allow me to be reading more from the Amergus Runes when he was very old." Gabriel pulled the parchment closer and placed two candles close, but never close enough to drip wax on his treasured parchments. "Here it be. 'Romans came to be killing all Druids, with untrue stories of Druid sacrifices and be using human offerings. This be a Roman lie, to be hiding the true reason, to kill all of us. In time of 60 Passing, Rome hath transfer of souls. These transferred souls became   leaders in Rome, now they come to be killing all Druids, to be killing Druids with transferred souls."

"Did ye catch all that, Lad?" Asa asked, "Someone had their consciousness transferred from the future back to Rome in 60 AD and used their knowledge to be getting ready for the *next* Passing, and then be killing those people in the next Passing, by claiming that they be exercising human sacrifice."

"I understand the plot, Asa, but did Amergus say who was transferred back to Rome in 60 AD?"

"No," Gabriel answered, "we be having only the dates and locations of these Passings. We also be having someone, or a family, who be using their knowledge for evil, and that be what we be up against today. That be why this table be built and why it be in the basement of a monastery."

"That's why ye be in grave danger, Lad," added Asa. "Just as we of The Consciousness be knowing a Passing was going to happen, so did our King. And he has his soldiers searching for so-called crazy people within the month, for a Transferred Consciousness dunna spake, think or act as the locals. We be learning enough to know that whoever be transferred be in Southern England but it be not likely they spake the King's English, or English at all, and they be easy to find."

Gabriel added, "The Consciousness' be hoping for transfers from years beyond yers, Raffe. We be hoping they be knowing which families had transferred members from the past and other helpful information for us."

I asked, "Will your group try to do the same things with this information that others have done in the past, Gabriel?"

Gabriel answered, "It appears that the answer to ye question lay in the fact that ye ne'er heard of the Passing or The Consciousness, in 2016, Raffe." Gabriel's tone implied that I had much to learn.

From my first introduction, I felt that I could trust Gabriel, but his words here required pure faith on the lack of evidence, rather than trusting in evidential records of any kind. Why was Asa constantly reminding me of impending danger when, so far, everything has been verbal threats from men in fancy uniforms?

Two bumps... one bump... two bumps ... were heard on the thick oak ceiling of this chamber, the floor of the main Chapel.

"The monastery has a visitor," Gabriel interpreted the coded message for me. Reading the concern in my eyes, he

64

added, "The soldiers have a code of their own. This could be anyone, for any reason."

"Do the monks here keep watch all of the time for anyone approaching?" I asked.

Asa answered. "The watch be kept both day and night without fail, Lad, for hundreds of years. The faithful be keeping the watch in this monastery and several others of The Consciousness."

Gabriel and Asa returned their focus on the parchment for only a few seconds before we heard the shuffle of footsteps on the floor above us. The distraction made it impossible to do anything but listen for their direction of travel.

Gabriel whispered, "I be fearing this may involve us. I be hearing someone coming." A very soft but fretful voice spoke through the door in Latin and Gabriel's face grew anxious. When the message was delivered, the messenger shuffled away.

Gabriel looked at me sternly and said, "Raffe, ye *must* be staying in this *room*." Then he looked at Asa and spoke a single word, "Come!" Gabriel ran out and Asa closed the door, behind them both.

I listened for the sound of a bolt or lock because I did not want to hear one. I did not care to be locked in a cellar chamber of a monastery by myself with nothing but my imagination for company. Suddenly, I could hear excited men's voices, but they were too muffled to understand, and some shuffling of feet.

Finally, a familiar voice rose above the others and roared out, "The Lad has a right to *know*! If *ye* won't tell him, I *shall*!"

Gavan! I *knew* that voice! How did he get here? What do I need to know? I was torn between trusting and obeying Gabriel and wanting to see and hear Gavan. I thought I should stay right where I was and wait. Once again, I found myself listening to the unfolding event of my life through that big oak door. I listened to the approaching of footsteps down the old wooden steps, by several men, and the short walk from the bottom of the steps to this door. I wasn't quite sure how to greet Gavan, my constant friend and guide, in 1690, until Asa and I fled Ramsgate. We never learned what happened after we left. No news is good news? I stood back in anticipation of seeing my new old friend again.

When the door opened, I wasn't at all prepared for Gavan's condition and I was stunned by his appearance. His left arm was in a black-with-blood sling and his left leg was wrapped with an equally nasty looking bloody-rag.

Gavan answered my question about how to greet him. He grabbed my shoulder and then gave me a wrap-around bear hug with his right arm. Tears of joy, which he made no attempt to wipe away, rolled down the round cheeks and disappeared into his beard. I was still standing like a corner post with my arms at my sides.

Gavan said, "I be the only hugger in this room?" He leaned in to administer another half-bear hug. This time, I threw my arms around him, being careful of his obviously injured left arm.

I gushed, "Oh *WOW*! I can't tell you how good it is to see you, Gavan." I gave his wounds a quick survey.

Gavan made his way towards one of the chairs. Asa and Gabriel helped him ease into it. "Things not be looking good for us in Ramsgate, Lad." Gavan began his story with gasping breaths.

Asa chimed in, "Gavan, run ye mouth while Gabriel and I tend to ye wounds. I be looking forward to hearing this *tale* of yers so don't stop spaking if ye feel a little pinch now and then." I sat next to Gavan to try and divert his attention as Gabriel and Asa began unwrapping the bloody rags.

I could see Asa's eyes wincing and welling up, as he surveyed Gavan's wounds. They were deep, dirty, several days old, and no one had tended to them before now. Gavan tried to talk as smoothly as possible, as his breathing was still labored.

I had to ask, "Is there nothing for *PAIN*."

"NO," quickly stated, "Gavan, keep spaking..."

"*YES*," announced Gabriel, as he got up and went to the back of the room, pulled out that ring of keys and attacked the cabinet. He rushed back to Gavan with a small bottle and placed it in his thick hand. "No questions, just *drink*, Gavan."

Gavan tossed the contents into his mouth and after his eyebrows jumped and he coughed a few times, he laughed, "Ye be an old dog with a bone... hiding yer prize brew from yer brother and friends!"

"Keep *spaking*, Gavan, we be needing to hear what *happened*." said Gabriel.

Whatever was in the small bottle Gabriel gave Gavan, it had an immediate effect. I was expecting Gavan to wince and complain as his arm and leg were being scrubbed and re-opened to prevent infection, but he didn't seem to notice.

I tried to distract Gavan's focus with the obvious question, "How did you get out of Ramsgate?"

"As ye and Asa left," Gavan began, "I looked about for me own best way to leave in another direction, if there be trouble, so... OW... so I quickly make a hole in the back wall, where the soldiers not be seeing me... AH... should I be needing to skedaddle." Apparently, Gavan was feeling some discomfort, but he didn't want to surrender to it.

Asa said, "We stopped long enough to be seeing the town gossip directing the soldiers to your home."

"That he did, Asa, and it cost him *dearly,*" Gavan responded, with a slight tone of remorse in his voice. "I waited just inside my door and as they got close, I shouted, 'Ye've already *been* here. No *needing* to check here *again.*'"

Asa couldn't resist, "And ye be thinking they would just turn on their heels and leave?"

Gavan shot back with a friend's dirty look and continued, "NO, Asa, they didn't go away, but the leader of the soldiers did send the Gossip in, rather than one or two of his soldiers. Once he was inside, I whispered, asking what the hell he did. He spake of his fear and he all but cried with fear as he be telling me. He said that he spake to the soldiers of Raffe be spaking strange for a couple weeks and he lived with me. I dunna be knowing, at that moment, that the leader of the soldiers be listening on the other side of me door.

The first words I heard from outside were, 'Pierce the door!' from their leader, and four swords rammed through me door! Two sword blades be thrusted on each side of the door.

The lad died before me eyes, in a silence he ne'er practiced in life, with one sword through his neck, and a second one through his heart. I be the more fortunate by my quick movement away from the door, but I still received these wounds from the tips of their blades."

"How did you get away?" I repeated. I could see that Gabriel was not taking this story very well, but he focused on tending his twin's wounds rather than panicking over the near loss of his brother.

"Patience, Lad!" Gavan chided, "I be doing the best I can. I lay Gossip's body against the door and pushed the table against it, as well, before I made my way to and out our new back door. I ne'er looked back to be seeing who or how many soldiers be behind me, until long after dark."

This is when Gavan gave Gabriel a knowing look and said, "I stopped at several Consciousness families along the way, but ne'er stayed longer than be needed, for water, food and information sharing. All be well and secure between here and Ramsgate, Gabriel, this area be completely secure."

What was that all about? Completely secure. Is this monastery some sort of safe zone?

Asa asked Gavan, "Be there something else ye need to spake to Raffe?"

"Yes. Ye may like hearing this, Lad. This Passing may be a major event. The consciousness of thousands may have been transferred. There are monks and peddlers searching for them all through the Southern half of England."

I'm sure the awkward look on my face was enough to cause Gavan to turn to Gabriel and ask, "Have ye not *told* him yet?"

"We be doing exactly *that* when ye dragged yer well-pierced self in here and interrupted us," teased Asa.

Gabriel, in his strong manner, spoke up, "We be needing to get ye to the Apothecary, Gavan, afore any more time passes. I be sure their medicines will be having ye back to health in a few days, but they must be starting immediately. Ye have lost a lot of blood."

Gavan was visibly comforted in the presence of his twin, but he had definitely been through an harrowing ordeal. My heart ached at the sight of Gavan's wounds and it was even more painful to recognize that his wounds were for my protection.

This Consciousness and secure area around this monastery sure had my curiosity revved up. I could see that these new friends, and me, by transfer, were all part of something much larger than a few monks in a secluded monastery.

Asa broke into my thoughts about this 1690 world I was in, and the familiar feelings I was beginning to enjoy with these men. They seem to know much more about me and my new life, than I do.

"Raffe, Lad, be giving me some help getting Gavan to the Apothecary," Asa requested, "and I will be spaking to ye, more about The Consciousness, as we go." I was more than eager for both and as the three of us were about to leave, Gabriel looked directly at Asa and gave a gentle warning.

"Not all knowledge be healthy to be knowing, at this time. Do ye agree?"

Asa looked back at Gabriel and then into Gavan's face for his response.

Gavan answered his twin, 'We fear no knowledge afore we be knowing the intentions, Gabriel."

Gabriel acknowledged this with, "It is true that we 'fear no knowledge afore we know the intentions,' Gavan, but me fear be for Raffe's safety and life, not be the result of knowledge we share with him. Raffe be far too recognizable as a stranger here and should he be discovered by the King's men, he'd be tortured to reveal everything we share with him. But, we be wasting time, Asa," his voice was most sober and sincere. "Please be extremely careful with my brother's safety."

Asa didn't respond verbally; we just let the big man put some of his weight on each of our shoulders as we exited the room. Asa looked as if Gabriel's request was almost an insult since he loved these twins equally, as though they were his own brothers.

Nothing could have made me more curious than to openly deny my information. This was a moment of faith for me. A moment I knew I had to trust my new 1690 friends with my life.

Gavan grew quiet as the three of us made our way along the long dormitory style annex of rooms which lay behind the main structure of the monastery. Every surface was kept tidy and the floors swept daily by the assignments given to monks, and guests alike, to justify the claim that, 'everyone in this Monastery be a working member of it.' Little did I know, at this moment, that this simple claim was to be a lifesaver for me.

We must have passed half a dozen doorways that looked very much alike before coming to the first one that was fully open instead of closed. The interior of this room was surprisingly bright with whitewashed walls that made a distinct contrast to everything else about this brick, stone and mortar building complex.

Asa didn't need to announce it but said, "Here we be, Lad. How be ye feeling, Gavan?"
Gavan admitted, "I felt a lot better and not long ago," and managed a little smirk for his friend.

This was not like anything I was expecting from 1690, not in the least! The floor was smooth hard-wood planks which had been coated with some sort of wax that gave the appearance of a linoleum or vinyl surface. The walls were lined with very neatly cut shelves which held finely crafted small clay and glass jars with identifying labels on every one of them. In the center of the room was a large examination table with a surface as smooth as the Grand Table of Consciousness. Every surface was brilliant white, except the floor, which made the two unusual features in the ceiling all the more noticeable. Centered above the examination table were two large trap doors, each about a yard square, with ropes and pulley systems for opening them. Waiting just inside the door was a young monk and standing beside the examination table stood a second.

The younger monk, Asa addressed as David, asked, "Be rhe safe?" as he looked at me.

Asa simply replied with one word, "New."

Gavan wrapped his arm tighter around me and glared at David, "He be with me and he *stays* with me. He be just fine. *I* be the one ye be needing to be concerned with right now; and by *right now*, I mean, *RIGHT NOW*."

The older monk, who had introduced himself as Matthew, gave a single command, "Come." With this word, David, Asa and I helped Gavan onto the examination table.

Gavan's wound on his arm was exposed when his shirt was removed. Both his arm and leg wounds had been left untreated for much too long and the flesh around each was bright red — not a good sign. It didn't appear that any serious infection had begun but the healing was going very slowly and there were obvious blood clots deep inside his muscles that the swelling and shirt had concealed.

As a former firefighter, I knew a few things about wound treatment but none of the equipment or medicines, familiar to me, would be available here in 1690. All I could do is watch and hope these ancient *healers* weren't about to pull some sort of weird mojo on my friend.

Asa asked the older monk, Matthew, "might this kind of wound be healing with light?"

Matthew looked at me, as he asked Asa, "*He* be having the knowledge of the healing light?"

Asa replied, "No, but ye be fixed on the task afore ye, for he be quick to learn, first-hand."

Gavan also answered, "He be about to be learning, but I be liking ye to be getting *on* with it, Brother Matthew."

Asa said Gavan's name slowly but with an odd tone, "Gaaavannn..."

"Oh, forgive me manners, Brother Caseous," Gavan said curtly, as a third man, wearing a white robe, entered the room. This 'Brother Caseous' was considerably older than Matthew and David. His white robe immediately set him apart from the others as did his stately demeanor and long black hair. Unlike the other members of this monastery, Brother Caseous, didn't shave the top of his head. If 1690 has taught me anything, it has taught me that *I have a LOT to learn.*

The monks and Brother Caseous knew exactly what to do. They began with shutting and bolting the door to the Apothecary, before opening both ceiling trap doors which let two brilliant beams of sunlight flood into the room from the mid-day sun.

Brother Caseous, attempting to humor Gavan, said, "Ye picked the best time of year to be getting yerself stabbed, young man, these herbs be all fresh-picked only a few days ago. Ye be the lucky one!"

If that was humor, I'm the Pope. I couldn't tell if Brother Caseous was teasing, tormenting or trying to make small talk. Gavan only gave the man a surly side glance as he mumbled, "Dunna ye be having more urgent need of ye medical skills than ye jester skills?"

It was obvious that this Brother Caseous had used this sad line of humorless wit so many times, that it was delivered like a plate of cold fish over stale rice.

The young monk, David, began to collect a series of mirrors, lenses and handmade brass frames which were stored in drawers, shelves and secreted places around the Apothecary. When he appeared to have everything ready, he told Brother Caseous, who was busy flattening the dried and fresh plant leaves, for what I assumed to be a poultice, the 'Light Healer' was ready for assembling.

Brother Caseous moved with well-practiced smoothness and speed as he assembled the mirrors and lenses in the brass frames. Once all of the pieces were together, the assemblage rose well over half way between Gavan and the open hole in the ceiling. After a couple small adjustments, he drew another small brass frame, containing a lens from a pocket in his robe and placed it in the brass framework.

After adjusting Gavan directly beneath one of the shafts of sunlight, Matthew opened a drawer and withdrew six small objects. He handed each of us one of these devices and when I examined the one I was holding, it had the appearance of sunglasses made with leather frames and thick mica lenses. I held mine up to the sky light and could immediately see that this was something like a welder's mask. Matthew and Brother

Caseous placed the poultice of new and dried leaves over the sword wound in Gavan's left arm. Then they moved part of the brass framework with the mirrors and lenses into the other shaft of sunlight as the initial shaft of light continued to illuminate Gavan's arm. Whatever they intended to do for Gavan, it was a total mystery to me.

Asa noticed me staring, and he held up the mica sunglasses, and advised, "Ye may be wanting to have these over yer eyes and squint a bit, because it be getting very bright in here, Lad."

Matthew and Brother Caseous continued making small adjusts to the mirrors and lenses. With each adjustment, the 3' circle focus point of a beam on Gavan's arm and the poultice began to grow brighter and brighter. Brother Caseous asked Gavan, "Be ye alright with this?"

Gavan mumbled with satire, "Feels just fine."

Matthew and Brother Caseous made some very minute adjustments and the beam intensified.

Once again, he asked Gavan, "Be ye in pain?"

Gavan said, "I'll tell you when to stop... um, Brother Caseous."

I thought these men were ready to finalize this healing project when Brother Caseous lifted a chain from around his neck. At the end of the chain hung a brilliant cobalt blue gem. It was translucent and amazingly beautiful.

Asa leaned close to me and spoke softly, "That be the healing stone. Only one like it in the world." That caught my attention.

The young monk, David, piped in, "Be advising that all here protect yer eyes... *now.*"

This is when I noticed that the lens which Brother Caseous had pulled from his pocket was not in use with the other lenses. Brother Caseous inserted the blue gem immediately below the larger clear lens as he warned Gavan, "Here be coming the Healing Light." He lifted a small wooden screen which had blocked light from passing through these last two lenses and the entire system of mirrors and lenses burst

73

with brilliance that could clearly be seen through the thick layers of mica shielding our eyes.

The color and intensity of the light in the room became far too dazzling for me to keep my eyes wide open. Through the tiniest of squinting lids, I could see a beam of bluish-green light on the poultice.

"How much *longer*?" grunted Gavan.

"That be doing it." Brother Caseous said, as he replaced the small wood light screen and slid the brass framework out of the sunlight. It took several seconds for my eyes to adjust to the well lit room.

Of course, I had a million questions but right now, Matthew and Brother Caseous repeated this entire process to apply their Healing Light to Gavan's wounded leg. I had no trouble standing silent and still because I was awe struck by what I was witnessing. The monks, David and Matthew, disassembled their healing device and placed every piece of it in pre-determined drawers or shelves. The blue gem was ceremoniously returned to Brother Caseous' neck and tucked out of sight.

I was still frozen in place when Asa, in a low voice, offered some advice, "Silence yer thoughts, Lad. We be spaking of this later."

David and Matthew began to dress Gavan's wounds with simple wrappings. I could see the distinct circle where the healing light was shone on the leaves darkened by the intense light but not burned.

Brother Caseous looked at me for a while before responding, "I guess ye be thinking this be magic because ye be coming here from 2016. Be that correct?"

I assumed Asa or Gavan told him, so I just nodded. This Brother Caseous was quite arrogant, and the moment he taunted Gavan, I really didn't care to know him better.

"What ye be knowing from 2016," Brother Caseous continued, "be our ancient medical knowledge, which ye just be witnessing, comparable to what ye be knowing in 2016? I shall be giving yer friends the pleasure of explaining the details, but this knowledge of healing with light be from the year 2994 and we be having this wonderful treatment for hundreds of years. Yer friend's wounds will be healed in less than three days, the time it takes for his body to generate new cells, at the immediate locations of the wounds. I be seeing in your eyes that this be confusing. Allow me to simplify it for ye. Humans are composed of the same basic elements and we need only those elements to be healed. In the leaves of certain plants, be the healing elements we be needing to speed up our body's healing. The use of the Healing Light be to transfer these elements from the leaves into the body without being invasive or destructive."

I appreciated his explanation, but Brother Caseous was still much too arrogant for my comfort. "But how could... " I started to ask.

Asa cut me off. "We be explaining this and more, later, Lad, but right now, everything must be put away to look as it did before we be getting here. The king's servants have been searching for this knowledge for hundreds of years and the king's soldiers would slit your throat for it."

My head was spinning with questions and every question had a halo of fear about it. My fear tended to overshadow my questions to the point of creating waves of panic, every time I heard distant footsteps or mumbled voices.

By observation I was convinced of the amazing technology contained in objects on a 326 year Passing, but what did Brother Caseous mean when he said, 'We had knowledge of the healing light that came from 2994?' And they have *had* this knowledge for *hundreds of years?"* If these people, living in 1690, can accept the fact that I came from 2016, then am I to believe that the year 2994 has already happened? This is a really weird concept of time for me.

Gabriel mentioned 'The Consciousness' as a group. I wonder how many are in this group. Are they just the monks in the monastery? Of *what* are the members of Gabriel's group 'conscious'? What other advanced knowledge from 2994 do these people possess? If The Consciousness has had this knowledge for hundreds of years, how have they been able to keep it a secret from their king? What about other places around the world where transferred consciousnesses have taken place? What affect has this had in those areas?

Questions, questions, questions!

Gavan broke my freight train of thought with one of his own. "Am I to be getting any help here?"

Asa was already under his wounded arm and I quickly took his other side as the three of us made our way back to Gabriel's chamber of knowledge. We delivered Gavan to Gabriel who helped him into one of the chairs around the Grand Table of Consciousness. He invited me to sit in a second chair beside him. Asa needed no invitation to occupy the third chair, as Gabriel studied my face.

Gabriel commented, "I be imagining how many questions ye be having in your mind, Raffe. Any question ye be liking us to answer first?

I asked eagerly, "Has the year 2994 already happened?"

Gabriel smiled and looked at his twin and Asa before responding. "That be a very good question to begin with, Raffe. I suspect there be having many more years after 2994 but we have never encountered any record of a transferred Consciousness from 3320 or later."

Asa, true to his mischievous nature, tossed me a question of his own. "Ye be having time to wonder how we of 1690 be knowing things in your past that ye be having no knowledge of?"

"YES!" I almost shouted back. "This has been a nagging sub-topic to many of the things I have heard you talking about, as well as, the medical technology used on Gavan."

Gavan was first to respond. "The Healing Light, Raffe, be not from *your* past. It came to us through the 1364 Passing. It be a medical treatment discovered long after 2016 and it be many years before the bronze framework, mirrors and 'healing stone' were assembled."

Asa added, "The king's family got knowledge of the 'healing stone' when it was used to heal an injured traveler, and they be searching for it e'er since. We be concealing its location and be spreading rumors that it does not exist. But they be continuing to send their soldiers and spies. They hang posters offering very handsome rewards for information about the 'healing stone' several times a year."

"Why aren't there more?" I asked

"Why there not be more... what?" Gavan echoed.

I clarified my question, "Why aren't there more people who know about, or are the descendants of us, who have had our 'consciousness' transferred?"

"Most be killed immediately," Gabriel stated as factually as he could. "Like ye, Raffe, when they transfer their consciousness, they transfer their language. Most found themselves in countries of another language, and their people not be understanding them. Mystical fear and cultural prejudices be killing them or casting them out to die. These cultures be thinking they be possessed with evil spirits or crazy. The Druids be a very open-minded and curious culture, who accepted Amergus, or Lynn Wayne of 2994, and he be able to survive and become a *leader*."

Gavan added, "Some of those who be transferred used their knowledge to become powerful in business and politics. We strongly suspect the King's family to be descendants of a transferred consciousness. Or, they be persuading someone, with pain or gold, to reveal this knowledge, but this be ne'er proven. We be suspecting them of being lucky in guessing which year will be a year of a Passing."

Asa offered, "About the Blue Healing stone, it be found in India, centuries ago, and may be not from earth. It's legend be saying it 'fell from the sky.' How to be using the Blue Stone with specific herbs, came from the famous transfer, Amergus, who be using 2994 medical knowledge to apply its properties to healing."

Chapter 6
The Discovery of the 'He-She'

As the days turned into weeks, the weeks became months. With the help of every safe person within the monastery, I worked on my speech mannerisms to help blend with the monks and locals. I sat by the hour listening to Gabriel read the Rune parchments. My fascination and curiosity grew as I absorbed, and patiently practiced, his word pronunciations.

Asa interrupted Gabriel's reading with the urgent request for me to help him, with a situation in the sanctuary. I didn't know how unprepared I was for the task before me, but I had learned to trust Asa and followed him without question or hesitation.

Long before we reached the sanctuary, I could hear shouting and screaming of male voices echoing through the ancient stone corridors. I began to get some old but quite familiar pangs in my gut that told me that I wasn't the only novice in this monastery. What both Asa and I were not prepared to see, was a young peasant, dressed in filthy rags. He was screaming at four monks. They were trying to help this young villager remove his clothes and take a much-needed bath before eating the evening meal. This newcomer was quite short, for a man, maybe 5'2", or less, with spindly arms and legs that clearly showed a body at near starvation. Most obvious and striking were the sunken dark eye sockets from which wild black eyes glared about.

My first thought, even before I felt any sympathy, was that he was as dangerous as any bobcat in a trap.

The physical confrontation with the novices wasn't what concerned me, and I gave Asa a knowing look which clearly said that I knew why Asa has sought my help. The young man in rags was speaking in 21st century American English and he had a clear Spanish accent.

Hoping to help, I spoke with a very poor imitation of his American mannerism as I asked, "Wa's-zup, bro?" Every monk, as well as the unwashed stranger, froze at the sound of my words. I took advantage of the silence. I attempted to give some assurance to the obviously terrified visitor. "Please don't be afraid of these monks, they only want to help you."

The scruffy young stranger's eyes fixed on me and what came out of him was not the expected calm gratitude I was hoping for.

"And who the hell are *you*, BRO?" Came from the dirty villager.

Knowing what I did, I thought it best to simply answer the question. "I'm Raffe, and like you, I'm new here, too."

"Here?" came the retort…"and where the hell is '*here*?'"

The attending monks left the sanctuary in frustration as Asa and I thought about how to deal with this young man.

My mind raced for truthful as well as comforting answers, so I started with a question. "If you're like me, you have only been 'here' for a few months, right?" The amazed and puzzled look on the stranger's face told Asa and me what we needed to know. "From the look on your face," I offered, "you really don't need to answer. Allow me to give you some information that may not be comforting to hear but will give you the truth."

Asa offered the counsel, "It be helpful to be giving this man just enough facts, at this time, to be comforting, since there be so much to share."

"*Man?*" the stranger blurted out, "I'm *not* a man! … At least I *wasn't* a man.

Asa and I looked at the stubbly beard on his face and his hairy forearms before Asa asked, "What do ye be *meaning*? Are you saying that ye be *not a man*?"

The stranger went silent, folded his arms around his stomach and slumped to the floor. I started to re-ask the question, but was stopped with the terrified eyes of this new visitor.

"My name… "He hesitated, and we quietly waited for the rest of the sentence. He continued, "My name is Maria, I live in Pueblo, Colorado."

Asa's response was simple and immediate, "What did ye just spake?"

Clearly, and more confidently, she repeated, "I said, my name is *Maria* and my home is in Pueblo, Colorado! Can you understand that? You talk weird."

We stared at each other for a couple seconds before I stated the obvious, "You don't look like a Maria, at least no Maria, at this *time*."

Maria snapped back, "What do you *mean*, 'at this time'?"

I took a couple seconds to formulate the answer. "What I meant, Maria, is that we are no longer in the place or time that we were in, a few months ago."

Maria's puzzled face demanded more information, so I started with, "If you and I had similar experiences, about four months ago, we also had a very strange experience of waking up in a completely strange place. A place where everyone recognized us but didn't know our names. Am I right, so far?"

Maria's face turned from fear and panic, to a doubtful and worried expression, when he/she asked, "Where are we *now*?"

I explained, "The 'now' is 1690 and the 'where' is Southern England." I let that sink in for a few seconds as all three of us waited in complete silence.

Maria spoke first, "Who are you, and where are you *from*?"

I gave the simplest and honest reply, "I'm from Denver, Colorado. I had just graduated from the firefighter's academy and was on a camping weekend with friends when everything changed."

Maria's next question sent all of us into silence again, "Were you a girl then?"

"No," I replied, almost afraid of what I might hear.

"Well, I was," Maria whimpered. "And I'm about to go crazy with this new world, new time and *new body*."

I looked at Asa and commented, "Gabriel never mentioned anything like this."

"This be new to me, as well," Asa replied.

It was only then that the thought occurred to me. I looked at Asa and said, "Lynn Wayne. Is it possible that 'Lynn,' a name that can be given to a man or a woman, was a woman in 2994?"

Asa was as surprised as me at this possibility. "Let us be asking Gabriel if he can think of such a possibility. Right here, this Maria be far too much of a mystery for me to respond."

I asked Maria to share the events that brought her to the monastery.

Asa commented, "You may be wanting to come up with a new name. Something more fitting to yer... appearance." Asa's concern for all of our safety was obvious in his voice. I felt it too.

Maria ignored the suggestion for a new name and began to relate the events of her last three months of trauma and fear. "I was a clerk in a convenience store, trying to make enough to pay for my night school classes. I went to bed that night, as usual, but without warning, I was awakened in the middle of the night. The first thing I noticed was the strange smells: mud, fish and manure, and my bed was gone... I was lying on a filthy mat filled with straw. There wasn't any light anywhere and I thought I was having a bad dream, so I curled up and went back to sleep. I was hoping to wake up, in my bed, and tell my friends about this horrible dream. Of course, you know... it wasn't a dream. I was in a small shack with two strange women and small girl. The moment I tried to speak to them, they looked at me like I was a monster and ran out of the shack. I wanted to get out of there too, so I pushed open the crude door. The first thing I saw was not a village or the countryside, I saw my *hands*! They were not *my* hands. I had just paid thirty five bucks for a manicure, and these hands were rough, calloused and my fingernails were *ruined*! The people in that village just stared at me at first, but they soon became hostile. They threw everything they could find at me, with screams of, 'Demon, ye are possessed.' And someone shouted, 'KILL him!' and I took off running. I had no idea why they hated me so, and I felt as if I were going crazy." Maria's emotional release at finding someone who didn't hate her but actually wanted to help, brought on a flood of tears and sobbing.

In an attempt to comfort her or him, Asa placed a hand on her shoulder and Maria jumped into his uncomfortable embrace. Asa starred at me with eyes that begged... 'please save me,' but he remained calm for the sake of their new friend. To help Asa's panicked look, I asked Maria to continue with her story.

After a couple minutes of recovering her or his emotional composure, she apologized to Asa and went on telling us of how she had survived by stealing vegetables from gardens. Not knowing where to go, she wandered to avoid persecution and admitted that she thought about suicide every day. At one point, about a week after her first horrible morning, while raiding a garden, she heard villagers telling men in fancy armored uniforms that they had seen me, and where they thought I might be hiding. "It scared the hell out of me that they knew where I had been spending my nights and the path to my hideout."

She explained, "I intentionally ran in a different direction from that path and avoided all humans for what felt like months, until hunger forced me to approach someone to beg for food. To my surprise, this village was kind and they treated me as if I were very special. They told me about this monastery and sent a young man to fetch the monks you saw me arguing with a few minutes ago."

Asa brought up the subject of a new name for the new resident of 1690 by asking, "Knowing what ye do, have ye be thinking of a more fitting name than 'Maria?'"

"No," was her blunt reply, "I've been trying to stay alive and couldn't care less if my name and body are a miss-match."

Trying to help further, Asa asked, "Would you like to hear a few suggestions? The Bible names be popular for ages."

With a few seconds of thoughtful silence, Maria took a long look at her, his hands, arms and legs before she replied, "How popular is '*Luke*?'"

"Luke it be! and Luke ye be from hence forth!" chirped, Asa, quite pleased with the progress, "But first, a hot bath... a clean garment... and a hot meal... in that order!"

Neither Asa, nor I, had any idea of the depth and breadth of complications which lay before us as we continued to answer all of the questions Maria/Luke could think to ask. I instantly felt a very sincere sympathy for Luke. How terrible his existence must have been since the night they both experienced a permanent nightmare. The image of the camping trip with Jake and the sight of that black object in the night sky flashed through his memory. Admittedly, Luke's experience in England had been much more difficult than his own. Thanks to Gavan, Asa and Gabriel, this amazing transition had been easy, in comparison.

As often as I remembered hearing gay people, back in 2016, complain about 'feeling like they were women trapped in a male body,' this transfer of consciousness produced that exact problem.

Asa and I knew that we had a lot of work to do if we were to keep Luke alive in a time where being different was enough to get you killed... along with everyone who tried to *help* him.

Luke was, obviously, very intelligent since he learned quickly to accept the facts of his transfer back to 1690, but the speech mannerisms were a challenge for him. When surprised or stressed, he reverted to his original *Spanglish* which held the potential of death and imprisonment for the entire monastery.

A fortnight had passed since Luke entered the monastery and he was making excellent progress, but even I could clearly hear his strong American accent during unguarded moments. Both of us had taken to wearing the same burlap brown robes worn by the novices and the monk. Compared to the soft cotton clothes of 2016, these course garment's itchiness was bearable, but only for the camouflage needed to blend into the monastery's community.

Luke's Spanglish accent was more pronounced to Asa, Gabriel and Gavan, who were becoming impatient with his English lessons, and I could hear the sharpness in their interruptions and corrections. There was cause for concern, in my mind, because they had been so patient with *my* intense training.

Even though Gavan and I had our beds in the same sleeping quarters, I never inquired of Gavan or Asa about missing the original Raffe. I wondered if my advantage was that the original Raffe was well known and loved, that they showed more patience. Could it be the fact that Luke was female in her/his first life. Maybe it's time to bring the subject to the surface. I fell back to sleep listening to Gavan snore in the lightless chamber.

Morning brought with it the same cleaning, prayers and simple breakfast that every other morning did and like previous mornings, Luke was repeatedly chided about his 'Spanglish' accent. The three Englishmen had created the combination of English and Spanish into a single word. The word was entertaining enough to use when attempting to joke about Luke's speech. No one thought that it might pose a threat.

Luke was not only intelligent, he was very kind and patient, and not once had he tried to defend his poorly spoken words, so when the first real-life challenge came, no one was expecting the direction from which the threat came.

The comfort of our daily routines had given everyone a sense of safety, so the visit to the monastery from a local villager was met with casual conversations. The villager asked Gabriel if they had any new novice monks to help with the many chores around the monastery.

Gabriel responded, "No, just be the same faithful few." To Gabriel's surprise, one of the elderly monks, who was sweeping nearby, spoke up.

"We do have the new 'Spanglish' novice. I believe his name is Luke."

A terrible silence filled the vaulted ceiling and every pew of the chapel. The kind of silence that screams louder than all other sounds. The villager pretended not to notice the strange new word 'Spanglish" and stretched his lips into a very small smile as he began to make excuses to leave. Gabriel was keenly aware of the villager's suspicions. He knew that even this single

84

strange word was enough to earn the villager a handsome reward, and the monastery, a threat of death to all who resided there. Gabriel suggested that the visitor stay for a meal and more conversation, but he flatly rejected the offer. He was now on a mission to get away, and get to the nearest soldiers he could find. Gabriel wanted to insist that he stay but that would be much too obvious, so he walked the man to the great doors through which the villager made his polite and hurried exit.

Once the great doors shut, Gabriel turned and leaned against them. He looked at the elderly monk, who was now on his knees, weeping bitterly into his hands, mumbling, "I be so sorry, Brother Gabriel, I be not thinking. I be so sorry."

Gabriel knew his regrets were sincere. He looked about the sanctuary, and then, the large statue of the Mother of God. "Dear Lord, help us," spilled from his lips. Just then, Gabriel noticed his friend, Asa, standing in the small doorway which led to the lower chambers. His eyes met Asa's and Asa gave Gabriel the slightest of nods before turning about and disappearing. Gabriel felt the raw and wretched grip of nausea crawl over his flesh, for he knew that Asa, as a loyal friend, would eliminate the threat very quickly... at least, he hoped.

Asa had his plan before he left the courtyard of the monastery. He had been needed for this kind of task before, and had trained his mind to think only of what he *must* do, to *save his friends*. He overheard the villager tell Gabriel what direction, and which roads, he would travel, *if* he was headed home. Asa also knew the roads leading to the nearest military billeting, so he ran as fast as his legs would carry him, to a rise that allowed an overview of roads threading through the region. He needed to wait only a few gasping moments before spotting the villager casually walking towards his village. Asa instantly left his observation post and sprinted for the visitor's village, taking an almost parallel route. His plan was to get far enough ahead that he could join the same road the man was traveling on, walking from the opposite direction. Asa would appear, to the man, to be *leaving* his village. If his plan worked, Asa would be back in the monastery, long before the villager was missed.

Once Asa was between the villager and his target, he had a moment to reflect on how much he hated being able to carry out such a mission, but he quickly refocused on the man approaching him. With just a glance, Asa could see that the only travelers in sight were the villager and himself. Asa picked up a casual stride away from the village and toward the traveler... as casual as a man who just ran a couple miles could manage. When the villager was only a few feet in front of Asa, the man noticed the sweat beads on Asa's face just as Asa was becoming aware of his eyes being stung by his own sweat.

The villager began to stare at Asa, so Asa said, "Hot day it be for a stroll, be it not?"
The villager responded, "Yes, it be, but..." The man never finished his sentence.

Asa drove his concealed dagger into and through the man's heart while clasping his open mouth, to capture any scream. The villager never made a sound. Asa supported his collapsing body, and dragged him into the brush, at the side of the road. Asa had been trained in this kind of work and he took care to keep almost all his victim's blood from soiling his clothes. He was successful except for the cuff of his left sleeve. He ripped off the frilly cuff and used it to clean the blade and handle of his dagger. He retraced the route he has used to intercept the villager, and stopped only long enough to wash his hands in a stream, and bury the bloodied cuff from his shirt.

When Asa quietly opened the door to the lower chamber of the monastery, he was startled by Luke standing inside with tears running down his cheeks. Like a woman, Luke made no effort to hide his emotions and he softly said, "I'm so sorry that you had to do this, Asa. Thank you. You are a very brave man."

Initially wanting to deny what was obvious to Luke, Asa asked, "Of what doth ye spake?"
Luke simply whispered, "Asa, I understand the need and you did the right thing. I want you to know this." Luke was looking at Asa's cut away cuff.

Luke looked as if he was about to collapse so Asa wrapped an arm around him for support, forgetting the man was a woman, inside. Luke instinctively put his arm around Asa and the two walked along in mutual support and understanding. When they were close enough to hear the sounds of Gavan and me practicing my English, they separated to walk independently into the chamber.

Gavan had known Asa since they were boys and needed no words to understand the mission Asa had just completed. The instant Gavan's eyes met Asa's, he saw the pain and pride of a valued friend and mate. No matter how successful Asa was with such a mission, he never became cold or emotionless. Gavan knew his friend was going to need some time to tell his best friend exactly what he had done. Asa needed to feel Gavan's and Gabriel's understanding and supportive recognition of the necessity for the taking of one life to save many lives.

It took only three days for the first rumors of a murder just outside a local village to reach the monastery. The stories ranged widely about robberies, unfaithful wives, secret lovers and the recent mystery, to some, of many people going crazy and soldiers rounding them up. It was this last topic of rumor which seemed to be the most logical and eventually became accepted. The local villagers, even the dead man's own family, agreed that he had been acting strange and must have been confronted by soldiers on the road, since he wasn't robbed or beaten. He was just killed for acting crazy and left to rot.

The rumors of soldiers killing the villager were very comforting to the inhabitants of the monastery and repeated on to any who visited the ancient compound. Asa, more than anyone else, was pleased to hear the stories about how cruel and brutal the soldiers were towards any crazy person they found.

It would have been to the liking of everyone at the monastery if their lives remained unchallenged and unchanged, but in a time of such turmoil, every day was overshadowed with the imminent threat of discovery and harm. There were even wild stories of family members, strangers and even a few soldiers, being found to be crazy.

Brother Gabriel asked Luke and me to join him in the chamber which contained the Grand Table and the parchments filled with Rune tracings. Gavan, Asa and Gabriel stood behind the great table and presented a somewhat formal atmosphere to the room which had held hundreds of hours of discovery for everyone present.

Gavan spoke first, "The time for a few changes hath arrived, Lads, and ye and Luke be needing to make a risky journey, for the sake of two transferred souls."

My heart sank in my chest like a rock in water. These three men had been the first true friends I found in this new 1690 world. Seeing them every day, even listening to Gavan snore in the night, was my anchor to sanity and security.

Luke blurted out, "I clearly remember what my life was like out there, and you want me to return to that existence?"

I shared Luke's emotional reaction but chose to be quiet until we heard more from the men I trusted. The thought of leaving the monastery without, at least, one of these men, was deeply troubling.

Gavan asked us to sit at the Great Table and the three most important people in my new world sat where they once stood. The few seconds of silence felt much longer. Gabriel broke the silence with information the monastery had just received from their sister monastery, on the island of Anglesey. I immediately recognized the name of this island. It was the island on which the Rune caves were located. The mention of it captured every tingling synapse in my mind.

"The message be short," Gabriel stated, "as the parchment be easy to conceal."

Luke was well focused on Gabriel. I glanced among all three of my mentor's faces and what I was reading was a mix of sadness, fear and affection for Luke and me.

Asa spoke softly. to Gabriel, "Are ye *sure* this be the right time to share this?"

Gabriel turned to Asa and replied with a quirky smile, "It be almost funny that ye should ask about *the right time,* in this matter." All three smiled while remaining quite serious.

"*Please*, Brother Gabriel!" Luke pleaded, "what news do you have for us?"

With a warm and fatherly smile, Gabriel began. "We be notified that several new Rune inscriptions be found inside a recently discovered cave on the Isle of Anglesey. The note claims these Runes to be the work of Amergus, who be also known as Lynn Wayne."

The mention of Lynn Wayne sent an uncomfortable chill through me. I didn't know why the mention of this name should affect me the way it did. Gavan, being the closest to me from my first day in 1690, took note of my reaction.

"Steady, Lad," said Gavan, "the gale winds be just beginning to fill ye sails." With these words from my most trusted friend, I literally shuddered with anticipation. The next few words from Gabriel's mouth shook Luke and me, like leaves in that gale.

"The message," Gabriel continued, "states that two names were found among these newly discovered Runes. The names be of Maria and Broderick." Gabriel never tried to be dramatic but his pause after speaking our real names filled the chamber with a chill that no blanket or fire could warm.

Immediately, Luke and I asked for more information. but Gabriel explained that this was all the message contained. My mind was spinning to find something to put the pieces of information into some sort of logical sequence.

Amergus, formerly Lynn Wayne, was transferred from the year 2994 back to the year 60, the same year in which Rome killed almost every member of the Druid culture. From all of the other Rune inscriptions, it suggests that this Amergus must have been the person who transferred back to 60 AD, but where did the original consciousness of Amergus go?

Luke's voice was shaking. "How could our names *possibly* be scratched into the wall of a Druid cave?" He was gasping for breath, as the weight of Gabriel's words crashed upon his mind.

"No one be sure of the how or why a transfer happens," said Gabriel, "just the number of years between events." He continued, "We be guessing that Wayne, before he be Amergus, be a historian or student of English history since he be familiar with events in Wayne's history which proved to be prophecies in Amergus's immediate future. How Amergus be knowing what year he transferred to, be a mystery that we be hoping will be revealed in the newly discovered Runes.

"Ye know, now, as much as we be knowing," Gabriel said in his softest voice. "We be spaking about this... and the surest, quickest and safest way to be getting the answers, be for *all of us* to make the journey to these caves, and be reading them for ourselves."

Luke's dread of leaving this monastery swelled up even stronger than before and he sat silently with tears running down his face.

I was so ready to get going that my first question was, "*When*, when can we get started?"

This is when Asa spoke up to state the obvious, "It not be as soon as ye may be wishing, Raffe, since neither of ye spake English well enough to avoid detection and deadly suspicion."

Luke was very pleased to hear Asa's words. He wasn't at all comfortable with a journey outside these walls, for any reason.

The best thing we can do right now is to continue your daily language lessons as well as some training in living off the land. I knew that my experiences with camping had prepared me for survival, but the real teacher of such skills will prove to be the very tough teachers called necessity and hunger.

Chapter 7
Preparations for the Journey

All of us were excited and deeply concerned about the journey we faced, and Luke and I dedicated our waking hours to carefully listening to the speech mannerisms of every monk, and studiously practicing 1690 English. Asa introduced some lessons which made Luke all the more afraid. He told both of us that we needed to know how to use a knife in combat. Luke was very squeamish about even *holding* a dagger in a threatening way, at first. The time spent, learning from Asa, eventually bore fruit and he began to practice every day. I had some experience with a hunting knife but, like Luke, I was a novice who learned quickly from a demanding teacher with Asa's skill and experience.

Asa taught his two pupils more than combat knife skills. He was a wealth of knowledge in survival skills which included fishing with his bare hands, or making a fish trap. Asa taught us how to make rabbit snares, which provided fresh meat for the monastery.

Three, then four months had passed since the message about the newly discovered cave had arrived, and I was anxious to begin the journey. Luke, however, was just as terrified as the first day he heard about his original name, Maria, being carved into the wall of a cave 1630 years before now and 1956 years before her/his consciousness was transferred from 2016 to 1690.

"If all of this wasn't good cause for a headache, nothing was," he muttered out loud.

"I be *hearing* that," Gavan growled, "Let someone be hearing ye spaking like that and we be *all* in danger."

This was all Luke needed to put his mind in a panic mode. "I don't want to go to any Druid cave," Luke whimpered, "I want to stay right here."

Asa responded to Luke's complaint. "Do ye actually be believing ye be safer here in this monastery than ye be in the forests of Britannia? Dunna be wastin me time with an answer, Luke. Our journey will be taking us *outside* of the realm of King William and his brutal wife, Mary. *No* monastery will be left unsearched for those who supported King James II, and the time of this Passing will only be serving to make this area and monastery compound *un*safe." Asa's words didn't give Luke much comfort, but it was now quite clear that going was a better choice than staying.

I had a question that I wanted to ask of Gabriel and the response I received was far more revealing than I ever expected.

I asked, "Why was the message about the discovery of a Druid cave sent to you?" It was a good thing that I asked this question of Gabriel while sitting at their evening meal, because the answer was extensive.

Gabriel began with a reference to the gigantic table in the basement below the sanctuary. "The Grand Table of Consciousness be made shortly after Lynn/Amergus be transferred back to 60 AD. It was built by others who be *also* transferred into *that* year, from *other years* of the Passing. Some experienced hostility and some be simply accepted into the culture of that time. A few of those transferred found others from their *own* years, liking to the two of ye. Having the bond of their original times, be forming a covenant for protection, as well as communication."

"Brother Gabriel, are you a part of this covenant?" I asked.

Gabriel calmly replied to my question, "We *all* be. Gavan and I, as twins, be members by birth, just as Asa and every monk in this monastery. The twist in Asa's membership to the Covenant be that his father be the King, but his mother be not the queen, so he be not claiming his father's bloodline."

"What?" I interrupted, "I already knew that Asa was an illegitimate son of the king, but you just said that he is a *descendant* of a *transferred consciousness* and that means the king is *also*."

"Yes," replied Gavan, "but, as Gabriel be explaining, not *everyone* who be transferred be even sympathetic of others they be knowing to be transferred. Some be using their knowledge of history to gain great wealth, or other selfish reasons. Most be choosing to be part of a Covenant of the Transferred in mutual support, information and protection."

When Gavan finished this fascinating history lesson, I was so enthralled that I stopped chewing my food and that was sufficient cause for a roar of laughter.

Gavan continued, once the laughter. and blush in my face, had settled down. "Gabriel be taught to read the Runes by the descendants of the few Druids who survived the 60 AD slaughter by Rome. There be not many of them left, today, but they be managing to pass their written language from generation to generation."

"We hope to be learning a lot more from the Runes recently found," added Asa, "but, even if we be only discovering why Amergus named the two of ye, it will be making the journey worthwhile."

Luke came up with the next question; "How far is the Isle of Anglesey from here?"

"Our journey be taking us less than a fortnight," replied, Asa, "if all be going well and we be having good weather."

"What **could** *possibly* go wrong?" was Luke's obviously satirical question.

Asa seemed to be expecting this question. He explained that much of the region had been hotly contested during the battles between William and Mary and the defeated King James II. Although the fighting was over, the local population was still divided in their loyalties and it was a tender and dangerous subject.

"My advice," said Asa, "be that politics, of any kind, ne'er be discussed after we be leaving the monastery. "

Luke added, "Excuse me, but what is a 'fortnight.'"

I grabbed the opportunity, and whispered, "Fourteen days."

"Gracious a Dios," Luke whispered and quickly slapped a hand over his own mouth.

* * *

Another two weeks had passed. The daily lessons from Asa grew longer and more intense, until the afternoon that Luke's dagger fighting lesson drew blood. It wasn't a serious wound, but it was the que that told Asa, that Luke and I were ready. Once again, Gabriel had Luke and I summoned to meet with Gavan, Asa and himself in the Grand Table chamber right after morning chores.

Spread out on the Grand Table were two groups of duplicate items which included hand drawn maps with the names of villages along their route, cold weather cloaks, oiled canvas slickers, an extra pair of pants, and new shoes, on top of handmade backpacks. What caught my attention was the short swords and daggers next to each stack of supplies. They were not at all ornate, but they appeared to be new and made especially for this adventure.

Gabriel could see the surprise and delight in our eyes, as he asked, "Do ye be feeling ready for this journey?"

I immediately replied, "We'll be more prepared to answer your question when we get back. When do we *leave*?"

Gavan answered my question, "Immediately after an extra *big breakfast* tomorrow morning." Gavan's face became very solemn when he added, "I be having a list of names for both of thee. The names be the members of our descendants of Transferred Covenant who be trusted friends in the villages we be passing through. If we be separated or anything happen to Gabriel, Asa and myself, these be the names ye must use to be safe. Of course, we do not expect ye be needing them, but ye must be keeping these lists hidden, on ye body, just in case."

The fear that flowed through Luke was very easy to see. Asa took a moment to assure Luke that they were not expecting any trouble. "We just be wanting to be well prepared, that be all."

Luke's trembling hands told all of us that he wasn't the least bit comforted by these words. It seems that everyone, except Luke, had forgotten that there was a young woman inside the body of a young man named Luke. He had done well with Asa's lessons, *physically*. *Mentally*, however, he had never encountered the need to fight, or even defend herself, before 'her' consciousness had been whisked back to 1690. As comfortable as Luke was with these men, there was a very powerful dread of repeating the weeks he had spent of near starvation.

Sleep didn't come quickly for me or Luke, that night, but it did come, and it was very welcome. I woke before daylight and was initially surprised when I noticed that Gavan was already gone from the room. Gavan was almost always up early so I wasn't concerned as I made my way to the dining hall. There standing along the far wall, was Gabriel, Asa and Gavan. Each man was holding a staff and Gavan and Gabriel held two staffs, one in each hand. All three had their travel packs on their backs and Gabriel had a small dagger strapped to his hip which looked out of place on a monk's robe. Gavan and Asa both had short swords and daggers on their belts.

A booming voice welcomed us. "Good morn, Lad. This staff is for *ye*, Raffe." Luke made his appearance right behind me, and he was greeted the same way, by Asa. Neither of the us had given any thought to carrying a staff, nor had we been given any training in the many uses of a staff. I assumed these lessons will be taught as we travel.

Two large bowls of steaming porridge were set out for us. Asa chirped, "We already be having our porridge, Lads. As soon as ye be through eating, we will be *on our way*." Asa's voice was a bit too excited for most men of his age and experience. Luke and I barely let the porridge cool before consuming every drop.

It was obvious that Asa was in his element when he was in open country and for him, this journey was going to be a fun time. We were only a few minutes away from the monastery when I noticed how small our packs were and asked Gavan where we would be finding or purchasing our meals.

"We be having no need to do either, Raffe," replied Gavan, "As a member of the monastery, Gabriel will request food from the villages we pass through. As for ye and Luke, we be needing to present a bit of a ruse... spake to all we meet that the two of ye be novice monks, taking a journey while under a vow of silence."

This seemed simple enough as long as we were not challenged by any of the king's soldiers or were overheard by villagers as we walked. Asa assured us that he, Gavan and

95

Gabriel would keep a close watch on us to be as quiet, as needed.

Each day of trekking brought the threat of blisters and aching muscles as our bodies soon adjusted to the long days. Luke and I welcomed breaks and the knowledge dispensed as we rested... lots to learn. The villager's provided meals as we moved along. Their gifts were blessings, not just food. And by genuinely gracious villagers whose goal, it appeared, was to help us, in any way they could.

On the sixth day of our pilgrimage, we passed close by a military outpost and decided to travel at night, to minimize the potential of contact with any soldiers. We could hear the barking of big dogs and suspected there might be a kennel of trained war-dogs at this outpost. None of us wanted to have anything to do with those huge trained killers. Asa warned Luke and me to say nothing, no matter what we saw or heard. All went well and we swiftly and silently passed the outpost without incident.

As the Eastern horizon turned from ebony to gray and then to impending sunrise, Gabriel asked Asa if it was safe to rest a while.

Asa replied, "As long as we be within patrol range of that outpost, we not be safe, but I do believe it be safe enough to take a short rest." All of us were glad to find a soft spot of earth and rest our legs.

Trying to communicate without words, I motioned to Gavan that I was hungry, and Luke agreed with a vigorous rub of his stomach.

Gavan whispered, "I be hungry, too, but we not be taking the time or risk a fire. There should be a village about a mile ahead and we can stop there."

"What did ye see?" Gavan whispered. As I attempted to answer his huge hand covered my mouth with a force that rocked my head back. With his face so close to mine that I could smell his breath, he asked in a whisper, "What do ye see or hear?"

Knowing that I could never communicate with hand gestures, I softly whispered as I leaned close enough to Gavan's ear to feel his whiskers against my lips. "I thought I saw something large and black moving through the forest behind you."

Both of us flinched slightly as our entire company heard the distinct sound of steel clinking against steel. Then, the forest went silent. I slowly looked at our group to confirm that Gavan and I weren't the only ones to hear this sound. Moving as quietly as possible, I reached up and gently pulled Gavan's big hand from my face. I grew more alarmed when I saw Gabriel's hand squeeze his staff so tight that his knuckles turned white. Asa was gripping the handle of his sword and slowly drawing it from the scabbard. In stark comparison, Luke sat surprisingly relaxed, with his eyes fixed in the same direction as the rest of us.

We all jumped an inch off the ground when Luke called out, "Come here big boy! Don't be afraid, we won't hurt you."

Several extremely tense seconds of silence followed as I tried to focus my eyes on the motionless black object which lay on the forest floor about 40 yards away. With the vow of silence clearly broken by Luke, I asked, "What is it... a bear or a horse?"

Asa mumbled something about the possibility of it being a small horse and Gavan whispered that it could be a bear, but the only moving human body parts, from any of us, was our lips. We just sat on the ground like four discarded statues.

It was Luke who, once again, shattered the petrified silence with, "Here boy. Don't be afraid, we won't hurt you." If my reaction to the beast rising from the forest floor was anything like Gabriel, Gavan and Asa, all of us will need to spend some time in the next river we cross, washing out our pants.

The black beast slowly began to rise... and rise... and rise some more, before it stood on all four legs to quietly assess us as a group. Then, he focused on Luke before slowly taking a few unsure steps toward us. Asa immediately drew and presented his sword and this quick movement halted the beast's approach.

Luke, again, assured our unexpected visitor that it was *safe*, as he slowly moved towards the great black beast on his hands and knees.

Asa whispered in his deepest voice, "Spake for yourself, Lad, I be seeing a great beast and a mortal threat afore us."

Luke quipped, "What *threat*? It's just a big *dog*."

Asa snapped back, "There not be any dogs as big as a horse around here!"

The response from Luke triggered my own memories of large dogs and I whispered, still quiet, intimidated by the large form before us, "There are such dogs, Asa. They are called Great Danes and they were bred as war-dogs. We heard the barking of such dogs as we passed the soldier's encampment."

Asa glanced over his shoulder at me and whispered, "I suppose that bit of information be intended to bring comfort me?"

It was Gavan who first observed, "He be having gentle eyes and I be seeing a long chain about his neck."

Luke spoke once again to all of us, before addressing the gigantic black beast before us, "He's someone's pet and isn't making any signs of hostility toward us." Luke once again called to the huge beast, "It's OK big fella, we're your friends." At Luke's plea, the huge dog took a few more steps toward us and sat down as if waiting for further instructions. Even in the sitting position, the beast's head was as tall as Luke's head when he was standing.

Luke suggested, "I have a piece of bread here. Let's see if he wants it."

Before Asa could finish saying, "Be ye MAD?" the sight of the small piece of bread in Luke's hand was all the encouragement needed to bring the beast directly to Luke... where it laid down and gently received the morsel of bread like a puppy. Asa remained at the ready, expecting the dog to tear into any and all of us... but he relaxed in amazement, as the great beast snuggled next to Luke's leg, rolled onto its back and gave out with a few tiny whimpers of affection.

"I be believing that he likes ye, Luke," observed Gabriel.

Asa mumbled, "I expect he be liking fresh meat, most likely."

The sight of Luke and the gigantic dog getting acquainted was both amazing and tender to see. After a few minutes, it became obvious to the rest of our group that Luke was crying.

Gavan, ever the big burly tender-hearted friend, asked Luke, "What be having ye crying over this dog, Luke?"

Luke didn't answer right away but kept rubbing and petting the big dog who was, obviously, enjoying every second of it. Finally, Luke replied, "Our neighbor had a chocolate Lab named 'Bosco' and he used to spend a lot of time in our yard. I often wished that Bosco was *my* dog, but even if Bosco *was* my dog, he wouldn't be here now."

Asa and Gabriel made eye contact and I got the distinct impression that they were communicating something without speaking a word. I had to ask, "What are you two thinking?"

Gabriel looked at me in silence for several seconds as Asa continued to look at Gabriel. "I be not certain of how to share this," Gabriel began. "Among the Rune parchments, in the monastery, be a few reports of Transfers who be claiming they recognized the personalities of animals they be knowing afore being transferred. These claims have ne'er been confirmed or investigated."

Upon hearing Gabriel's comment, Luke said, "Up Bosco!" We were all stunned when the great beast instantly leaped to its feet and stood face to face with a startled Luke, still sitting on the ground. Luke found a small twig and tossed it with the command, "Fetch!" Like an arrow loosed by an archer, the great dog bound after the stick, snatched it up the instant it struck the ground, and he bounded back to Luke. He dropped the stick in Luke's lap and sat upright with a delightfully pleased with himself look in his eyes.

Again, Luke's eyes teared up and the big dog gently leaned forward to softly lick the tears away. "Could this be possible?" Luke asked, as his gaze focused on Bosco. It was obvious that Luke didn't see the tears in all of our eyes.

"Whoever ye may be, big fella," commented Asa, "ye not be needing that awful collar and chain around your neck." Senescing that he was being addressed, the big dog turned to face Asa, and he laid down with his massive head in Asa's lap. With calm and gentle hands, Asa worked the locking mechanism which held a spike filled collar about the dog's neck. Upon releasing the links of the collar, Asa discovered a ring of puncture wounds which had been inflicted by the inward facing spikes. The dog let out a few little whimpers but never moved until the hideous collar fell to the ground. Asa was stunned and sickened by the number and severity of the wounds created by such a cruel device. Taking his que from Luke, Asa said, "Up Bosco!"

Not only did the dog leap to its feet, he began to run in tight circles with puppy-like whines of joy. To counter the welling of tears, we all laughed without censorship of any kind. Asa, thrilled to have a new friend, who was bigger than any man he knew and must have weighed more than any two men... and yet sweeter.

Asa said with a flourish, "I dub thee 'Bosco, the Dane of Kings.'"

The next hour was spent fixing breakfast and getting better acquainted with Bosco. I wondered how we were going to travel with such an animal, but I never asked any questions since our vow of silence was once again, in affect. When we approached the next couple of villages, Asa, Gabriel or Gavan took turns entering the village to request or purchase food.

The next week of our journey was uneventful and all of us were pleasantly comfortable with Bosco to keep watch through the night. Only twice did Bosco give us any cause for alarm, when his ground shaking growl was both heard and felt. Whatever brought on his alarm must have thought it wise to move off in the darkness. Having Bosco with us gave all of us peaceful nights of sleep and we never needed to coax him to stay with us. It was of his own nature to walk among us all day and sleep in the center of our camp each night.

Bosco did have an appetite every bit as big as he was, and we found ourselves getting meals for seven instead of five when one of our group procured food. It was Asa who suggested that Bosco might be able to hunt for his own food. Asa knelt and with both hands embracing Bosco's head, had a face to face conversation with the massive dog, as if he was a child.

"Bosco," Asa advised, "it be time ye hunt for some meat to feed yerself." Bosco sat stone still, and stared intently into Asa's eyes, for several seconds before bounding off into the forest. This was the first time Bosco had been out of our sight in days and the look on Luke's face implied he was suffering the pain of abandonment. Asa seemed quite confident and assured Luke, "He be coming back."

A couple hours passed, and we continued our journey westward. It was getting toward evening, and Luke kept searching the forest for any sign of Bosco. His concerns were contagious enough to cause all of us to search for our new friend. Gabriel announced that we should make camp soon, which gave us enough light to gather firewood and make bedding plots. Luke's whispered plea, "What about Bosco?" was met with a stern frown from Gabriel.

"I be knowing not about Bosco's location, Luke, but I do be knowing that he be well able to care for himself, and he be having no trouble finding us," offered Gabriel.

Just as our first encounter with Bosco had played out, we once again saw a large black object moving swiftly through the trees. In only seconds, the great black form of Bosco was bounding into our midst; and this time, he came bearing gifts. In his jaws were three dead rabbits! Bosco had not only supplied dinner for himself, his belly was obviously full, but for us, as well. Even more comforting was the presence of our loved watch and guard dog, Bosco. We all slept soundly that night, after a feast of roasted rabbit.

It wasn't many days before the child-like question began to be felt and occasionally asked, "Are we there yet?" Patient as ever, Gabriel seemed able to give estimated answers and, having previously traveled here, I trusted him to know. One afternoon, when Gavan asked if we were on the right road, I whispered, "Yup, just checked my GPS." To this, Luke and I had a little chuckle before being frowned back into our 'vow of silence'.

When Asa asked, "What be a GPS?" Rather than reply to Asa, I gestured to my mouth and shook my head to imply my inability to speak. Luke and I laughed a little more at Asa's puzzled frown. I knew that our little joke was unfair to his limited knowledge of 21st Century technology.

I whispered to Asa, "I'll tell you later," and he was comforted... a little.

That evening, when we stopped to make camp for the night, Asa once again sent Bosco to fetch a few rabbits and the dog bounded out of sight. Being certain that our group was alone, Gavan asked the question, "Does anyone be having a guess about who Bosco belongs to?"
Luke took a quick breath as if he had been kicked in the stomach, and declared, "He belongs to us!"

Gavan replied, knowing how much Luke had taken to Bosco, "He may be our dog *now*, Luke, but he be wearing a collar and dragging a chain when he be finding us."

Luke responded with hurt in his voice, "I find it very awkward to call the torturous device around his neck, a collar."

"No argument with ye opinion, Luke," agreed Gavan in a soft and fatherly way, "but there may be someone who be feeling differently. Dogs are property, and their owners be doing with them, as they wish."

Luke replied in a calm voice, because he knows that Gavan, Gabriel and Asa liked Bosco. "As much as I can understand such a rule or law, Gavan, I can never agree to it, as a *just* law."

Gavan, attempting to address an issue, and not let it turn into an argument, replied, "We be in England, Luke, and the year is 1690. These are facts which, like universal laws, must be recognized and obeyed."

Luke was silent for several minutes, not only for his respect of Gavan, Gabriel and Asa but because he had, like me, grown to love these men. Unable to argue, Luke asked, "What are we to do? Bosco has adopted us, as surely as we have adopted him and we are many miles from where he found us."

Gavan dropped his voice to a very fatherly tone and replied, "I not be knowing, either, Luke. I just be feeling that we be needing to discuss this, before a crisis arises."

Luke, a bit pouty, stated, "*You* guys discuss this. I have already made up my mind that I will *not* lose anything *more* from what I remember before landing in 1690." I'm sure I understood Luke's words better than the others, but I chose to be silent, at this time.

Gavan addressed Luke's word choice of 'guys' again, but saying nothing on the issue of Bosco. "I still be hearing some words which may present a threat. Ye said, 'you guys,' and no one, in this time, be using such an expression."

Luke was still feeling a bit defensive but replied "Okay... I'm sorry."

Asa snorted, "We not be saying *that* either."

Luke fired back, "Ye Lordships, I hunbly apologize to thee." His frustration was manifest with a folding of his arms and silence.

Gabriel commented, "This be much better." and the three shared a smile.

Trying to end the strained silence, I softly stated, "We may not have... be having any meat with our meal this evening, but I do... be hoping Bosco gets back before dark."

"Me, too," added Asa. "I really be liking the way we sleep when he be amongst us."

It was a quiet evening without so much as a breeze to stir the leaves.

I heard a distant short and sharp sound that, even though it had some familiar features, it was unfamiliar. I notice Asa's body language focusing on the sound, as well. Our eyes met.

Asa asked, "Ye be hearing what I be hearing?"

"Yes, but I don't know what it is," I whispered.

Luke replied, "I think it was Bosco yelping in pain." I hated to recognize his words because they were exactly what I was thinking.

Asa nodded, "I be *certain* that it be Bosco, but he will be needing to come to *us* rather than us wandering in the night to find him."

The entire group was frozen and silent, listening for any more sound clues, for what seemed an hour, but was actually a few minutes. Once again, a whimper came through the trees and it sounded much closer. As we fixed our eyes as far as our camp fire lit into the trees, a dark form could be seen moving slowly in our direction.

Luke broke the agonizing silence. "Here, Bosco. Come here, big boy." Almost imperceptibly, the black form corrected its movement and staggered into our camp and laid prone at Asa's feet. It was Bosco and the feathered shaft of an arrow protruded from his flank. As before, Asa went into action, as Luke and I stared in shock and disbelief.

"Someone be sitting by his head and comforting him as I be inspecting the damage," Asa ordered.
Luke sat on the ground and Bosco laid his big head in his lap, as if he knew what to do. Asa very carefully lifted Bosco's arrow pierced leg. Bosco attempted to resist but never made any sound or act of fear.

"The arrow has passed through one leg and cut the inside of the other," announced Asa. Not knowing how long Bosco could be trusted to lie still, Asa explained the steps he intended to take, and he expected all of us to help.

The cut on the inside of Bosco's leg needed to be protected from further injury, and the pierced leg needs to have the arrow removed. Gavan produced a small piece of thick leather. It looked like the sole of a sandal and placed it over the lesser wound as Asa held the pierced leg up high enough to prevent the point of the arrow from doing further harm. Asa told Gabriel to wrap the arrowhead with his fist and grab the long shaft of the arrow on the outside of the pierced leg to prevent the movement of the arrow in the wound. Bosco laid in silent obedience, with Luke talking to him and gently stroking his big head.

Asa used his dagger to cut the shaft of the arrow and tossed it aside. Asa then carefully lifted Bosco's leg to allow

Gabriel to remove the shaft with the arrowhead clasped in his fist. Once the arrow was removed, the wounds of both legs were wrapped.

"It certainly be most fortunate that no large blood vessels be damaged," said Asa. As Bosco lay so trusting and obedient, all of us were silent but each of us admired how patient he was during the removal of that arrow.

"I'm beginning to marvel at how intelligent and trusting Bosco is." I noted, "every dog I've known would not be so trusting as this."

Asa replied, "He be an amazing dog. I be already questioning as you, Raffe, and I, have no answers. He be the most likable beast, ever afore my eyes."

Gabriel spoke up to pose the obvious question, "Who be shooting him, and why?"

Gavan observed, "I be believing we be finding out. Cometh, a man with a bow and arrows." Everyone, except Bosco, snapped their head to where Gavan was focused. It was from the direction where Bosco had returned to us, earlier.

A tall man stood some 40 yards distant and looked at us with very curious eyes. He didn't have an arrow nocked and he was leaning on his bow as if it was a staff. He appeared more curious than threatening. Asa adjusted his red scarf to be fully visible, and stood up. He waved to the archer to come forward, who neither responded with words nor complied.

Asa spoke loud enough to be certain that he was heard, "We be friendly travelers in this region. Ye be having no need to fear us or the dog you shot! The dog will be fine once he has had time to heal."

More silence came from the stranger for an uncomfortable span of time. Trying to demonstrate his sincerity, Asa held up the metal point of the arrow and said, "Ye be wanting this back since metal points be expensive."

To retrieve his arrowhead, the archer carefully walked forward until he stood just a couple feet from Bosco's hind feet. Bosco looked up at the stranger but made no indication of fear or aggression. This deeply affected the young archer and he said he shot out of fear because he had never seen any beast as large, except an ox or horse. Taking notice of Gabriel, Luke and me and our monk's robes, he assumed us to be priests.

The archer blurted out, "I be so sorry! I be having no idea that this great beast be a dog or that it belonged to the Church. Please, forgive me?"

With his warmest voice, Gabriel used this moment to say, "I forgive ye, my son. I be seeing how ye mistook 'Bosco' for a wild beast. With the quick thinking of our friend, Asa, the dog be recovering and be as strong as ever."

Everyone, except Luke, understood this incident as a misunderstanding and fear-motivated action. Luke was glad that he was under an oath of silence and it gave him the excuse to not say the angry words boiling inside him.

The young archer, to show his sincerity, removed his quiver of arrows and leaned it, and his bow, against a tree before asking, "Do ye be thinking Bosco also be forgiving me?" Gavan spoke saying, "I not be knowing of any dog be willing to forgive the man who shot him, accident or not."

"Even if Bosco *does* snap at me," proclaimed the archer, "I wouldn't blame him." With these words the young archer knelt next to Bosco and he gently stroked the great beast's head. We all held our breath because we had no idea what Bosco's reaction would be. After a few soft strokes, Bosco raised his head and licked the hand of the man who shot him.

It was Asa who spoke up with the observation, "There be an example of Christian love, unlike any I be seeing from a human."

"My wish be to help," offered the archer, as he continued to stroke the rich soft fur along Bosco's head and neck.

"As a hunter," Gabriel responded. "ye may be bringing us some meat to help Bosco recover."

"I will gladly do that," the archer said with great relief. He was given a task he knew himself to be well suited for. "I be trying to get you a rabbit before nightfall and hunt again tomorrow, for more." With this encouragement, the archer got to his feet, recovered his bow and arrows, and set off into the forest.

No sooner than he was gone, I asked, "Did anyone get the archer's name?" Gabriel, Gavan and Asa looked at each other with questioning eyes and then back to me. It never occurred to anyone to ask.

Luke softly said, "His name is Oliver and he's the eldest of four sons."

We all joined in staring at Luke, still holding Bosco's head while looking at his own feet.

Asa, being the most curious among us, asked, "Please be spaking to us how ye come to know the name and family situation of the young man ye just met!"

"I guess I should be more understanding," Luke began, "of you men forgetting that I was a woman before my consciousness was transferred to this time and body."

"What doth that be having to do with this situation?" asked Gavan. "How doth ye previous gender affect anyone today?"

"I certainly don't know *how*," Luke replied, "but I *do* know that when I looked at him, we had some sort of instant connection. He whispered some information into my mind, without speaking a word." None of us had anything to say as we processed the strange information Luke was relating to us.

It was well past sunset but not quite dark when the voice of Oliver called to us as he approached our camp. He had only one rabbit and we all agreed that it should go to Bosco. And Bosco agreed. Once skinned, the rabbit was thoroughly enjoyed for several seconds before Bosco completely consumed it.

Turning his focus on Luke, Oliver said that he had to get home, but he promised to find us tomorrow and bring more rabbits. The young man bid us all a farewell and then a singular, "Good Night," to Luke. It was too dark to be sure, but I think Luke blushed a little.

Since Bosco was in no condition to keep watch, we decided to take turns keeping the fire stoked and stay alert for the potential of any intruders... man or beast. With such wounds, Bosco passed the night with more sleep than any of his human companions. Long before dawn, Luke and Asa woke and silently moved about in preparation for breakfast. Then they readied supplies for whatever traveling we might be able to do, IF Bosco was able to walk.

All of us were awake before the first rays of light illuminated the tops of the trees and the topic of conversation centered around Bosco, our journey and the surprising connection between the archer, Oliver, and Luke. The first time Asa mentioned Oliver, Luke grew uncomfortable and turned the conversation to Bosco and his needs. Not wanting to create any conflict, the others let the subject of Bosco fill our concerns and plans. Gabriel said that we were within three days of reaching Anglesey Island and this pause in our travels would be a good time to share his expectations with all of us.

I thought it a little discomforting that we were so far into a journey before the final details were revealed but also anxious to hear what he had to say. With mugs of tea, far too hot to drink, we warmed our hands as Gabriel began his lecture.

"Please interrupt if there be anything that be needing an explanation," Gabriel began. "In my years of learning the Druid writings, and reading many parchments containing their sacred and secular stone recordings, on several occasions, read of hidden texts which, according to the writer, be *not* Druid and ought to be *heeded* because the words be about a distant future."

Upon hearing Gabriel say, "distant future," Luke spoke so loud and fast that Bosco awoke with a lurch that became like a bolt of lightning traveling through all of us.

Luke challenged, "What do you *mean* '*distant future?*' How *far* into the future?"

Asa, acting like a referee, held up both hands with his palms toward Luke. "Be giving him a little time to spake," Asa said. "I suspect he be telling ye." It seemed obvious that Asa had heard the contents of Gabriel's lecture before and didn't want to waste any time.

In an assuring tone, Gabriel said, "It be quite alright, Asa. We be only imagining what this transition be like for Luke and Raffe, and I intend on using our stationary time to inform and comfort them."

I had a tornado of questions swirling in my mind, but Gabriel's words were so assuring that I knew I would have fewer questions if I waited. Gavan sat silently leaning against a tree as the rest of us exchanged words and gestures. Maybe it was Gavan's calm demeanor that motivated Bosco to crawl to his side and lay his massive head in Gavan's lap. Gavan welcomed the big dog's warmth and affection and the two appeared to be enjoying that special moment as Gavan's thick fingers gently stroked Bosco's head and neck. Apparently, the old wounds made by the cruel collar had healed or they were much more comfortable than his new wounds from Oliver's arrow.

Without recognizing my present surroundings, I said out loud, "I wish I had a camera. The sight of Bosco and Gabriel is definitely a 'Kodak moment.'"

Luke replied, "I guess your mind just made a trip back home, Raffe."

I immediately felt very foolish for speaking and regretful of the thoughtless danger to which I exposed all of us. I quickly looked around to be certain that we were alone and sat down to hear what Gabriel had originally wanted to share.

Gabriel began again, "Both of ye, Raffe and Luke, already know that ye names be scratched into the wall of the cave we be going to visit in a few days. There be much more written in that cave, and I be hoping that yer knowledge, from ye previous lives, will understand what ye hear and help us preserve this information."

I sat in silence as Gabriel continued.

"Asa and I be caretakers of the parchments ye saw stored in the basement of our monastery. We also be given the responsibility of protecting the cave sites in which the Runes be found."

Luke spoke again, and asked the exact question I was forming in my mind: "Who or what organization *assigned* the two of you to this task?"

Gabriel appeared to welcome Luke's question and replied proudly, "The Grand Master of the Grand Table of Consciousness be giving each of us responsibilities which supports and protects the order. Every one of us be either descendants of transferred consciousness or, like both of you, transferred people who are struggling to survive in a very strange and hostile time. Asa be knowing more about the threats facing thee, and I be turning this subject over to him to be explaining." Asa may have lacked the leadership qualities of Gabriel, but he wasn't lacking in courage and the skills needed in a fight.

"It be all about ye family," Asa began, "in the Passing of 1364, a young man's consciousness was transferred to a young peasant-farmer. He be treated like some   divine messenger by his family and the villagers, when he claimed to be from the year 2994. He initially lived a comfortable life because the peasants brought him gifts to hear about the future and his strange manner of speaking. The initial special treatment went well until he heard reports of other transferred people, and took it upon himself, to eliminate the competition for fame. The gifts brought to him be enough for him to be hiring thugs to quietly murder anyone who made claims to be from another time. Upon eliminating his known competition, he reaffirmed his special knowledge and increased his wealth and power. Eventually, he be making himself a local king. This new king increased his fortune and power by marrying into a wealthy family and decreed that every one of his descendants be considered a divine bloodline."

"With bounties being on their heads," Asa continued, "it be assumed that all of the transferred people be killed. What this self-proclaimed king *didn't* know was that long before his year of transfer, others be transferred in the years 1038, 712, 386, 60 and even 266 BC. Enough of these previous transfers had met with the ignorant fears and folk legends for the secret organization to be carefully established and prepared for the next anniversary of *The Passing*. Knowing the years of The Passing, we, the descendants of previous Transfers, locate and protect people like ye and Luke, from the king's solders who be having orders to *kill, on sight,* anyone who be acting differently."

"How can someone be killed without good reason?" asked Luke.

Gavan sat up and pulled up the sleeve of his shirt to reveal the large scar made when he covered Raffe's escape. "Just be like this, Luke," he said, "and they be even deadlier with another villager who be having no idea of the danger he be facing." It was obvious that Luke was very impressed with Gavan's long scar and he returned to sitting quietly, absorbing all this information.

"Like any family," Asa continued, "this ambitious new *king* be wanting to protect his little kingdom and be providing for his heirs. He be making laws protecting his descendants, and rewarding anyone who be finding and reporting others thought to be transferred. The unfortunate result of such evil laws be the unleashed slaughter of anyone who behaved differently, or be *claimed* to be acting differently, to conceal a murder. It be still a common suspicion when someone be murdered, and reported to be acting strangely, it be the *old laws* being used as a justification for their crime."

"Are the years of a Passing common knowledge?" Luke asked.

Gabriel replied, "No. Both sides of this issue, the descendants of the king and the Order of Consciousness be keeping the anniversaries secret. We keep it a secret to protect transferred people from bounty hunters and the king's descendants keep it a secret so they can prepare for the next Passing."

"This is a most fascinating history, Gabriel," I interjected, "but how does this affect anything about Luke and me?"

Gabriel didn't answer me immediately. He sat quietly studying the small flames of our breakfast fire for several minutes before lifting his gaze up, past all of us and into the treetops which were now awash with brilliant sunlight. He tilted his head back and allowed the brilliant light to flood his eyes until they began to shed tears which rolled down his cheeks. Closing his eyes and wiping them with his sleeves, Gabriel brought his face down to meet Luke's and my transfixed stares. "Ye be having a right to be knowing that Amergus not only be naming both of ye, but she/he wrote about a manner of death one of ye will suffer."

"And the manner of death is... ?" I asked.

Gabriel, looked at both Luke and I, and softly said, "I not be knowing, *yet*."

"Wait!" grunted Luke, "Are you telling us that a woman, transferred from the distant future back to 60 AD, wrote something on a cave wall about two people transferred in 2016 back here to 1690: and we are supposed to believe our 'manner of deaths' is written on that cave wall?" Luke looked like he didn't believe or comprehend his own words.

A simple and whispered, "Yes," was Gabriel's reply, "but not *both* of thee, just *one* of thee."

I looked at Luke for a few seconds and neither of us could do anything except blink. I then studied Asa, Gavan and Gabriel's faces before asking, "Does anyone know what it is that 'passes' every 326 years to bring about these time-transfers?" Asa looked as if he was about to speak but Gabriel spoke first.

"No one be knowing," Gabriel began, "but the most recent discovery of Rune writing implies that the answer to yer question may be found in these texts. Since none of the monks who be knowing of this cave can read the Rune words, we be interpreting them after we be getting there."

Luke let Gabriel's words sink in before observing, "If the Runes cannot be read by any of those monks, how does anyone know that Raffe and my names are written in that cave?"

Gabriel looked directly into Luke's eyes and said, "Because that portion of the chiseled words be written in American-English, Amergus' first language, before she or he be transferred."

I don't know how long we might have stayed there with blank expressions on our face if Bosco hadn't taken that moment to attempt to stand. His first two efforts failed, and he let out some very sad whimpers when his hind end refused to support his weight. He lay on his side for several minutes as Luke and Gavan gently stroked his head and back, before struggling to sit up. With a mighty heave forward, he was standing, quite wobbly, on all four legs. It took him several more minutes before he attempted any steps and they were tiny shuffles with his hind legs, as most of his weight was supported on his front legs. Bosco had only moved a few feet before he tenderly lowered his frame to the ground, closer to the fire. Luke knelt next to Bosco's head and Bosco gave his knees a thorough wash with his palm-sized tongue.

All of us were in a melancholy mood as Luke stroked Bosco's head. It was Asa who stated the obvious, "We not just be staying here for a week while Bosco mends. We be within a few days of our destination, and remaining anywhere, other than in a monastery for more than a day, be very risky."

Gavan asked the group, "Anyone be having a suggestion of what we should be doing?"

Asa used this question to emphasize his initial concerns by saying, "Anything be better for us than staying here, in this open forest. The monastery be our safest lodging, yet even a friendly village be an advantage."

My contribution to this conversation was to state the obvious, "Luke and I may be key elements in this journey, for the reasons Gabriel has told us, but neither of us know where we are going, and we increase our danger if we talk with anyone outside our group. I can only speak for myself when I say that I am committed to finishing our journey, and I trust every one of you with my life."

Once again, it was Asa who brought up the painfully obvious topic of Bosco being able to travel. Gavan cleared his throat, as he suggested making a stretcher. This idea didn't last very long.

Asa asked, "Which two of us ye be thinking strong enough to be carrying one end of a stretcher with a dog weighing well more than two men?" No one answered because all of us knew the idea was impossible.

"Good morning!" came a call as Oliver strode between the trees, and pulling a handcart, as if he was an answer to our current dilemma. Oliver pulled his cart up to our camp and sat down to catch his breath. As curious as I was about this man's ability to communicate without words, I was more interested in his potential friendship with our enemy. Oliver was a tall man with broad shoulders and powerful arms which hung on either side of a deeply defined chest. I was familiar with the draw-weights of English longbows being well over 100 pounds, and shooting such bows develop the upper-body muscles, so I assumed his use of a longbow be credited for his muscular physique. His affinity for archery, however, had no connection with his long blond hair and very precisely sewn clothes. The stitching of his shirt was very carefully done, almost as consistent as a sewing machine might produce. I couldn't shake the impression of Oliver coming from a very well educated or wealthy family. This was a man who needed to be watched!

"What be all of this?" asked Gavan, as he stood to admire the appearance of a handcart at such an opportune moment. His face grew even brighter as he saw that the cart was packed with fresh vegetables, loaves of bread and a freshly killed chicken.

Oliver's face beamed with delight, as he explained, "I be telling me parents about shooting yer dog and how understanding all of ye and Bosco were. Then I told them that ye be traveling from the monastery to the Isle of Anglesey."

"How be ye knowing where we be coming from and where we be going?" interrupted Asa, with a suspicious and interrogating tone.

Luke volunteered, "I told him," and looked at his own feet to avoid Asa's frown.

Oliver could easily see that his words had stirred a bit of trouble for his new friend, Luke, and continued his explanation. "I assure ye that yer information be safe with me, and me family. Many years ago, the good monks on Anglesey came to our village when a sickness be raging among us. Several children, including me, took sick and two children died before the monks came with food and medicine. The monks be staying until the danger be past. The village be wanting to thank them, by helping the four of ye to finish your journey. I also have some honey for Bosco's wounds and clean bandages."

114

It was Gabriel who spoke first, by saying, "I not be knowing what to say! This is most kind and timely of thee."

Oliver added, with a broad smile on his face, "Me parents be saying I could travel with ye to help pull the cart, and return the cart, when ye be finished with it."

"That's wonderful," said Luke, as he realized that he shouldn't be speaking at all.

It was Gabriel who chuckled and put a big arm about Luke's shoulder for comfort. "I be guessing that it be from you, Luke, that Oliver learned of our origin as well as our destination. The ruse of being bound by an oath of silence be long broken."

Gabriel announced, "Oliver be traveling with us but the oath of silence, for ye two, must be observed when anyone be present."

Gavan asked Oliver if he had already eaten because we would soon be on our way. It would be most unkind, to ask the bearer of such fine gifts, to pull a cart on an empty stomach.

"Yes, Brother Gavan," replied Oliver, "and I am very anxious to be on our way."

It took a few minutes to re-arrange the vegetables and secure the chicken out of Bosco's reach before the great, gentle dog could be hoisted by all of us onto the cart. The huge dog nearly filled the cart and seemed quite content to lay quietly as Oliver gently rolled the cart westward.

As our small collection of souls walked along at a pace that wouldn't shake Bosco too severely, I asked Gabriel, in a whisper, "How much information should we share with Oliver? He seems like a nice lad, but we have only known him for one day."

Gabriel leaned slightly in my direction and softly replied, "I be still bothered some by how much Luke be telling. I be thinking we should learn that first, afore deciding what else he be needing to know."

That may be difficult," I replied, "since Luke hasn't left his side for more than a few minutes."

"I hope this not be a problem," whispered Gabriel. "We be only watching and waiting."

The rest of our travel that day was uneventful. I was expecting that Bosco would want to jump off the cart to relieve himself but, to the joy of us all, he just lay quietly. Each time the cart was stopped to exchange the job of pulling, Bosco raised his head to look about and then laid back before the cart began to move. Near the end of our day, we selected a small clearing near running water for our night's camp.

Asa was pulling the cart when we stopped, and he called for assistance when Bosco stirred. He wanted to exit the cart. Gavan was close and he was able to get one arm under Bosco's belly as the big dog slid his front end to the ground. With Gavan supporting much of his weight, Bosco was able to stand on his lesser injured leg. Apparently, Bosco decided that this was as good a place as any to relieve his bladder and bowels.

Standing patiently by, as the necessities were completed, Asa declared, "I guess we can travel a little farther before making camp." Gavan chuckled and pulled the cart a couple hundred yards and we stopped again. Bosco made the noble effort to walk on his one hind leg by gingerly hopping on three legs. Even this short distance was exhausting for Bosco and when he caught up to the cart, he slumped to the ground, and the rest of us walked around him.

"I be believing Bosco thinks this be as good a camp site, as any," Asa said. A fire big enough to roast our chicken was made and we all, except Bosco, enjoyed a stomach-filling dinner.

The morning was cool and gray and the breeze came out of the West and carried the smell of a salty mist. Knowing that we were approaching the West coast had all of us in good spirits with the thoughts of sleeping under a roof and enjoying our meals at tables in the monastery. Bosco made several good efforts to walk on his own and each time he reached his limit, the party had to stop and lift him onto the cart. He never complained or even hinted at being afraid. The dog seemed to be so comfortable and compliant that he was the topic of several conversations which all focused around the loving and trusting nature of such a massive beast.

In camp that evening, I listened as Gabriel, Asa and Gavan discussed their plans for crossing over to the Isle of Anglesey. Gavan suggested that they hire a local fisherman to carry them over. Asa protested that such a passage was much too dangerous because of the bounties on the heads of transferred people. The group hadn't noticed Luke and Oliver walking up to listening distance.

Oliver volunteered, "Me brother be having a boat and I'm sure he be helping us. He be one of the children the monks saved."

Asa, always a little cautious and, by experience, suspicious, asked Oliver, "How ye be so sure of your brother's help? How long it be since ye last be seeing him?"

Oliver studied each of the men's faces before responding, "My brother be trusted for the same reason as me. My parents be trusted, and our entire village, too. We be descendants of Transferred Consciousness. That be why the monks worked so hard to save the children in me village. We be knowing that there be a recent Passing and there be people who be needing of rescue from the king's men."

Gabriel began to chuckle, and his chuckle turned into laughter, as he excitedly put together the pieces of the *chance* meeting with Oliver, and the generous help offered by Oliver's village.

Gabriel asked, "How did ye be knowing that Luke and Raffe be recent Transfers and why did ye keep yer knowledge a secret from us?"

"It be *yer* secret, not mine," replied Oliver. "Luke be saying ye not be wanting anyone to know, so I not be mentioning it."

"That be making good sense," chimed Gavan, "Ye be a good lad for keeping our own secret, a secret from us. Please be telling us about yer brother's boat. Be it big enough for all of us? As a fisherman, I know a few things about boats."

Oliver shared all that he knew about his brother's boat, but he also admitted that he had never actually seen the boat. He was just sharing what his brother had told him, two years ago.

"Whatever it be taking," Asa commented, "once we be getting onto the Isle of Anglesey, we'll be out of the king's realm of power. Our discovery of what be inscribed on the walls of that cave will have some answers for us."

Gabriel added, "We already told a few very interesting pieces about the inscriptions, but pieces of information not be meaning much, without the context of the whole message."

I looked at Luke for a moment and, without words, we both felt the sensations of fear and discovery fighting for dominance in this bazaar journey. I had many questions in my mind vying for dominance as severely as they were screaming for answers. One haunting thought kept boiling to the surface of my consciousness. What could I do with the knowledge I already have, from someone born centuries after Luke and me, with technology neither of us will understand.

Gavan read my face like a book and commented, "Ye not do *anything* with information ye not be *having*, Raffe. Allow not the *fear* of the *unknown*, to prevent ye from *learning more* than ye already be knowing."

Asa and Gabriel gave Gavan a very surprised look, as Asa teased, "When ye become such a deep-thinking philosopher, Gavan?"

From the very corner of his bushy eyebrows, Gavan squinted as he replied, "I be always smarter than ye be expecting of me. It be giving me the slightest of advantages, most of the time."

With a soft and big-brotherly voice, Asa replied, "I be believing you, Gavan, and I shall always be hoping for ye to be close by, in any threatening situation."

Our growing troop had only traveled a quarter of a mile before Bosco began to give little whimpers with each painful step he took. I was surprised that he had been able to take more than a single step. We halted the cart, and Bosco, as if on que, hopped next to the cart and stood quietly, waiting for us to carefully lift his massive frame onto the soft blankets. His wounds were not bleeding,.. an indicator that he was healing very quickly.

I had been thinking about the situation which lie shortly ahead of us. On several occasions, both Gavan and Asa mentioned that our destination was on an island but neither gave any clues about how we were going to get to this island.

As if he was reading my thoughts, Asa asked Oliver, "Do ye be knowing anything about yer brother's uses for his boat?"

Oliver gave some thought to Asa's question and said, "He spake of using his boat to ferry people and supplies to and from the Isle of Anglesey, but, as I be telling ye, I not be seeing it or learned any specific details about his boat."

Asa, trying to gather more information asked, "What kind of things did ye brother be ferrying?"

Again, Oliver thought before responding, "He be telling me that he ferried cattle and large sacks of wheat and barley by planking two boats together... lashing long planks to be making a platform over and between two boats." To this Asa, Gavan and Gabriel gave a smile and grunts of relief.

Even with this encouraging new information, I found myself wondering how the presence of a giant dog was going to be perceived by the owners of the boats. I had a question for Oliver and asked as we walked, "What's your brother's name?" Oliver appeared a little troubled by what I thought to be a very simple question.

"Well," began Oliver, "his given name be Andrew but, he might not be using his real name when working his boat. There be a rumor, for several years, that another Passing was coming. Most people from our village, when conducting business with outsiders, be using a false name. When we be getting to the crossing, it may be best if I be making some inquiries afore the rest of us be showing ourselves."

Gavan, along with everyone else, heard Oliver's words and made an offer. "How about I be traveling with ye, Oliver," Gavan suggested, "I be familiar with boats and sea-faring men and I be of help if boats need to be rigged for a crossing." Oliver was instant in his acceptance of Gavan's help and appeared genuinely pleased to have the big fisherman for a companion.

Gavan asked Oliver, "What be the sort of people we be likely to encounter at the crossing?"

"It be difficult to put everyone into one group, Gavan," Oliver began, "Some citizens in that community be only there to cheat, rob and kill. These ruffians be found in the taverns during the day and in the allies after dark. Most there be like anyone else and be hardworking, honest people who only wish to live in peace and safety."

"How be it that ye know so much about a community which ye not be visiting before?" asked Asa.

Oliver was very open and comfortable with his reply. "Many living at the crossing come from me own village, and that means they be descendants of Transferred souls. We all have a bond of trust which be keeping us separate from the others, even when we be living amongst them." Oliver spoke about Transferred descendants, in a manner that implied some sort of identity method, which was unfamiliar to the rest of us.

I had to ask, "Oliver, how can you distinguish between a descendant of a Transfer and others?"

My question put a questioning look on Oliver's face, as he looked at each one of us very carefully. "By yer *aura*," he replied, as if surprised that we should even ask this question. All of us stopped, exchanged eye-locks and finally all of us were looking at Oliver with blank but curious expressions.

Gabriel was first to speak. "What ye be meaning by the word 'aura,' Oliver?"

Oliver didn't respond immediately but chose to look at each one of us, individually, before answering Gabriel. "This question has me a little fearful. I be using the words, 'aura,' because each of us be having a soft blue or pink aura around our bodies so we can instantly identify descendants of Transfers. The auras round Raffe, Luke and Bosco be much brighter than the auras round Gavan, Asa and ye, Gabriel." Oliver again looked at the rest of our troop with bewilderment that such a question was asked.

Asa was first to recover from the stunning revelation of Oliver's words, and as always, challenged what he heard. "Ye be telling us that we *glow*, like a choir of angels?" Asa asked.

Oliver began to smile with the dawning of his memories of information he had been told years ago. "That not be accurate, but very nice, Asa. My parents be telling me, when but a child, that the members of our village be all direct descendants of Transfers. Our pure bloodline has allowed us to see the remnant aura of Transfers and their children, if both parents be having pure blood."

"Ahah!," spouted Asa, "I be hoping I be not the only one here who finds this report so amazing that my brain be wanting to *reject* it!"

The silence about us was growing louder by the second, and I felt as if I might wake up and discover that this was all a bad dream. The sharp sound of Asa's question snapped me back to the present situation.

"If this be the ability of yer 'true bloods,'" Asa asked, "how be it that neither Luke nor Raffe be seeing it?"

Oliver answered with a soft and apologetic voice, "I not be knowing, but me patents be telling me that it be only found in those who be having *both parents* who are descendants of Transfers, and neither be having such parents, if they be recently transferred."

"This be some amazing information to process," Gabriel observed. "It *does* explain why ye be so comfortable round us when we be but strangers." As the question was forming in his mind, Gabriel continued, "What about ye be shooting Bosco? Why would ye *do* that if he be having an aura?"

To this question, Oliver's face grew bright red as he stared at the ground and
confessed. "I be thinking the big dog killed and be eating someone from our village. I not be seeing an animal be having an aura afore."

As before, each answer from Oliver left us slightly more shocked than the last. I had a lot of questions dancing in my mind, but I couldn't organize my words, so I remained silent.

"TMI," said Luke. His face blushed the instant he realized that he had spoken out loud and used language that was unknown to everyone except me.

Asa asked, "What be the meaning?"

"It's an expression commonly used a long time from now, Luke explained. "They are the first letters of a three-word expression, meaning, 'too much information,' and it will, one day, be a common form of communication."

"That's nice to know," quipped Asa, "but in 1690, it be enough to get all of us killed."

Asa's sharp reminder brought us all back to the present reality, the present mission and the ever-present threat.

Our small troop began to move forward once again as Gavan pulled the cart. Oliver walked close beside Gavan so they could quietly discuss plans for meeting Oliver's brother, Andrew, and securing some floating transport to the Isle of Anglesey. I kept looking from body to body among us, straining my eyes in hope of seeing the strange aura Oliver claimed to see. The idea of having an aura that only the right people could see, sounded like a great way to be safe... if, those with an aura were trustworthy. I thought it would be good to talk with Oliver about this, as soon as possible.

Evening arrived long after all of us, except Bosco, were ready for a rest. Through the warm day, I had formulated, and then rejected, dozens of questions... for dozens of reasons. When a fire was built and our sleeping plots prepared, we gathered as the evening meal was prepared. Even Bosco found the strength to exit from the cart and lie with his big head in Luke's lap, anticipating every scrap he could solicit, with his big soft eyes.

I said, "Now that the amazing information you shared with us has had a few hours to digest, would you help me with a few more questions?" I didn't expect Oliver to know everything, but all of us were certain that he knew a lot more about this aura stuff than he had already shared. "You told us that everyone in your village has the ability to see the aura of other Transfer descendants. Can you tell which people are from your village and which are descendants of the original king?"

"Yes," replied Oliver. "That be very easy, since they not be having an aura, at least none that we be seeing. My parents be telling that this is because the first king be so greedy for wealth and power that he married the daughter of a wealthy landowner. The descendants, ever since, be having no aura. Several of the Transfers from the 1364 Passing be living on a small farm where the village now stands. Couples from this farm be having several children, and it be through those children that the ability to be seeing our aura be discovered. These children remained isolated and as adults, they had children with their neighbors, and a community began. After a couple of generations, it be decided that young people, who be seeing an aura, to be matched. Now, the entire village, about 150 souls, be seeing auras, as well as, being committed to marry to preserve the gift." Oliver continued, "Our elders be predicting that another Passing be about to happen; and men from our village be searching for those here from the Passing, and they be bringing them to our village."

This information caught Luke's attention and he interrupted Oliver to ask, "How many new Transfers have you found?" We all waited for the answer.

Looking a little sheepish for his lack of knowledge, Oliver answered, "I not be sure. Those we found , be carefully brought into our village and assigned to a home. Once inside the village, no one spakes of them and no one be asking. This process be planned and prepared, for many years. If the king be having even a hint of this, it would be the death of everyone in my village."

I didn't sleep very well that night. Thoughts about my own strange experience due to the Passing, thoughts about how Luke and I presented such a lethal threat to these brave friends, and pondering thoughts about the transferring of animal consciousness, refused to let my mind sleep. Sometime long after laying down, and even longer before dawn, I heard Luke whisper.

"Are you still awake, Raffe?"

I spoke as low and soft as possible to respond, "Yeah, ain't this a bitch?"

Luke didn't say anything, but I could hear him quietly sobbing.

I thought, this must be even worse for Luke. He's trying to live in a man's body with a woman's thoughts and feelings."

123

Luke leaned on one elbow and wiped the tears from his eyes. "I've been talking with Oliver," he started, with almost a whisper, "and when we are finished on the Isle of Anglesey, I think I'd like to stay in Oliver's village rather than return to the monastery. He said that there may be families who could use some help with the children. I told Oliver who I was before the Passing and he thinks I could be helpful, especially if they find recent Transfers who need a place to stay. I'm sure I can be helpful in some way."

I didn't answer immediately to consider his words as well as his potential future. Before I spoke, a deep male voice interrupted.

"Me thinks that be a great idea, Luke." It was Gavan.

"I think it be, too," Asa piped in.

Gabriel waited several seconds before mumbling, "I think it be a good idea too, Luke... and I also think getting some *sleep...* is a good idea."

After breakfast, it was agreed that Oliver and Gavan would make the one-mile journey to Bangor to find Oliver's brother, Andrew, and procure what was needed to cross over to the Llandegfan side of the Menai Strait. The rest of us will stay put in this camp, which was well off the primary road to Bangor. This plan will also give Bosco more time to mend since we still had more than enough provisions in Oliver's cart.

Chapter 8
Finding Andrew

It was a clear day with a slight breeze from the South when Gavan and Oliver prepared for the walk to Bangor. Oliver made no secret of his excitement to see his brother and he packed a few items into a sack for Andrew that their parents had included in the cart. Without giving much thought to it, Oliver grabbed his bow and quiver, which had lain unnoticed in the cart, wrapped in a blanket.

"WHOA!" exclaimed Gavan, "where ye be thinking ye be going with that weapon?"

"I carry this with me everywhere I be going," explained Oliver.

Asa was quick to add, "What do ye think the king's men be doing to ye ifffen they see ye carrying a weapon able of bringing down one of the king's deer?"

Oliver looked a bit puzzled and explained, "I've never shot a deer, only rabbits and a couple birds."

"Oh, I believe you, Oliver," continued Asa, "but I be having every reason to doubt that a group of soldiers, looking for trouble, be so quick to believe ye."

"Asa is right, lad," Gavan added, "ye be having no need of a bow and arrows in the town." Oliver had learned to trust in the counsel of these men and returned his bow and quiver to the cart.

"If it be giving ye any comfort, Oliver," said Asa, "I be having a small dagger that ye be welcome to carry."

"That be alright, Asa," replied Oliver, "if Gavan be armed, I feel safe, and me brother be there, as well."

Gavan and Oliver were barely out of listening range when Oliver spoke without turning his head. "There be something else I be needing to spake about the people from me village... not shared with everyone because I don't believe I have any answers.

Having captured all of Gavan's attention, he continued walking, but turned his head toward Oliver and inquired, "What, under heaven, might be that new secret?"

Oliver, trying to act as if the words were nothing special, said, "The people of my village can talk to each other without speaking."

The two men continued walking for several seconds before Gavan began to slow his pace and then came to a stop. He waited for Oliver to stop and face the big man's flushed face. Leaning heavily on his thick staff, Gavan asked, "Ye be needing to explain this to me, lad. Me thinks I understand what ye just spoke, but be needing a few more details."

"I expected that ye would," replied Oliver. "That be why I be wanting to wait 'til there be only one person to be loading me with questions rather than the whole group."

"Aye," said Gavan, "ye have your one person and I do be having some questions for ye. To start, how do ye learn to spake without words?"

"We be using words," explained Oliver, "but, we not be using our mouths to spake them. Afore ye ask... our minds be hearing the thoughts of others *when they want to be heard.*"

"Be you reading my mind?" asked Gavan.

"No, Gavan," replied Oliver, "we be only reading the minds of other members of our village; and e'en then, only when the person thinking *wants* the thoughts heard and *only* by the person they be wishing to *address*. It be the same as two people whispering in a room full of people. And, if it be comforting ye, only people from our village, and maybe transfers, be communicating this way."

"Ye be right about one thing, Lad," huffed Gavan, "it be *giving* me great comfort to be knowing that me thoughts be safe from ye."

Oliver looked a little surprised by Gavan's comment and asked, "May I be asking ye what ye be meaning by that?"

"Sure, ye can, Lad, but *not today*," Gavan replied. "*Today*, we be having many other issues to be exploring and goals to achieve."

126

"I be understanding. That be why I be sharing with ye the method I be using to find Andrew. Ye not be needing to ask... I be explaining as we walk." said Oliver, anticipating Gavan's next question.

Gavan snapped a question, "Did ye just be hearing what my mind thinking to ask ye that?"

"No," replied Oliver, "it just be seeming logical that ye would ask." Both men laughed but Gavan's laugh was a little more uncomfortable than Oliver's.

"People from my village be easy to identify by the aura we be having. When we be getting to Bangor, I be finding a slightly high position and be searching for auras in the population. When I be seeing someone from my village, I be waiting for them to be making eye contact. Then, I be asking of them, if they be knowing Andrew, and be helping us to finding him."

"How do ye know that ye be trusting everyone from yer village?" asked Gavan.

Oliver took on a very serious expression, before answering, "We *not* be knowing, Gavan," he admitted, "but, there be a little trick we be using, as children, that requires yer help to hide us until we be certain. As children in the village, we be playing a game of hide and seek. In this game, we be learning that just having eye contact need not be revealing our identity, and we practiced hiding behind an object with a tiny hole in it. This be allowing eye contact without showing yer face! This works e'en better when a third person be between us, and we be using this third person as a place to hide."

"How I be doing this?" asked Gavan.

"All ye need to be doing, Gavan, is to stand still, and be allowing me to stand close behind ye and peek over yer shoulder, or under yer ear lobe or through yer hair. They be aware of someone communicating with them, but they not be able to be seeing me when they look at ye. Me thoughts be different than yers, and the confusion be giving me the few seconds needed to determine if they be helping us."

Gavan walked without speaking for a short while, before commenting, "It be sounding strange to me, but if this worked

127

for ye as a child, it just might be giving us the edge for secrecy we be wanting."

The two men were entering Bangor and it became increasingly obvious that there were very few people walking the main road to and from the boat docks. Gavan quietly asked, without turning his head, "Ye be seeing any auras?"

"Not e'en one, so far," Oliver replied. "I be preferring that we be in a large crowd, making us harder to identify."

"It be your game," Gavan said, "just be letting me know what to do, and what not to do."

As expected, the closer Gavan and Oliver got to the center of Bangor and the docks, the larger clusters of humanity milled about. Fortunately, Bangor was a busy port with traffic to and from the Isle of Anglesey. This meant there were many visitors and pass-through vendors. Again, Gavan inquired about seeing people with auras and Oliver gave a one-word reply,

"None." As the water's edge and long docking platforms came into sight, Oliver suggested, "Let us not be getting any closer to the docks. If Andrew be there, I be seeing and spaking with him, from here."

It was Gavan's turn to give a one-word reply, "Amazing."

The two men stepped onto a plank walkway for a few inches of elevation and a little shade from the mid-day sun. Gavan was about to make an observation about the weather, rather than stand like a couple of silent statues when...

"There!" Oliver whispered, "About halfway to the docks, I be seeing an aura, but I be not seeing who be making it. Stand right where ye be, and I be moving behind ye."

"Not too close, Lad," teased Gavan, "that will draw attention for sure."

Oliver looked a bit puzzled because he failed to recognize Gavan's kind of humor. Gavan made several attempts to look casual and comfortable as he quietly waited for information from Oliver. Seconds that seemed like hours passed before Oliver leaned forward...

"We be needing to get *out of here* and *right NOW*. We *not* be going back the way we came, so we must be finding our way into the forest to the North. I be showing how and where to travel, so follow me without spaking."

The two made their way as casually as any of the people around them and found a path paralleling the water's edge. They were soon away from the center of Bangor and Oliver abruptly turned East into the dense foliage. They still hadn't exchanged a word and Gavan was growing more anxious to know what frightened Oliver into making this retreat. They arrived at a slight rise where the trees presented a thick canopy and a good vantage point to watch their back-trail. Oliver stopped and turned to look toward the water which was long out of sight.

"This be a good place to pause and watch for anyone following us," whispered Oliver.

Gavan was breathing a little heavier than he would admit.
Gavan asked, "This be a good time to ask..."

"Yes," interrupted Oliver, "and, no, me not be reading ye mind." At this, both men smiled, and Gavan waited for Oliver's report.

To get Oliver to start talking, Gavan asked, "Ye be knowing the man ye saw?"
"It was a woman," Oliver said, "I be remembering her not from village and, she had a strange accent, also not of me village. It be frightening. When she be not answering *my* questions but wanting me to be answering *her* questions, I be knowing we needed to get away."

"What ye be meaning... she be having an accent?" asked Gavan.

"I be not traveling like my brother, Andrew." Oliver explained, "It may be meaning nothing at all that she be wanting to know about us, instead of answering my questions."

Gavan, attempting to grasp the concept of a conversation, between minds. that was several hundred yards apart, asked the first question on his mind, "Ye be thinking ye be frightening her with yer questions?"

"Ye may be right, Gavan," Oliver thought. "I be assuming that she be from our village because I be seeing her aura. Possible that her parents left our village to be living in Bangor and she be thinking like the locals. Some spake with a different language."

"I be having to take your word for that, Oliver," chided Gavan, "since the conversation be between ye and her."

"Iffen we be waiting here for a while," Oliver noted, "we be knowing if anyone be following us. If it be safe, we be returning and try again."

"Be it possible that someone else be able to hear what the two of ye spake?" asked Gavan.

"Me be thinking not," replied Oliver. "I ne'er be looking away from her and both must be having eye contact to communicate."

Gavan didn't look as if he was completely comforted by Oliver's explanation, but he had no better plan of his own. "Ye be wanting to give it another try?" asked Gavan.

"We might be well to try, Gavan," Oliver replied, "we not be wanting to waste the rest of this day sitting here."

They stood and looked around for a couple more minutes before descending to the path that paralleled the water's edge, and slowly made their way south. They had only passed a couple small empty shacks, which appeared to be remnants of some destitute outcasts from decades ago. Gavan had increased his stride as he grew more confident that they had not been followed.

Just as he stepped past the corner of a shack, a very large man stepped in front of him, as two equally large men, came around the same shack and took a broad-legs stance behind him. Gavan, holding his staff in one hand had his other hand on the handle of his dagger, under his shirt. He prepared himself mentally for combat. No one spoke, but the man in front of Gavan looked passed him, and in the seconds that followed, Gavan saw his face soften and his eyes began to tear. He didn't need any words to tell him, that this was Andrew, and he was so pleased to see his brother. By the time Gavan turned to see Oliver, the two men had also relaxed their faces and postures. Gavan felt total relief, like a rabbit loosed from a snare.

Gavan asked Oliver, "Ye be telling them who I be?"

Oliver said, "Already spoke to him."

Gavan asked, "Ye be telling Andrew why we be here?"

Oliver said, "Already spoke to him."

Gavan asked, "Ye be asking about a boat to cross to the Isle of Anglesey?"

Oliver replied, "Already be asking him."

Gavan, feeling a small rush of frustration at the speed of Oliver's and Andrew's communications, started to ask...

Oliver replied, "Yes, Gavan, I spoke to him about everyone in our group, including Bosco."

Gavan opened his mouth to ask another question, but decided to simply wait and listen. The perplexed expression on Gavan's face brought friendly smiles to the faces of the three, hopefully, new friends.

"What to do now?" was the only question that finally found Gavan's lips. He was a little surprised when he heard the robust and refined voice of Andrew addressing his question.

Andrew started, "There be quite a few tasks afore us, Gavan, the least of these be the procurement of a second seaworthy boat."

"Seaworthy?" asked Gavan. "I be seeing the far shore and expect yer brother be shooting an arrow into the far bank."

"Having no doubt that he could, Gavan," replied Andrew, "but it be costing him his life to retrieve it."

Gavan was thoroughly impressed with the young man named Andrew. Gavan never expected anyone he met to be as tall as himself, or Gabriel, but the well muscled man before him carried himself with dignity and articulation when he spoke. How ironic that a man who could communicate without speaking, was so precise with his words. Like Oliver, Andrew was very powerful in his upper body and Gavan attributed the requirements of an experienced seaman to his powerful physique.

The puzzled look on Gavan and Oliver's faces prompted Andrew to explain. "That water may be having all of the appearance of a calm flowing stream... right now. What ye be seeing be one of two low-tides that visit the area every day. For the Menai Strait to reach high tide, it be rising greater than the

131

height of three tall men, with the entire ocean pushing a tidal surge to swamp any river boat. We be needing to have our vessel ready, to cross completely over, before the tide begins to return to the ocean. Iffen we fail, we be all swept out to sea, or tipped and drown on the way."

"How difficult be it to cross if we cooperate with the tides?" asked Oliver. Andrew glanced at Oliver who instantly took on a very surprised expression.

Gavan noticed the change in Oliver's face and asked, "If it not being too much trouble, I be liking to know the answer to Oliver's question meself."

Andrew apologized. "I be very sorry, that be rude of me. I be so accustomed to spaking with Oliver that I failed to recognize ye, Gavan." Andrew continued, "The high and low tides only be lasting long enough for stout and experienced men, working as hard as possible, to make it the far shore. There be no room for any delay, for any reason, or the entire venture be lost. We shall be trying to cross two boats, at the same time. The drag caused by this be making our progress a little slower, and the danger of being swamped, much higher."

After Gavan's expression relaxed a little, Andrew suggested, "Let's be getting the two of ye out of the sun and away from suspicious eyes. I expect ye be liking something to eat and some tea, as we be spaking about our plans."

"All of that sounds most welcome, Andrew," said Gavan, "There be so much for us to learn and share with ye, if Oliver not be filling ye mind with everything about us."

Andrew smiled because he was aware of how his and Oliver's mental communications caused others to be uncomfortable. Gavan's mischievous nature made its appearance when he asked Oliver and Andrew to keep their abilities a secret from the rest of their group for a while. Gavan was formulating some teasing fun he wanted to use to torment his brother and Asa.

Gavan and Oliver were very pleased to rest in the comfort and seclusion of Andrew's home. Just being away from the probing eyes and ears of locals, who immediately recognized them as strangers, was a big emotional relief. Oliver, after looking around Andrew's home, quietly shared his thoughts with Gavan concerning Andrew's home.

"Andrew doesn't live alone," Oliver reported, "as this place be much too clean and organized."

Gavan was about to ask Oliver if he knew who kept Andrew's home, but he paused at the sound of approaching footsteps. The front door swung open and there stood the woman Oliver had initially made eye contact with in town. She was a tall slender figure with very smooth bronze skin, straight black hair and dark brown eyes that appeared to be black when out of the sunlight. Gavan's first impression was that she might be Asian. No matter what her ancestry, she had a lovely kind face.

She didn't say anything, but she and Oliver just looked into each other's eyes. Several seconds passed before Gavan, feeling very uncomfortable, cleared his throat.

"Excuse me." Gavan asked, "I be missing out on a long conversation?"

Oliver's face turned red and he quickly apologized, "I be extending my apologies, again, Gavan. I be not meaning to be rude. This is Rose. We encountered her this morning and, due to me fear, caused us to waste time fleeing out of town. Rose be liken to Andrew, me and our village, for both of her parents be descendants of a transferred consciousness. I not be recognizing her because her parents chose to live in Bangor, instead of our village. Her father died while attempting to cross the Menai Strait several years ago, and this home be her mother's. She be the second of four daughters, and..."

Gavan interrupted with a puzzled expression, as he asked, "Ye be telling me that she shared all of this information in the few seconds the two of ye looked at each other?"

"Oh no," replied Oliver, "we spoke about her whole family, where her sisters live, their husband's name, and the names and ages of the 14 children her sisters have birthed. She also be sharing with me about some of the cautions we be needing to consider in this area, but Andrew had already shared all of that with me."

The only thing Gavan could do was stare and blink as he tried to absorb and process the unfamiliar way that so much information could be exchanged without a word spoken. "How ye be sharing so much information, so fast?" was Gavan's grasping question.

Oliver looked passed Gavan at the wall, as he thoughtfully considered a reply. "Ye may or may not be thinking of this, Gavan, but ye think much faster than ye spake. Yer mind must select from thousands of words, to spake only an appropriate few to be making up a sentence. Ye mind works many times faster than ye jaw and tongue. When we spake with our minds, we be spaking a thousand things at the same time we be listening to the thousands of things being spoken *to* us." Oliver paused because he knew Gavan was struggling with new ideas that he had witnessed but couldn't comprehend.

Trying to be as careful and considerate of Gavan's limited knowledge, Oliver asked, "Ye be liking to hear more?" Gavan's eyes revealed a hint of fear and Oliver wanted to be certain that this man, he so admired and respected, wasn't offended, so he asked again, "Iffen ye be wanting to learn more, I beseech ye to ask. Nothing be holding from you."

"Honest, Lad," replied Gavan, "I do be wanting to know more but I be feeling a kind of fear that be more frightening than thy strange words. I be fearing my head be bursting if too much be put in there."

"Ye not be needing any such fear, Gavan," Oliver said softly, "our minds seem to be like the ocean for room to be swimming round, they just not be overfilled."

Gavan considered Oliver's words but requested, "Let me get some food and rest afore we be spaking of this again. We be having more than enough work and thinking afore us and these tasks be requiring our best efforts."

After a warm meal and a couple hours sleep, Gavan announced, "One or both of us be needing to return to our camp and report our findings."

"And ye recommend... ?" asked Oliver.

"Returning to our camp site," offered Gavan. "Surely yer brother be using a few more sets of hands with preparing the boats for our crossing, and I can tell our friends about our adventures in Bangor and the potential dangers. What I *not* be revealing to them be anything about yer spaking without words. I be thinking that it be requiring a demonstration... and a little fun." Oliver flashed a quick grin before setting off to find his brother, as Gavan thanked Rose for her hospitality.

It was easy for Gavan to retrace the path that he and Oliver used to find Bangor. The day was very warm and humid, and it required Gavan to walk slowly to prevent overheating.

Gavan's slower pace was most fortunate since it allowed him to hear strange angry voices coming from their camp site, before he revealed himself. The stranger's voices sounded rough and threatening, as well as a bit afraid.

Gavan looked for something he could throw, as a weapon. His staff was sufficiently stout enough to use as a club, but he wanted a little more range. He leaned his staff against a tree and carefully picked up a round rock slightly larger than a child's head, and held it in front of his chest, with both hands. He inched forward until he could see what and who was confronting his companions. It was a pair of highway robbers that didn't look to be more than 20 years old. They were dressed in tattered rags and each held a hefty club which they were using to make threatening swings through the air. It appeared that Bosco was quite content to lie on the ground at Luke's feet. The would-be thieves were standing with their backs toward Gavan as he carefully moved closer. Asa didn't appear to be as concerned by the clubs each thief held, and stood very relaxed with his right hand firmly wrapped around the handle of his sword.

When Gavan was about ten feet behind the larger thief, Asa warned the thief!

Asa said, "Ye best be careful. My big friend be walking up behind ye." Gavan froze; he couldn't believe Asa would give away his advantage, at a moment like that.

Instead of heeding Asa's warning, the elder, stronger thief mockingly replied, "I not be falling for a stupid trick like that!" and maintained his fixed glare at Asa while making a couple more wild swings with his club. Gavan, pleasantly surprised by the rejection of Asa's warning, moved forward to an arm's length away. Gavan held the cannon ball sized rock tensely between his big hands and waited for the right instance to launch it at the head of the thief.

Again, Asa spoke with a calm voice, "I be warning ye, Lad, the man be standing right behind ye now, so just drop your clubs and run away."

The inexperienced thief made a very weak impression of a mocking laugh and asked Asa, "How stupid do ye think I be, old man?"

Gavan took this que to say, "*Very stupid.*"

The thief jumped straight up and spun around at Gavan's words. Gavan launched his ancient missile with muscles as taunt as a bowstring, like a professional basketball player making a cross-court pass. The hapless thug saw the large rock approaching the center of his face like a gray cannon ball. The nose crushing splash knocked the would-be thief clean off his feet. The thief lie flat on his back, out cold... as cold as last week's camp fire. Beside the thug's head lay the rock with the distinct image of a blood-spattered nose at it center.

"Bullseye!" exclaimed Gavan.

The second thief wasted no time assessing his situation, and the loss of his accomplice, and he ran headlong in panicked flight through the trees. The unconscious thief lie face up next to Bosco, who leaned forward to lick the rivulets of blood from the man's severely flattened nose.

Luke appeared ready to faint and Gabriel asked him, "Be ye alright?"

Luke didn't answer but held his staff with both hands and stood erect to draw in a deep breath to regain his composure.

Asa commented, "I be glad, for sure, it turned out this way, Gavan, I be expecting him to turn round the *first* time I warned, and then stick him the instant he turned."

Gavan had a small frown for Asa before he replied, "I be not believing ye tried to expose my perfect stalk... *twice.*"

"He was too stupid to succeed," observed Asa, "no matter which one of us got to him first."

Gavan said nothing out loud, but he immediately thought of the advantage Oliver and Andrew, or anyone from their village would have had in that situation. They could have communicated the instant they could see each other's eyes.

Gabriel, being Gavan's twin, read the expressions crossing Gavan's face and asked, "What ye be thinking, Gavan?"

Gavan thought it best to evade the true answer and replied, "I be only thinking of how this situation could be going badly and I be very glad that it not be so."

The five of us stood facing each other with the limp form of a skinny young thief between our feet. At the sound of faint moaning, we all looked down in silence, to await the conscious recovery of the thief. The moment he began to stir...

"Bosco, don't let him get up," Luke ordered. As if he understood perfectly, the great beast crawled forward several feet and lay his huge bulk over the man's chest. From this superior vantage point, Bosco continued licking the blood which freely flowed down each side of his crushed nose. Asa picked up the thief's club and Gavan retrieved his big blood-stained rock.

When the thief's eyes opened, the first image he saw was the massive black face and teeth of Bosco. He let out a scream, as he impotently flailed his boney legs. The screams sounded more like a young girl than a hardened thug. Bosco continued to hold the thief flat on his back and licked his face repeatedly. Both of the thief's arms were pinned under Bosco.

"Should we help him?" asked Luke.

"Not yet," replied Asa. "Let Bosco finish cleaning his face so we not be having to." Bosco was enjoying himself, but when that big tongue began to lap across the center, of his now disfigured face, the pain was more than he could bear. The thief began to howl and scream so loud that we were concerned that the noise could draw unwanted attention.

After a careful look around, Luke said, "Up Bosco!" and the dog sprang to his feet only to, once again, feel the pain of his wounded leg. He laid down facing the thief. The thief lay motionless, his wide-open, tear filled eyes, staring up at the huge black form that loomed over him... waiting for another opportunity to lick his face.

"What we be doing with thee, young thief?" asked Gabriel. Thinking that this would be a good opportunity to instill a fear of continuing a life of crime, Gabriel chose to make good use of Bosco's presence. "Do ye be seeing this great black beast afore ye, Lad?" Gabriel began. The thief fixed his eyes on Bosco as he blinked away the tears welling up in his eyes. Gabriel growled, "I be having *thousands* of them... some much *larger* than this pup. And I be going to command them to be watching ye, from every shadow and in the darkness of night. Should ye e'er steal again," Gabriel continued with a bigger and more intimidating voice, "I be giving them permission to *tear ye apart...* eat every *piece* of ye... both flesh and *bone*, until *nothing* be found to be showing ye e'er *existed*!" Gabriel paused. He could see the terror in the lad's eyes as he fixed his gaze on Bosco. "Ye *understand* me, lad?" Gabriel asked and waited for an answer.

His first words came out in tiny little squeaks that couldn't be understood, so Gabriel asked again, "Ye hear me? I be having yer promise to ne'er steal again, to be saving yerself from being devoured by my great beasts?"

This time, the thief's voice was audible but still shaky. "Yes, monk, I swear to ne'er steal again!" He was still transfixed on the ominous black form next to him.

"Then be *gone*, young thief," roared Gabriel, "I be setting my beasts to watch ye e'ery move. Ye not be *seeing* them, but they be *watching* ye e'ery *step*! GO!" With Gabriel's final instruction, the thief slowly got to his feet and Bosco, also, slowly got to his feet until both were standing, still eye to eye. Bosco whipped out his great tongue and gave him one more lick — right across his crushed nose. The pain shot through the thief as he scrambled through the forest, on the same path his smaller friend took to escape. When silence had returned to the forest, no one felt any need to disturb it, until...

Luke observed, "Where is Oliver?"

Gavan eyed Luke a moment before asking, "Ye be missing him already, Luke?" Luke's crimson face was all the answer we all needed. "Sorry, Luke," Gavan said with a kind voice, "I be having not made that sound like a tease. We all be knowing that Oliver is a wonderful lad and we be happy that ye are friends. To be answering yer question," Gavan continued, "Oliver be choosing to stay with his brother, to work on a boat suitable for a crossing."

Gabriel asked, "What kind of crossing be ye expecting this to be? Heard many wild tales about the Menai Strait being a very dangerous body of water to be crossing."

"Those wild stories might all be true, Gabriel," began Gavan. "The strait is not very wide since ye be seeing the far shore at about the distance a strong bow be casting an arrow. The danger be the speed and number of tides." Noting the puzzled looks of his companions, Gavan gave the following details, "Unlike anywhere else I be seeing, the tides here change *four* times a day instead of the normal two. The rise of the rushing water from low to high tide is over the height of three grown men! The rushing and deadly surge be having a well-earned reputation for sinking unwary travelers."

"Alright!" chided Asa, "Now that ye be giving us the *good* news, what we be expecting in the way of *bad* news?"

Gavan smiled but continued sharing the information that he and Oliver had discovered. "Oliver be having no trouble finding his brother." Gavan lied because he didn't want to explain the 'speaking without words' that Oliver and Andrew had revealed to him. "Andrew be a fine man, like Oliver," Gavan shared, "and he quickly came up with a plan to be lashing two boats together for safety and larger cargo. We be choosing a single crossing, with all of us, would be safer and quicker than trying to be making two crossings on separate tides."

"I have been to the banks of this strait," Asa shared, "but ne'er be considering crossing because of the risks involved. I be secretly dreading this portion of our journey, but ye comments about creating a double-hulled craft be giving me some comfort."

"I have to admit the same kind of fears," Gabriel confessed, "I be believing that a safe way to cross be found, and yer words, Gavan, have given me comfort."

"Hate to be robbing ye of yer optimism," Gavan addressed his words to all, "but the time allowed for us to be making our crossing be very short because we only be navigating during the few minutes of a high tide. This be giving us just enough time, to work very hard, to complete the crossing afore the tide begins to retreat, where we be swept out to sea or drowned." Very sober faces held their silence once again as Gavan's report was pondered.

"I can't think of any alternative," I commented. "Luke and I have memories of vast bridges that make crossing the most violent of rivers a simple task of walking or riding." I looked at Luke and it was obvious to me that he was thinking about steel bridges, cars and motorcycles when I used the word, 'riding.' Upon hearing my voice, Gabriel and Asa immediately looked about to be assured that there wasn't anyone within hearing distance of us.

Trying to sound optimistic, I asked Gabriel, "How far is our journey, once we cross the Menai Strait?" Gabriel gave my question a moment of thought, before answering. "Two or three days."

"You have been there before, haven't you?" I asked.

"Yes," was Gabriel's reply, "but I not be crossing the Menai Strait to be getting there. I be traveling by ship to the East shore when I be but a novice monk to study under Brother Ashton, an old monk who could read and write in Runes. How I be wishing he be alive today to be helping us when we be reading Amergus' messages."

Wanting to explore all options, I asked Gabriel, "Would it be a reasonable alternative to finish this journey by ship?"

Gabriel had a very quick reply, "Certainly, it be quicker and much more comfortable, Raffe, but every port and ship be likely to have soldiers, and maybe out of uniform, onboard ships. Remember, when I be traveling as a novice monk, there was a different monarchy. And no massive black dog." I had no reason to doubt Gabriel's wisdom and told him exactly that.

"Let's be getting back to the challenges at hand," observed Asa, "We be not able to read anything if we fail in crossing this strait afore us."

Wanting to be an encourager, Gavan spoke, "I be getting a very good impression of Andrew. Physically, he be looking like he could cross without anyone's help, but he be having two stout lads with him. All three be giving me the impression that they crossed many times. I suggest that we be camping here again this night. On the morrow, we be entering Bangor in two small groups to draw as little attention to ourselves as possible. It may be best if the *first* group travels through Bangor, find Oliver and be asking him to be coming here to escort the *second* group through town. Already I be through Bangor," observed Gavan, "so I be traveling with the *first* group. Oliver be not long to be coming back, for the *second* group."

There were no arguments or questions, and our stomachs were reminding us of the need to prepare our evening meal. Each of us had many questions rolling around in our minds, but we knew that it was only a short while before the big question, 'Will we safely cross the Menai Strait?' is answered. Gavan shared our concerns about this crossing, but he was much more interested in understanding the wordless communications used by Oliver and his village. With Bosco feeling stronger, we were assured to sleep soundly tonight, confident of his diligent watch.

"Bosco," exclaimed Luke, as he sat staring into the dying fire. "What are we going to do with Bosco? How can we walk him through Bangor without creating a panic?"

"Do you think he will stay flat in the cart?" I asked.

"A few days ago, may be," commented Asa, "but he not be trusted to stay on his side while we be wheeling him through hundreds of people and thousands of smells." Answering this question was more important than sleep so we all sat up, built up the fire and thought about a solution.

"How be this idea..." began Gavan, "when the first group contacts Oliver and Andrew, we be asking both to return to our camp. One can guide the second group back through

141

Bangor; and the other, be taking Bosco through the forest where he not be seen."

"That sounds fine with me," offered Luke, "Oliver and I can take Bosco through the forest. And, yes, I *do* want that time to be able to talk with Oliver, when the rest of ye aren't around."

"Good idea," said Asa. "Now, I be going to sleep, right?" Silence returned as the light from our stirred fire flickered through the lower leaves and a couple distant owls called to each other.

We were all awake before the hints of a cobalt blue Eastern horizon turned to gold. Asa was preparing a breakfast over a fire that appeared to have burned all night.

Gabriel asked of all of us, "How be everyone's sleep?"

Echoed mumbles of "good" came back in a staggered pace.

We were loading the cart and cleaning up our camp area when Bosco's attention focused in the direction of Bangor. He didn't growl, he just stood rigidly with his eyes straining to detect any movement. Bosco's focus caused the rest of us to stop what we were doing and look to the West. After a couple minutes, Bosco let out a single "WOOF!"

An unseen visitor immediately shouted back, "It be me, Bosco! We be friends." At the sound of his voice, Bosco galloped into the trees; and an instant later, we could hear a man scream, and the scream was followed by a roar of laughter. The laughter was still strong as Bosco, with Oliver at his side, stroking his back, came walking into sight. Immediately behind the great beast, appeared the now ashen-faced Andrew. Oliver had to gain control of his laughter before he could tell the rest of us about the cause for the scream and his laughter.

"I not be telling Andrew about Bosco," Andrew said, still chuckling, "for I be wanting to see his reaction at first sight." More laughter followed until Bosco, thinking he had done something very special for Oliver, wet the whole side of Oliver's face with a single lick. It only took Andrew a couple minutes to warm up to Bosco, and Bosco was only too happy to have another friend.

142

Seeing that Andrew was the younger, yet larger of the brothers, Gabriel introduced himself before Oliver had the opportunity. Typical of the village traditions, Andrew looked directly into Gabriel's eyes, as the two men shook hands.

With a single glance and greeting of, "Good Morning" to Gavan, Andrew commented, "Twins?"

Gavan gave a pleasant, "Surely, we be."

Oliver introduced me to his brother, and then put his arm around Luke's shoulders and said, "This be *Luke*, Andrew."

The brothers looked directly into each other's eyes, for only a second, before Andrew said, "I be very pleased to meet you, Luke. Oliver be telling me some nice things about ye." The blush on Luke's cheeks were bright enough to compete with the rising sun. Luke stood frozen as a flood of emotions, from Andrew's words, stirred within him. Gavan and Gabriel looked at each other and then at Asa. Each man raised their eyebrows slightly, to acknowledge that they had caught Luke's blushing face.

Wanting to come to Luke's aide, I asked the open question, "Did I miss something here?"

Oliver replied, first to Luke, and then to the rest of us. "It be alright, Luke. I only shared with Andrew about thy aura."

Not knowing what Oliver meant, I asked, "Didn't you tell us that Luke and I be having auras?"

"Yes, I did," replied Oliver, "but not be explaining that Luke's aura is pink, and the others be having blue auras." By now, Oliver and Andrew were accustomed to seeing surprised and confused expressions on our faces. I couldn't help smiling as I thought... wonder if that's where the tradition of 'pink for girls and blue for boys' came from. I was lost in my own thoughts when Oliver's voice brought me back. He looked at me as though I had missed something important.

"What?" I asked, "Did you ask me a question?"

"Not just of ye, Raffe," Oliver responded. "I be asking for the opinion of all of ye."

"I'm so sorry, Oliver. I was lost in my thoughts. Would you repeat your question?"

"Certainly," replied Oliver, "The question be concerning Luke's returning to live in our village, when yer journey here be finished." To say that I was unprepared for Oliver's question was obvious on my face. As usual, it was Asa who spoke first.

Asa asked, "Do we be needing to answer your question right now, or can we discuss it as we travel?

Gabriel offered, "Now that the subject be introduced, maybe it be an excellent topic of conversation as we be making progress on our journey."

Normal color returned to Luke's face and I took this as an indicator of his pleasure at the question being postponed.

Andrew stated, "I suggest we be making some progress on our travels, as we be discussing our personal destinations over walking feet."

"I agree," said Asa. "We already be making some plans, but now that both of ye be here, we be getting yer opinions on how a group as large as ours, be passing through Bangor, without drawing unwanted attention."

"This be the reason both of us came so early this morning," responded Andrew, "We be concerned that yer whole group might travel together, and we not be wanting that."

"What be your plan?" asked Gavan. knowing that Andrew was more experienced with the local population and countryside.

"I believe we be all traveling as a group, but not *through* Bangor. It be slightly longer, but we be knowing of a path that be taking us *round* Bangor where ye can wait for the right timing to be crossing the Menai Strait."

"That be sounding much safer," observed Gavan, "and it be keeping Bosco with us and out of sight from prying eyes."

Andrew addressed the group, when he said, "We be having the boats lashed together and waiting just above the high tide limits. We be making a comfortable camp behind me home and food be brought to you, so no needing to build a fire."

The walk around Bangor didn't seem to be very long since I had no idea how long the travel through Bangor would have been. We did see a few people at long distances and none of them seemed to have noticed us. When we stopped, Andrew pointed out the top of an exceptionally tall cedar and told us that his home, his mother-in-law's home, was beneath the lower limbs of that tree.

"How much control do ye be having over the movements of yer dog?" Andrew asked.

"He still be recovering from Oliver's arrow," chided Asa. "I not be expecting he will try to wander at all, at least for a week. Will we be here that long?"

Andrew thought before responding to Asa, "With two high tides e'ery day, I expect to be having you safely crossed by this time tomorrow."

That was the kind of news we all enjoyed hearing since every one of us knew that crossing this strait would put us safely away from the king's realm of authority.

"Oliver and I be getting some food for ye," said Andrew, "Ye be preparing yer camp for tonight."

"Let's hope we only need a one-night camp." commented Luke. I was a little surprised that Luke had found his voice since he hadn't spoken a word since we left camp this morning.

I looked at Luke and inquired, "Is this a good time to bring up your desire to live in Oliver's village?"

"It's as good a time as any," replied Luke. "All of you know full well that I was a woman before the Passing took me back to 1690. My body may well be that of a young man, but my mind hasn't changed at all and my mind likes Oliver, maybe even loves him. Oliver told me that his village would be the best place for me to live because everyone there can see my aura and recognize who I am... on the inside."

It was Asa, as usual, who asked what each of us was thinking. "Let me see," he started, "ye already know that we understand yer situation and we accept ye. Why ye be wanting to live in a small village, with another man?"

"If I stayed with you, my dear friends, I would still be a woman, on the inside, living with a group of men. With Oliver and his village, I will be with a man, who understands and cares for the person he knows, *as the woman inside* me. There will also be other women, who would recognize who I *really* am,

145

and can be the female friends I need." It was obvious that Gavan had a question and was struggling with how to ask it. Luke recognized Gavan's struggle. "What is it, Gavan, what are you wanting to ask me?"

Gavan's face flushed red, and more red, as he summoned the words and courage to ask, "What be about the... sex? Ye most certainly be a man, on the outside."

To my surprise, Luke wasn't the least bit uncomfortable as he responded, "Love is *love*, Gavan. It has been my impression that you and Asa are very *familiar* with the ways two men can express love... physically." Luke's words were so sincere and kind that neither Gavan nor Asa appeared surprised as they glanced at each other. I must confess that I was a little uncomfortable, for them, more than myself.

Gabriel spoke, "Sure be nice to be having *that* bit of information *out* in the open. We all be happy with this topic of conversation?"

I commented, "We started this conversation seeking and understanding of Luke's plans. I welcome returning to the subject of our *personal* lives when we have more time. I believe Luke has made his feelings clear and even shared with us the 'why' of his choice. I believe you already know this, Luke, but I want to repeat, my agreement, and my support for you."

We returned to the chores of preparing our camp and had just finished when Andrew and Oliver returned with steaming bowls of lentils for us and two large fish for Bosco. We ate in silence and, with full stomachs, we all relaxed in the warmth of the fire.

I asked of Andrew and Oliver, "Do you mind me asking you to tell us more about the auras you can see around people and beasts?" They were pleased that I introduced this subject as Andrew indicated that Oliver should reply.

"All living things be having an aura," Oliver began. "The aura around plants be very faint and almost always white or cream color. The aura round people be much more interesting because it varies in color and intensity according to the health, gender, moral and emotional state of that individual."

Andrew continued Oliver's description, "The presence of auras be the primary reason our village strictly enforces the purity of having both parents who be direct descendants of Transferred Consciousness. A few be choosing to find a mate outside the village, and moved away. There be no book or written records of this information and each generation teaches their children to look for, and identify, the meaning of auras."

Gavan spoke up, "I be making a trick of the ability ye two demonstrated while I be in Bangor, but thought it best to be asking ye two, to describe your ability to speak without words." The last three words captured the full attention of Asa, Gabriel and me.

"That be easy," replied Oliver. "Andrew, remain here by the fire, and I be walking as far away as possible. Be having someone whisper to ye and I'll shout their words from where I stand."

With these simple instructions from Oliver, he got to his feet and began walking. He was well past normal hearing distance, but still in direct sight of Andrew, when he stopped and turned to wait.

I leaned close to Andrew and whispered, "Cell phone."

Andrew got a confused look on his face and Oliver shouted, "Sell fone?"

Gavan was delighted with the stunned look on Gabriel and Asa's faces. He didn't notice that I was just as surprised as they were.

Asa sat up, thought about what he wanted to say and leaned close to Andrew, with his back towards Oliver, and whispered. Oliver began to laugh so hard, that he could hardly speak before getting his composure.

Oliver shouted, "I be *shitting my pants!*"

Asa was as amazed as the rest of us and said, "I be *believing* it, but I not be *understanding* it."

Oliver began to return when Gabriel motioned for him to stop. Gabriel turned his back to Oliver and softly whispered a few words into Andrew's ear.

Oliver's face turned crimson red. but he cupped his hands to his mouth, and shouted, as loud as he could, "I LOVE LUKE!"

This brought about a roar of laughter from everyone, except Luke, who matched Oliver's blush with one of his own. Oliver walked back to camp, sat down beside Luke and put one of his big arms about Luke's shoulders.

Gavan began the following dialogue with a request, "Please be telling us how ye be communicating this way?"

Andrew and Oliver shared as much information as they had time for, since the sun was low in the West and tomorrow's promised to be a very eventful day... crossing the Menai Strait.

Chapter 9
Crossing the Menai Strait

Sleep had come easily but it only lasted until we could hear the thundering of the powerful roaring tide rush in. It paused for what seemed like much too short a lull before beginning its chaotic roar when oceans attempt to cram far too much water through a narrow channel. Each time the roaring tide ceased, I imagined us struggling to cross before the next tide began. In my mind, we never succeeded. I envisioned our boats being tossed over and all of us struggling to reach the far shore.

The image that bothered me most was the struggle of Bosco's big head attempting to stay above water as his body was pummeled like a dried leaf in a tempest. His leg was healing very nicely but could he sustain the strain needed to reach shore. Each time I envisioned this, I sat up with tears in my eyes. I looked over to see if our loyal friend was resting and the sight of this massive beast snuggled next to Luke allowed me to make another attempt to sleep.

I was on my third or fourth attempt to sleep when I noticed Gavan sit up, bend his legs and wrap his arms around his knees. He looked over the smoking fire pit and used his head motion to invite me to walk away from the others. It was obvious that Gavan wanted to talk without waking the others.

We walked in silence until we were beyond hearing distance but still in clear view of the camp. Gavan pointed at a large tree which appeared to have fallen a couple years ago but still offered a comfortable place to sit.

Gavan's big round face was calm and his full black beard, in starlight, was very similar to the many renditions of Santa Claus that were a part of the Christmas season in the world I left behind.

"We not be taking the time for one-on-one conversations since we be starting on this adventure," offered Gavan. "Ye not be mentioning your family from 2016 and, as ye be making this journey with us, I be wanting ye to be knowing that I be feeling as close to ye as I be for the Raffe I raised. May be, I be loving ye more because ye are smarter, and wiser, and ye be placing yer greatest trust in me."

Of all the friends I left, back in 2016, I had never felt as secure in those friendships as I did in Gavan. I recognized that I didn't love him in the way Oliver loved Luke or Asa love Gavan, but I did love him dearly, as a brother and friend. So. I told him the exact thoughts I was feeling.

"Mates forever," was Gavan's simple words.

"Gavan," I began, "my life here has been so traumatic and full, that I have not thought much about my former life. Both of my parents died when I was just a baby and I was their only child. I was raised by very nice people who were older in my earliest memories of them. They both died while I was in college, so, for me, the transfer of my consciousness didn't leave many people behind."

"I be very glad ye be here, Raffe, and I be liking to remain yer best mate forever. This water-crossing be giving me some worry and I be wanting everything between us to be clear and good."

"You never need to worry, Gavan, I see you as the big brother I always wanted and, as you said, 'mates forever.' If it will make it any clearer, I do love you and I always will. This crossing may become a challenge, but it will never separate us." There was a pause. "How much has Gabriel shared with you about the cave writings we're going to explore?" I asked.

"No more than ye be knowing, Raffe," replied my friend. "I be knowing that we not be having to live under the sun and stars. After we cross, we will venture to an old but comfortable monastery very close to the cave they found. My concerns," Gavan continued, "be not about the cave or what we be finding there. I be wondering how ye be adjusting to this new, old world?"

I looked all about us and smiled at his new, old world. "As you already know, Gavan, my first reaction was fear, that bordered on panic, when I realized that this was not a dream. I have you to thank for the emotional support and steadfast friendship." I was beginning to think this log has witnessed about as much male mush as it could stand, but Gavan wasn't finished.

"My part in our friendship be a little easier than yours, Raffe," Gavan shared, "since I be knowing ye since a new born baby and be raising ye in my humble home ever since you be a tot."

Gavan's comment inspired a question that had not occurred to me, until this moment. "Gavan," I asked, "am I very different from the Raffe you raised?"

Gavan's bushy eyebrows raised as high as they could move, and his face grew warm and soft as he began his reply. "The Raffe I be raising was a tormented child and a troubled teen. He be not too smart, but he be conniving, and he ne'er be forgetting or forgiving of anything he be thinking done against him." Gavan could see the surprise in my face, at such a description, and he paused.

"If that Raffe was so bitter and mean, why did you look for me the first night we met?" I asked.

"Through Gabriel's studies of the Rune writings, we had a good idea that another Passing was due," Gavan explained. "When ye suddenly be dropping into a lifeless corpse afore us, in the pub, it was Asa who spontaneously gasped, 'The Passing,' and we be watching over yer body for near an hour afore Asa said, 'we not be waiting until daylight with a body at our feet, if this be *not* a 'passing.' We be carrying ye into that alley and propped ye against a wall. We met when I be returning to see if ye be still dead. When ye moved and I heard your voice, I quickly be knowing that a Passing be occurring... and the love I be feeling for ye as an infant welled up inside me as if it, too, be resurrected."

A closer bond was formed between us. Neither of us had noticed his approach as we shared this moment, long overdue, but the instant his big tongue soaked the side of Gavan's face, we knew that we were not alone. Bosco sat next to us and his big head was higher than either of ours.

"I have so many things about the world I left that I would like to share with you, Gabriel and the others, but I don't know how to describe things like TV, radios, traffic jams, air and space travel, or even the everyday items like fast-food and cars." I could see that every word I said was nonsense to Gavan. "I *can* tell you that some things have *not* changed at all, Gavan." I continued, "People. People are just as good and just as evil in 1690, as they are in 2016."

"I not be knowing if yer information be very comforting," Gavan replied. "I be expecting that people be better over time. There be a time, when we be having no laws, courts or governments, to help people live quiet lives."

I replied, "It isn't a matter of more laws," Gavan. "It has always been each person caring about the safety and comfort of others. No matter how many laws govern the land, there will always be a few who care more about themselves that anyone else. The first Raffe you knew, may have been a selfish soul."

"That he be, Lad," was Gavan's reply. "We be needing to try and get some sleep, Raffe," Gavan counseled. "We be talking about this again, on the west bank of the Menai Strait."

We walked quietly back to where the others were sleeping and I spontaneously gave Gavan another hug, which he affectionately returned. As I was covering my feet to lay down, I glanced at Gabriel and Asa. Both men's eyes were open and looking at me. Asa winked at me and Gabriel smiled and mouthed the words, 'Good, Lad,' and we all surrendered to sleep.

It was the movements of the others that woke me. I got up feeling as if I had not slept at all. It didn't take long, for all of us, to be well fed with the food Rose brought us, warmed with hot tea and feeling the energy of an exciting day before us. No one from our traveling group was aware of the schedule of the tides, so we were surprised when Andrew appeared and informed us that we could hurry and cross with the next high tide or wait for the following tide.

"I strongly recommend that we be getting ready" said Andrew, "and cross at the next slack tide because it be well passed dark for the next. That, or wait until tomorrow."

In only a few seconds of silent eye contact, all of us began rushing to clear camp and follow Andrew to the rising water's edge. None of us were prepared for what we saw as we approached the strait. The rolling torrents of ocean water be thrusting eight foot waves in every direction, as the immense power of the shifting ocean pushed waves upon waves, like a massive stampede of great watery beasts. I immediately thought of the muddy springtime rapids crashing between the rock walls of the Grand Canyon. The roar was growing louder by the second and if it were not for the fact that we were standing in an old growth of trees, I might have feared that we were all about to be washed away in the torrent.

Much quicker than its roaring ascent, the sound of the incoming tide subsided, and the thunderous waves settled into gentle rolls, as the moment of high tide approached. Andrew's two friends were standing by the water's edge, holding a rope which led to the stern of two sturdy boats, lashed together with long, thin poles. The platform created was about three arm-spans long and two arm-spans wide, covered about half of the boats surface from stem to stern.

It looked very safe and it gave me some relief after witnessing the raging tide.

Andrew told us that we needed to load up immediately and be ready to launch the instant the slack tide began. Everyone pitched in and the supplies were laid on the left side of the platform, the cart was turned over and placed over our packs and lashed to the poles. It only took a few minutes to secure everything and, as Andrew and Oliver and their two friends held the boats secure, we all climbed on board. Bosco impressed us all by leaping onto the log platform and laying down beside Luke without a word of coaxing. We sat or stood in imposed silence as we waited for Andrew's order to set off.

I noticed the stout rope that was strung across the strait and suspended with enough tension to keep the rope a few feet above the high tide level in the middle of this narrow portion of the waterway.

As I was looking at the rope, Oliver told me, "We be using that rope to be pulling our boats across. It will appear lower, as soon as the slack tide begins. If we all be pulling *hard*, we be well across during the two-hour slack tide."

I asked Oliver, "Has that rope ever broken?"

Oliver looked at Andrew until he looked back to me. "Andrew be saying it be broken once, but due to the toppling of an anchor tree and not be the rope itself breaking."

I asked Oliver, "Did you and Andrew just communicate all of that, in one glance?"

Oliver smiled and replied, "That and more. Andrew wanted to be knowing what your plans be for Bosco."

I was surprised by Oliver's words. "We assumed that Bosco would come with us."

Oliver looked over at Andrew, as his brother checked the tightness of his lashings and replied, "Andrew not be planning on that giant dog being part of the cargo. He estimates that Bosco be weighing as much as two grown men, and he not be helping with the pulling, as *everyone* needs to do, to cross before the tide begins to ebb."

I wasn't at all prepared for this. I looked over at Luke, who was sitting on the back edge of the platform with his arm resting on Bosco's back, waiting for the command to begin the crossing. It was obvious to all of us that the bond between Luke and Bosco was much closer than with anyone else, and I was immediately torn inside to have to tell Luke.

I asked Oliver, "Would ye please ask Andrew if Bosco could be included? It's very important to all of us."

Oliver looked at Luke and Bosco and he immediately knew that leaving Bosco behind would be devastating to Luke. "I shall ask," replied Oliver, "I know how much Luke loves that dog." Oliver looked towards Andrew and they made eye contact for a second. I could see Andrew shaking his head in rejection of Oliver's request.

Knowing the answer Oliver was going to give me, I told Oliver, "Please tell Andrew that I'll stay behind and cross later."

Oliver turned to me and asked, "Ye be *serious*?"

"Yes, I am," I replied. "I love that big dog, but I am more concerned for *Luke*. That giant puppy is her, I mean *his*, closest link to the life he left behind. Luke *needs* Bosco to *survive* here."

"I agree," said Oliver, as he turned back to Andrew once more. This time, Oliver and Andrew held eye contact for well over a minute before Oliver smiled and said, "Andrew agreed, Bosco be staying onboard but Andrew not be accepting any responsibility for Bosco's safety."

I took a deep sigh of relief and patted Oliver on his back, as I said, "Thank ye, Oliver. Ye and Andrew are good men."

Oliver smiled and said, "Let us all be getting to the other side before we be telling each other how good we be."

Andrew shouted, "Everyone be getting on board. I be telling each person where to be sitting to evenly distribute the load. Luke, ye be keeping Bosco where ye be, will he stay?" Luke was surprised by the question, but recognized the need of an answer.

"Yes," Luke replied. "I'm certain that he will sit or lie right next to me."

"Prove it," ordered Andrew, "I be wanting ye and Bosco to stay on the opposite side of the platform from the heavy cart and supplies. Yer only job be keeping Bosco in one place, during the entire crossing." Luke, sitting where he was assigned, let his feet hang above the boat's hull. Bosco looked about but remained fixed and calm next to his Luke, and made no further movements.

"*That* be *perfect*," said Andrew. "Time for the rest of ye to be getting on board. Gabriel and Gavan, I be going to be needing your broad backs and stout arms to be making this crossing as fast as possible."

"What I be doing?" asked Asa.

"I be wanting ye and Oliver to be on the ready to start pulling if we be needing the extra help."

Asa replied, "Aye, aye, Captain," and sat opposite Luke and Bosco where Andrew pointed.

"We be only a few minutes short of high tide," announced Andrew. "Let's be getting this boat a little distance off the bank, to be readying for some hard pulling the *moment* I be *saying* so. *Remember* to only be pulling on the *upper rope!* *Ye* will be seeing, on the other side, the *lower rope*... there to help us reach *solid ground* on the west bank."

Gavan, Gabriel and Andrew stood motionless with their hands around the large rope that spanned the strait. There was a little tension visible among us, but all were ready.

"*Start pulling!*" ordered Andrew, as his friends released their hold on the small rope at our stern. The motion was much swifter than I anticipated even with the very mild sideways motion from the last few minutes of the incoming tide.

"Not be wearing yer selves out by pulling *too hard,*" Andrew warned. "We be pulling for over an hour and ye be *needing* yer reserve strength on the far bank."

By the time our modified craft had traversed a third of the crossing distance, the water was as calm as a pond and the pulling shared by three men was steady and smooth. Luke took off his shoes to let his feet skim over the cool water. Bosco laid at his side, with his big head snugly against Luke's leg, as Luke slowly and tenderly stroked the giant's head, neck and shoulders. Bosco often sought out Luke's affection, at almost every pause of our journey. Luke leaned close to Bosco's ear and began speaking softly as the dog gave the impression of understanding Luke's words.

Oliver noticed this verbal interaction between Bosco and Luke and asked, "Luke, what ye be saying to that great beast that puts such a blissful expression on his face?"

Luke paused his communications with Bosco, and Oliver could see, even from behind, that Luke's ears had turned bright red from his blush.

Oliver, always keenly attentive to Luke's reactions, said, "Ye not be needing to answer me, Luke... not meaning to pry."

Luke continued to run his fingers through Bosco's fur, as he replied, "Oliver, I don't mind sharing this with all of you. I believe Bosco is a transferred consciousness from my neighborhood in 2016 and I quietly whisper popular songs that I remember. He always gives me the impression that some of those songs are familiar from *his* previous life. Even if he doesn't understand the words, maybe he understands the melodies."

I wasn't expecting to encounter such a sentimental moment while traversing the Menai Strait some three hundred years before my own birth. I let my sentimental tears flow knowing that the patient understanding of my friends wouldn't bring me any shame.

We were making good headway during this high tide calm and all eyes were on the slowly approaching west bank of black trees.

Andrew asked Gavan and Gabriel if they needed to take a break from pulling and I volunteered to take a turn at the rope-pulling. Gavan said that he wasn't tired at all. Gabriel admitted that he doesn't do a lot of physical work around the Monastery and a little reprieve, during this high tide calm, would be welcome. I gladly grabbed the opportunity to take part in the pulling... it made me feel essential to the group.

The change from high tide to ebb tide came much swifter than I expected. One second, the water was so placid that its surface reflected a mirror-clear image of the eastern bank of trees, broken only by our swiftly spreading wake. In the next, the water's surface morphed to a rippled and undulant turmoil generated by billions of tons of water demanding their return to the sea. It appeared that the entire strait was a turmoil of water demanding every drop before it move quicker than the impatient drop behind it.

Luke was first to see the small object floating slightly north of our boat's wake. He asked out loud, "Did we lose something? I can see something floating about 20 or 30 yards behind us."

We all looked in the direction where Luke was pointing, but no one was looking as intently as Bosco. The big dog was up on all fours intently watch the floating object.

Andrew said, "Believe it be one of yer shoes, Luke."

"Can we go back for it?" asked Luke.

Before anyone could answer, Bosco bound off the back of the platform, and began to swim for Luke's shoe, in an act of devoted love... just like he did every time Luke tossed a stick for him to fetch.

Luke was too stunned to make a sound for several seconds. These seconds were enough for Bosco to swim several yards closer to the shoe, as the increasing ebb tide carried him north at a pace much swifter than his progress towards his target.

When Luke called out, *"Bosco, come back!"* the dog was too far away to hear clearly over the now rumbling ebb tide and too focused on Luke's shoe to give up his quest.

Luke turned to Andrew and pleaded, *"PLEASE* turn back to get him!"

Andrew looked back at Bosco and then to Luke as he gravely replied, "We not be turning back for ye dog any more than we be turning back for ye." Andrew resumed his pulling on the rope with increased fervor and encouraged the others to *pull harder*.

Luke's tearing eyes were fixed on the now bobbing head of Bosco as he ignored the rising waves about him in pursuit of the only thing that mattered to him — to save the shoe of the man he loved more than his own life.

All hands were now pulling on the rope, except Luke's. He was transfixed on the quickly receding head of Bosco as the ebb tide rushed him north, beyond our view.

Oliver felt deeply sorry for Luke's loss but also knew that Luke needed to be busy pulling for the lives of all present. *"Help us pull!"* Oliver shouted, over the now raging rush of the ebb tide, as he placed his arm around Luke. Luke responded and all of us dedicated our thoughts to getting to the west bank as quickly as possible.

When we were about 100 yards from the west bank, I noticed that the rope we were pulling on, had a second rope lashed to it.

Andrew shouted, *"Pull on the lower rope* from here to shore!" We all responded and soon discovered that the rope we *had* been using was getting higher and higher until it was too far over our heads to reach. Andrew could see my surprise at the rope's elevation and leaned towards me to shout, "The tide here be over seven meters. The higher rope be anchored high up the trunk of a large tree and be within reach at high tide. This *second rope* be anchored to the *base of a tree* so we be pulling ourselves to shore, as the tide waters recede.

It was getting dark now and the approaching sight of the West bank was very welcome. With just a few more minutes of hard pulling, we could hear and feel the hulls of our craft ride against ground. Andrew jumped from the bow to secure our craft to a tree trunk just a few feet away. The rest of us, except Luke, were very happy to follow Andrew onto the solid ground of Anglesey Island. Luke asked to be left alone for a while, and we left him in his sorrow over Bosco. We made our way a few yards into the forest to build a fire and set up our camp for the night. Oliver quietly sat on a large rock within sight of Luke, to watch over him, without intruding at this grievous time.

A camp was made, and the late evening meal prepared with very little conversation, as Luke continued to sit in silence staring at the nearly empty channel that was the last place he had seen his faithful dog. When Luke, with Oliver at his side, joined the rest of us around the fire, he refused any food and lay quietly on the blanket Oliver has spread for him.

"What can we do to help Luke?" I asked Gabriel.

Gabriel appeared as upset as the rest of us when he replied, "Be a friend and allow Luke to be having his quiet time. I be remembering how Gavan and me be so heart broken when our first dog died. It be not as dramatic as this, for our dog died of old age, but we be kids and we, like Luke, loved our dog."

Asa was part of our conversation and said, "I not be owning a dog that I claim as me own, but I ne'er be enjoying the company of a dog, as much as with Bosco." Asa's eyes were just as red and teary as the rest of us.

Andrew, attempting to be sympathetic of the loss, as well as his brother's concern for Luke, offered some comfort by saying, "We not be certain that the dog drowned, we only be knowing, for certain, is he be still swimming when we lost sight of him. If we look for him in the morning, he may have made it to land." Andrew didn't make eye contact with Oliver because he didn't want his brother to perceive how little he believed his own words.

With only a few words shared after the evening meal, the darkness on the west side of the strait seemed thicker and foreboding. The glow from our fire lit up a few of the lower branches but the canopy over us seemed oppressing and much too close. Gabriel and Andrew walked a few yards from camp and began to talk quietly. I assumed they were discussing a search for Bosco or help with our travel plans. I learned that my assumption was wrong.

Gabriel walked back and sat between Gavan and Asa and told all of us, "Andrew be telling me that there be no way Bosco could survive the rush of that ebb tide." The three of us agreed with Gabriel, but none of us wanted to speak any negative words, so we just nodded our heads in agreement, as we stared into the fire.

Luke sat up and announced that he would keep the fire going so the rest of us could get some sleep. Being older and more familiar with dealing with pain, Gavan and Gabriel told Luke that they would stay with him during this time of loss. Luke appreciated their heart-warming counsel and curled up next to the fire like a child who had lost his best friend. In spite of his words and emotional loss, sleep finally allowed Luke to escape this horrible day.

When the eastern horizon brightened, all of us had felt the refreshing relief of sleep and we might have slept for another hour except for the joyous shouting from Luke. The marvelous sight of Bosco standing next to Luke, with Luke's shoe in his mouth, was a stimulus for all of us. The question, in my mind, was shared by all of us.

"When did Bosco *find* us?" I asked, hoping someone had an answer.

Luke replied, "I felt water dripping on my face and looked up to see Bosco standing over me!"

The big dog's bandages were gone but he didn't show any signs of bleeding. He still held Luke's shoe for quite a while, as if it were a trophy, before finally dropping it in Luke's lap. As the fire was rekindled and breakfast prepared, several speculations about Bosco's miraculous return were shared. Only Bosco knew the whole story and he didn't appear to be any the worse for his ordeal.

Like a shot of adrenaline, Bosco's surviving the tide of the Menai Strait energized Luke with a renewed passion for life, in his new world. I felt a bit of the energy, as well, and said a few words of gratitude towards that big dog. When we witnessed the two of them prancing and dancing together, all of us shared the joy. Oliver was now a part of their bond and the trio gave our mission new energy.

With these thoughts in my head, I spoke with Gabriel as we walked westward. "Gabriel," I began, "I have been wondering why this particular Rune is so important to ye."

"I not be knowing, yet," Gabriel replied, "I be sharing with you that Luke's and thy original names be inscribed in English and that be enough to be making me extremely curious. I be expecting it be affecting ye and Luke."

"My curiosity is very strong," I replied. "I just want to use this travel time to know as much as possible about the cave, the writer and the people who used Rune writing."

"The first thing, I be feeling confident to spake to ye about, be the Druids, Raffe," Gabriel began. "They be not the barbaric wild people who be practicing human sacrifice, as the Roman's described."

"Other than your parchments, back in the Monastery," I inquired, "what other sources of information about the Druids have you found?"

This brought a smile to Gabriel's face, as he prepared his answer. For the sake of everyone in our group, my conversation with Gabriel was intentionally loud enough for everyone to hear and share.

"Asa and Gavan are quite familiar with my discoveries," Gabriel began, "but, Oliver and Andrew may have some facts to contribute; so, I shall begin with the Roman lies." Mentioning Oliver's and Andrew's names brought their full attention on Gabriel's words. "The Romans," Gabriel began, "be no different than any other political power, in that, they present false information to gather support for their objectives and vilify their enemies. This be the situation when the Roman Emperor be wanting to be conquering more land and impressing his own people that his cause be noble and necessary. To do this, he be telling the Romans that the people, called Druids, were hideously evil and deserving of annihilation. The Romans, under his leadership, be having an obligation to eliminate this evil race of people."

Giving Luke a short glance to assure his attention to my next words, I commented to Gabriel, "That's a political trick that hasn't changed over time. Luke and I were taught history lessons of many rulers, from many countries, who have used the same kind of lies to justify many wars and genocides."

"Hearing this be very saddening," Gabriel replied, "But, it be not surprising me at all. I doubt the hearts and thinking ways of humans be changed much since our beginning. Getting back to Amergus," Gabriel continued, "he not only be finding the Druid people to be intelligent, he identified them as compassionate in the treatment of strangers. And they be willing to discuss intellectual knowledge, far beyond the knowledge of the first century understanding of the Universe... and the role of humanity." I was very impressed with Gabriel's comfortable use of the word, 'Universe' in context of what Luke and I understood from 2016.

Gabriel continued, "I be expecting to be learning a lot of new words and names that ye and Luke will understand... And I be expecting thy presence, while reading the Runes, will be every bit as revealing, as ye be, when we learned what the numbers and names of future inventions be. As ye may remember, the Runes are written to be making a vocal sound, and reading those sounds, often be resulting in saying words that be having no meaning to anyone except ye and Luke."

I commented, "I find it kind of sad that the lies, spread by the Romans, have survived through the centuries."

"That be most likely due to the profound truth... history always be recorded by the victor," Gabriel said. "Without any Druids, or anyone to read their history carved into the cave walls, there be no one to share the truth."

Gabriel could read my face like an open book, when he said, "Are you wondering, how did I learn to read Runes?" he asked, but it was a rhetorical question. "Part of the Roman lies be their boasting that they killed all of the Druids. They be devastating the Druid culture and slaughtering almost all of the Druids; but, like it so often happens, there be a remnant who be afore warned, by Amergus, on the Roman plans. This remnant be hiding, until the Romans left, and survived. When the wisdom and warnings of Amergus proved to be true, he be followed as if he be a god. It be saving their way of life and their written language, but only through a few in each generation there after. I be chosen to be one of the readers of Runes, in *this* generation."

Gabriel then placed his big arm around my shoulders and pulled me close to his side as he asked softly, "Let me be knowing if ye be liking to learn to read Runes, Raffe. The next generation be going to need someone to continue the skill."

If the expression "food for thought" meant anything, I just had a banquet spread before me and no idea where to start eating. Surely, the expression of hunger on my face, sent my answer to Gabriel. Gabriel's quick nod and a smile, confirmed it. I was flattered that Gabriel would put so much trust in me, but that wasn't the end of my thoughts. There was no way I could explain to Gabriel, or any of the others, that it really disturbed... no, *concerned* me, to be asked to learn a language, for a generation that will live and die, hundreds of years before my own birth.

To know about the Transfer of Consciousness was very much a part of knowledge shared by Gabriel and the others, but, Luke and I were living in one era, while our memories were all from a future time. I decided that this was a learning time for me, and Luke, if he choses. Our personal issues relating to something our friends couldn't comprehend wasn't going to be helpful, so, I decided to simply be a good student and help any way possible.

Initially, our journey on Anglesey Island had been on a dirt trail that appeared to be well traveled and wide enough for two or three people to walk abreast. Without intentions, we had gravitated into walking in pairs, except for Andrew, who pulled the cart with Gavan and Gabriel flanking him to assist in directing Andrew onto the correct path.

Our second day's walking began like the first, until we came to a distinct fork in the trail. The wider path led northwest and Gabriel took the southwest path which was markedly narrower and appeared to be seldom used. With huge trees on both sides of us, this smaller path felt a bit confining. The path worked *between* trees, instead of a swath of cleared trees, and we could only see a limited view ahead or behind us.

Asa took notice of my constant searching around and behind us and asked, "Be ye concerned for our safety, Raffe?" I felt a little embarrassed that my paranoia was so obvious.

I commented, "This forest is so thick, that I can't help thinking that *anyone* could walk upon us or simply wait in ambush."

"If it be helping ye relax, Raffe," Asa continued, "just be watching Bosco. He be seeing, hearing or smelling any threat, long afore any human." This was very comforting advice and from that moment on, I watched Luke, Bosco and Oliver, since they were never apart.

In the early afternoon of the third day, Andrew stopped pulling his cart and Gabriel announced, "We have arrived!" I looked about and saw nothing except more trees to the west and south, but north of us, just a few paces off the trail, an ancient stone wall was visible between the lower branches of the trees. Gabriel led the way and Andrew turned his cart toward the stone wall and followed a pebbled path which led to an opening in the wall that had the remains of two huge doors leaning against the stone wall, in their final repose. Just my guess, but those door fragments looked as if they had been off their hinges for many years.

Gabriel had told me of the attacks on monasteries during a religious purge throughout England and the state of these doors, in their charred and battered condition, was clear evidence that this ancient monastery had suffered some violent history.

We gathered around the opening in the wall and Gabriel held up his hand to indicate that we should stay where we were as he proceeded through the gap in the wall.

He was still in sight as he walked a few yards inside, cupped his hands on either sides of his mouth, and shouted several strange words. I immediately looked to Asa for an explanation. He anticipated my inquiry.

Without turning his head to face me, Asa quietly whispered loud enough for everyone to hear, "Be *patient*. Be *still*."

Gabriel repeated his words, just as he did the first time, but in a slight turn to his left. We all stood in statue-like silence for a few seconds which felt much longer.

The third time, Gabriel turned to his right, cupped his hands, drew in a deep breath, but he froze and never made his call. We could see Gabriel's reddened face soften, as his color returned to normal. A twinkling of delight shown in his eyes and a smile grew on his lips.

"Nycolas." Gabriel spoke. He looked like he was seeing an angel.

Nycolas was the same word he had already shouted two times. The voice of an old man echoed from inside the walls.

"For what reason ye be doing this shouting, Gabriel... ye thinking I be hard of hearing, in me old age?"

Gabriel's face was radiant with happiness to see his old master and mentor. The two men met and joyfully embraced for a long time, as if they had been apart for a terribly long time. The old man turned to face us, as Gabriel kept his arm around Nycolus' shoulders. Nycolus gave a warm greeting to Asa and Gavan, but, when he looked at Oliver and Andrew, he only smiled warmly, as all three nodded in recognition. Nycolas then looked at Luke in a wordless greeting, for just a second, and I could see Luke's eyes widen, as his face turned into amazed surprise. What just happened?

The old monk's face turned to me and our eyes met. I was initially afraid as I heard Nycolus' voice in my head, but his lips were only smiling gently. I could hear the flood of thousands of words entering my mind... all at once.

My fear faded as the first words I heard were, "Please, fear not, Brody, now known as Raffe. We be having much to discuss and I only be wishing to let ye know that ye be most welcome here." Many words followed but they came much too fast for me to process... like spoken words.

I was stunned and looked at Luke to see if he was hearing the same things as I was hearing. Luke's face was calm, but his eyes were red with tears and I knew that Nycolus had spoken to his mind, as well. We were both stunned into silence upon meeting Nycolus. In *my* eyes, he was the original *Santa Claus*. His head was covered with a thick crown of curly snow-white hair, which morphed into a remarkable white beard which trailed down over his chest. Like many older men, his body was full-figured from neck to ankles and his hands, thick and strong, yet soft, clean and well manicured. His voice was very deep and even a whisper could be heard by all of us. He spoke up using a sweetly teasing voice, "Ye be going to stand out here all *day*, or ye be liking to come in and relax, now that this part of thy journey be completed?"

Gabriel, still holding his arm around Nycolas, said, "Come on in. We not be traveling all this way to sitting, sleeping, and eating, on the *ground*."

The first simple door Nycolus lead us through revealed a large gray walled chamber with a few wooden beds. These simple beds had ropes lashed around the frames to create a surface in which to spread a burlap sack filled with straw or horse hair and a blanket. The next room, with the same mud stucco walls was a somewhat larger room with a large hand-hewn table and rough benches as long as the table on either side. Along one wall, a rough bench held what appeared to be a couple large pots and a small waist high fireplace. I presumed this area was a location set up for food preparation.

Nycolas stood next to the only door to this room and quietly watched his new guests familiarize themselves with these guest quarters. When Bosco walked past Nycolas, he gently reached out and ran his hand softly over Bosco's head and down the length of his back. We thought nothing of Bosco being comfortable with the touch of a stranger because he had always been accepting and gentle. Once everyone was in the room, Nycolas gave a big sigh of relief and said, "I be so pleased that Bosco, who still called Bosco, be *housebroken*." Luke's face lit up with delight as he heard the confirmation of his long-held suspicions and hopes... Bosco really *was* a transferred consciousness from his neighborhood in 2016.

"Ye not be getting too comfortable," Nycolas said to the group, "for these are *not* ye quarters. These rooms be where the occasional travelers be given a place to sleep until they move on. I believe ye be finding *yer* quarters considerably more spacious and comfortable."

I, like the rest of our group, waited in silence for Nycolas to continue his tour of this ancient structure. The smiling old monk walked back into the room filled with beds, and stood before a large wardrobe, and waited for everyone to enter the room. Once we were all together, Nycolas asked Asa to close and latch the door leading into the dining room. When Asa did so, Nycolas asked the group to back up two paces. He turned to the wardrobe, placed his hand on the top-right side, to locate and push a hidden button. We only heard a muffled click and then, the entire interior of the wardrobe quietly swung into the room, revealing a large passageway into another room.

Even before entering this secreted room, we could see that it was much larger, by far, and well lit with large glass windows on the north side. This room had nearly a dozen beautifully crafted chairs which all had padded leather seats, arms and backs. Between the windows were shelves of books reaching from floor to the 4-meter ceiling.

"This be the library," commented Nycolas. "There be much more to see afore ye be taking yer rest and yer evening meal." I heard Nycolas say that we had 'more to see' but his words, 'evening meal' was really something special. Like a small flock of sheep, we followed this charming and amazing old man through a couple sleeping rooms which were furnished with beautiful framed beds which had deep padded mattresses and soft linen sheets. The kitchen and dining room were every bit as large as the library, and cabinets filled with fine china. The finely crafted chairs, around the massive four-foot by ten-foot dining table, were also padded with leather upholstery. From the moment we passed through the passage behind the wardrobe, the only sounds heard by any of us was the occasional groan of amazement and several 'Wows' from Luke and me.

I looked at Gabriel and asked, "Did you *know* about all of this?"

Gabriel actually blushed a little, when he replied, "I be not knowing of these quarters when I was in *training* here, and I be not hearing any rumors of such a place on the Isle of Anglesey."

"That be because these quarters be not existing when ye be a novice here, Gabriel," said Nycolas.

Oliver and Andrew were as stunned as the rest of us, when they looked about these spectacular rooms. Andrew looked at Nycolas and the old monk replied vocally, "Let us spake our words, Andrew, for the sake of those present who be not communicating mind to mind."

"Forgive me," Andrew replied, "I just be finding it quite a surprise that someone, who be not from our village, be spaking mind to mind."

"Why make thee the assumption, Andrew, that only those from your village be having this ability, or that I, too, be from your village?"

"We be taught this," Andrew explained, "since we be small children, and we only met two people, from any other place, with our abilities."

"That be yer woman, Rose," injected Nycolas, "and her mother. Ye be having much to learn, Andrew, and I gladly be yer teacher, if ye wish," came the gentle and sincere offering from Nycolas. *"But,"* Nycolas continued, *"afore* any learning and discoveries," he said, with his eyes fixed on Gabriel, "we be needing to *eat, relax* and get a peaceful night's *sleep.* So, please select thy own beds and rest a little." He further announced, "dinner be soon served, and I be calling ye, at that time."

Like a busload of kids entering the first day of summer camp, we all looked at the beds and made our choices. There were no conflicts because there were more beds than travelers. The mattresses were as soft as clouds compared to the lumpy ground that had been our bed for much too long. I doubt it was more than a few seconds before all of us were asleep. It was the marvelous aroma of home cooking that woke me before I heard Nycolas' cheerful voice call, "Dinner be served!"

Nycolas sat at one end of the great table and, once again, reminded me of Santa Claus enjoying a feast given to his little helpers. He said, with a nod, "We be trying to prepare foods which would be most familiar for each of ye." As the novice monks served us on beautiful china plates, I was speechless when a thick, juicy cheeseburger with lettuce, tomatoes and onion slices was placed before me. I had to fight back strong emotions of appreciation as I looked into the grandfatherly eyes of Nycolas, who appeared every bit as excited by each visitor's reception of this mind-boggling meal. The novice who brought my plate was an exceptionally bright-eyed young man who, by his lack of a beard or mustache, looked to be in his mid teens. He never spoke, but it was very clear to me that he was intelligent and alert to everything around him.

After delivering my dinner, this novice walked to the side of Nycolas and stood quietly with his fingers interlocked before his chest, as if he were waiting for further instructions.

I wanted to learn what meals had been served to others in our group. I almost laughed out loud at the plate of steaming tamales, refried beans and Spanish rice was set before Luke. His face was a mirror of my own and no words were needed to see his delight. I was curious to try an experiment and watched Nycolas closely from the moment he and I made eye contact. In that instant, I concentrated on the thought, "Thank you. This is wonderful of you."

Nycolas' lips never moved but I distinctly heard his kind voice saying, "Ye be most welcome, Raffe. We be only at the beginning of a great friendship, for we be going to share many amazing adventures together. I be having someone quite special to introduce to ye and ye friends, as soon as all of ye have eaten."

I stopped chewing and Nycolas laughed with delight. Everyone around the table was involved in conversation and the pleasant din of voices was almost like a playground of excited children. My mind was a scramble of questions, but I was so thoroughly enjoying this remarkable meal and festive atmosphere that I didn't want to disturb it with questions. Nycolas' wordless hint that our futures were going to be connected was enough for me to ponder as I sank my teeth into the delicious cheeseburger.

Even Bosco was given a bowl of his own and it didn't take him more than a couple minutes to consume all of it. Once again, Bosco behaved in the most amazing way; when he finished eating, he laid beside Luke's chair and went to sleep.

Gabriel, just like the rest of us, was very satisfied as he leaned back in his chair to re-assess the room, the table covered with empty plates and the engulfing atmosphere of contentment and safety.

To Nycolas, Gabriel observed, "I not be having enjoyed a finer meal, at a grander table, with dearer friends. How ye be managing to create all this within an ancient structure on this remote isle?"

"To answer thy question, Gabriel," Nycolas began, "I would like to introduce to this company, the brilliant young mind responsible for the comforts we be enjoying. The man you see standing at me side, be Geoffrey. Geoffrey be born without the ability to hear, but his mind be far more clever than most. He be born to a high-blood family, but his father, feeling the shame of his not hearing, sent him to be raised by me, since his fifth birthday. An example of his genius: it was Geoffrey who designed all of the furnishings we are enjoying as well as the bed ye will be resting upon each night. It was Geoffrey's idea to leave the exterior of this ancient monastery unchanged from its condition after marauders attacked nearly a decade ago, for the sake of those who might pass through here for exploiting or greedy purposes. That is also the reason behind having the modest quarters for strangers, and *these* quarters for returning friends, such as this group here tonight."

All of us were very impressed and I immediately said, "Thank you, Geoffrey, this place and this meal be wonderful." As I said these words, it dawned on me that Nycolas had just told us that Geoffrey was 'born deaf.' I felt my face flushing and was about to apologize when I saw Geoffrey's hands moving about, as if his fingers were gesturing something.

As Geoffrey continued making hand-signs, Nycolas spoke, "He says, 'Thank you, Raffe, for the compliment. I be looking forward to be knowing all of you and the opportunity to be making yer time here very comfortable'."

Asa asked, "How he be saying all of that with only his fingers?"

Nycolas began to reply to Asa, but Geoffrey placed his hand gently on Nicolas' shoulder. Nycolas paused and watched Geoffrey's hands, as he began to interpret, "With the absence of my hearing, I learned to enjoy other skills and abilities. My father never wanted me to be seen in public, but my mother refused to let me be sent away, until I was five years old. I embarrassed me parents by making an appearance during a dinner prepared for royalty. I couldn't speak with my hands, at that age, and tried to beg food from the king and queen. I was sent to Brother Nycolas the next day. His love and patience with me, be giving me the ability to learn, and culture my mind with the things I love, like architecture, art, history and religious studies. When I heard that Gavan and Gabriel were returning, and saw the joy in Brother Nycolas' eyes, I wanted to be making this day very special."

Asa was amazed beyond words. I kind of liked seeing Asa stumped for words.

My eyebrows rose at the mention of Gavan being a return visitor prompted Nycolas to elaborate, "Gavan, ye ne'er be knowing that ye visited here afore, did ye? Ye and Gabriel be dropped here as new-born babes by a young woman who couldn't be providing for ye. A young couple asked to raise both of ye, and while still infants, left with the couple ye be knowing as yer parents. When they died during a plague, Gabriel was returned here and you, Gavan, were raised by in-laws of your adoptive parents." Most of this information only confirmed what both of the twins already knew, except for them having been left at this monastery as newborn twins.

Gavan asked the natural question, "Do ye be knowing who our birthmother was?"

To this question, Nycolas gave a few seconds of silence, before replying with one word, "BE."

The implications of this one word stunned both men and they looked at each other before repeating his question, "Do ye be knowing who our birthmother 'be'?"

Nycolas' countenance changed a little from an informative teacher to that of a consoling grandfather, as he softly replied, "Yes. She be a young girl when she came to us. She be assaulted by several young soldiers in Bangor, and left for dead. Monks carried her here so we be helping her recover. It be during that long stay that we be learning that she be with child, nay children. It was her choice to stay here until the two of ye be born. It be then, that she chose to find a good home for you and become a nun."

"When we be seeing her?" asked Gavan.

"I have sent a letter to her, informing her of yer intent to visit," Nycolas began, "but it be up to *her* to decide if she be wishing to see ye. I be hoping ye appreciate the terrible emotional trauma she be having to live with after being assaulted, and then giving up her babies to be raised by someone else."

Gabriel thought for a moment before asking, "I be here for almost fifteen years as a novice and monk! Why be this the first time I be hearing of her?" The disappointment in Gabriel's voice was painfully clear. He thought about all of the years, in which he was so close to his mother, and she never revealed herself.

Gavan reached his big hand across the table and placed it on Gabriel's arm, as he said, "I be so sorry, Gabriel. I ne'er be knowing about her, either, but I be not living as close as ye be."

Nycolas, as wise and experienced as he obviously was, counseled the twins, "Be not allowing any bitterness to grow because of choices made by a young girl who be the victim of the actions of cruel soldiers."

Gavan and Gabriel took a few seconds to study each other's face before Gabriel replied, "I be seeing no bitterness in Gavan's face, and I be knowing that there be no bitterness in me, for our mother. Everyone around this table be painfully aware of the treachery, pain and death left in the wake of drunk soldiers. Nothing be our mother's fault and both of us, for a while, had a loving mother figure. We be having no cause for any negative feelings. If we be having any feelings towards our birthmother, it be sympathy for the terribly frightening event which brought about our existence."

Geoffrey's fingers began to move very slowly as Nycolas patiently watched. With a face of tender patience, Nycolas began to relate Geoffrey's words, "It would appear to me, Gavan and Gabriel, that this monastery and the tender wisdom of Nycolas, has been a safe haven for children to grow up in. I would have been no more than a pampered babbling embarrassment if I had not been brought here."

I was very impressed with Geoffrey's ability to read lips and respond in a manner that seemed like a clone of Nycolas at his age. Both men had crystal blue eyes and a strong chin. I found myself wondering what Nycolas would look like without his beard. Then I flatly rejected the thought for that white beard was such a pronounced feature of his character. I looked back at Nycolas and he was gently stroking his beard... was he hearing me? I couldn't help blushing.

Nycolas glanced at Gabriel and Gavan with a warm smile of appreciation, as well as admiration for being so understanding toward their birth mother. "I be letting her know how ye received this information and encourage her to contact ye, but the choice be hers."

"As nice as it would be to meet our mother," Gabriel stated, "that be not the reason we left the comfort and safety of our monastery."

"YES!" replied Nycolas, with some emotional relief from a sad topic with a reminder of the exciting adventure before all of them. "If it will be acceptable with ye," Nycolas continued, "I be having plans for as many of ye who be wishing to join Gabriel and me, to visit the most recently discovered cave."

"How many of these caves have you found?" I asked Nycolas.

"There be hundreds of caves, Raffe," Nycolas replied, "but only a few be with written history recorded in them, and this cave be having a large amount of writings on its walls."

I asked, "Has anyone capable of reading the Runes been in this cave since it was discovered?"

Once again, Nycolas assured us that we will be the first to read what is inscribed in Runes, but not everything written in this cave is written in Runes.

"As ye already know," Nycolas continued, "some of the writing be in *English* and it be these few words that enticed ye to be making the risky journey ye just completed."

Around the table, heads were nodding in agreement, as some steaming pudding was placed before each of us, and all conversations ceased as our dessert was enjoyed. As soon as our desserts were consumed, the murmurs began with questions being exchanged. All of us shared the question: "What be written on the walls of this cave?"

Anticipating this, Nycolas spoke over the din of our conversations to announce, "I be certain that all of ye be having many questions afore tomorrow's adventures, and ye be having even *more* tomorrow evening. I recommend that we be retiring for the night and be allowing our personal discoveries answer as many questions as possible. Then, we be sharing our un-answered questions, when we be returning."

With overly full stomachs and weary legs, Nycolas' recommendation was followed with pleasure. I assumed that Oliver and Andrew's questions had already been answered with a few glances around the table. I went to bed with a demanding curiosity to discover and experience more about Nycolas' ability to communicate with me, mind to mind. I expected that falling asleep was going to be difficult but from the instant I lay on those soft sheets until I heard Nycolas' joyous voice calling us to breakfast, I had only a few seconds of consciousness.

Breakfast was hot, hearty and very short-lived. Everyone was ready to see the cave.

Chapter 10
To the Cave

I chose to walk with Luke and Oliver as we left the monastery because Luke and I knew that our names were inscribed in the cave, in English. I had yet to ask how he felt about this, and what other feelings he had about the entire journey. Luke was always friendly, but conversations tended to be something that had to be drawn from him rather than casually enjoyed. This, of course, is a description of Luke's sociability before he met Oliver.

I was glad to see that Geoffrey was traveling with us because I was already impressed with his insightful comments and his youthful energy was always needed.

Since that day in which Bosco limped into our camp with Oliver's arrow in his leg, Luke and Oliver spent the major portion of their days in private conversations. I still find it difficult to think of Luke as anything except the 'man' who has quietly lived with Gabriel, Gavan, Asa and me for months. I wondered if the others thought of Luke as a man or a woman. The more I thought of it, the less I expected it to matter to anyone, except Luke, and now, Oliver. I began my conversation with Luke and Oliver by asking Luke, "What are your thoughts about finding our names written on a cave wall over fifteen hundred years ago?"

Luke smiled and replied, "I've been thinking of a few ways of posing that same question to you, in an interesting way, which will describe the bazaar nature of what we are doing right now. We are walking through an ancient forest, on the Isle of Anglesey in the year 1690, to enter a cave which has been concealed since about 120 AD because a woman was transferred from the year 2994, into the body of a young man named Amergus in 60 AD. That

Amergus became a Druid Priest and warned his people of the impending Roman slaughter of their civilization, and inscribed the names of two of the members of our group, so we could read it today." I smiled as I saw Oliver's face twist into an amused expression of humor and amazement.

I replied, "That sounds exactly like the thoughts I've been having about this fateful day," I also commented, "I feel as if we are important but also very humbled, if our lives can have a positive effect on today's future and the history of the world we grew up in. I get the impression that we are links in a chain that, once completed, might affect our own lives in 2016."

Luke looked down at the path before us, before responding, "Maybe we can write something about today's discovery and hope it will have a positive influence. I would like to think of my own life, both before the transfer and now, as being a good influence instead of just another life, come and gone, through the ages."

"We certainly have an advantage of future knowledge, over everyone else in our group." I replied with energized enthusiasm to see that cave.

The words, *"Here it be!"* from Nycolas came much sooner than I was expecting because we hadn't walked for more than thirty minutes. I had this preconceived image of a cave being a black hole in the side of a mountain or cliff wall. But, here we all stood, looking down at two large flat stones, at our feet. Nycolas stood just off the narrow path we had been traveling, and pointed at the ground. The gash in the forest floor was only about four feet long and two feet wide at its widest point. A pair of large flat rocks were placed near the opening and Nycolas said that they had once covered the opening.

Nycolas also shared with us, that it had been just about a year ago, that a novice from the monastery was collecting wild berries and herbs along the path when his staff sank from sight between those flat stones.

We could see the end of a ladder protruding above the lip of the opening. It didn't look very inviting to crawl into this opening, or, in the situation of Gabriel's and Gavan's thick chests and broad shoulders, squeeze through.

Nycolas looked over our group and asked, "Who would be liking to go first?"

Geoffrey, reading Nycolas' lips immediately gestured with a finger pointed at his own chest. He was volunteering. Nycolas could see that the young man's body was the best for the task, but he would prefer someone who could shout up his findings. Geoffrey understood and patiently waited.

Asa asked the question that was in my mind, "How much room be there in that tiny 'ole?"

To Asa's question, Nycolas smiled and replied, "What ye be seeing here is like the narrow opening of an archer's shooting slot on the exterior wall of a great castle. So it be that this tiny portal be the introduction to a vast underworld."

Eyebrows arched on every face.

Gavan, still holding his face of awe, asked Nycolas, "Do ye be knowing of any other ways to be entering this cave?"

"Yes," Nycolas replied, "but this opening be the most accessible for us. Only a bird or mountain goat can use the other cave entrance."

Gabriel stepped forward and looked down into the blackness. "How we be going to *see* anything down there?"

"When ye be reaching the bottom of the ladder," Nycolas said, "ye be having enough light to see a bundle of torches, with a flint and steel to light one. When ye be ready, the rest of us be following."

Gabriel carefully sat on the rim opposite the ladder and tested a wrung before placing his weight on it. He tested each wrung until his stomach passed the opening and with a little manipulation of his chest, his shoulders and head slipped from sight. We could hear his deep breathing resonate from the black hole. Then the sound of his deep voice reverberating even deeper, he announced, "I be at the bottom of the ladder and be lighting a torch!" His voice was booming loud from his anxiety and excitement for this moment. He had been anticipating this, for nearly a full year.

From my tightly shared vantage point, we could see Gabriel's efforts to light a torch was very quick and both he and the cave walls were illuminated with the flickering yellow flame. Gabriel's first reaction was to glance around and as he did, he reported, "This cave be... huge. I canst see the far wall from here."

Nycolas told Gabriel to place his torch in the bronze holders that were along the wall, about shoulder high. Gabriel followed instructions and he could see the once black hole grow brighter and brighter as each torch was lit and hung along a wall. Gabriel cupped his hands and shouted, "Come on *down*. The ladder be *sturdy* and there be more than enough room for a *hundred people down here!*"

Anxious curiosity was like a giant vacuum that sucked each one of us descending into the small opening; each moving a little faster than the last with the confidence of safety and the fear of a dark unknown dispelled, with the torch lights.

The moment Luke placed his feet in the cave's opening, Bosco began to whimper at being separated from his closest friend. Luke stood on the ladder with only the upper half of his body exposed and comforted the giant dog.

Oliver offered, "I be staying up here with Bosco. I can be seeing the inside of this cave some other time." Luke was so grateful to Oliver, for allowing him to enter the cave. Bosco stood over the opening as Luke descended, but the loyal giant whined and pawed at the rock opening as if he could dig her out. Bosco quickly resigned himself to laying on his stomach with his head in the opening, watching Luke make his way down the ladder.

I was last to enter the cave. Bosco licked my face, as he watched, in puzzlement, as I sank into the ground. Oliver's gentle stroking of his back, neck and head was having the desired calming effect as Bosco laid his head in Oliver's lap.

I was not prepared for the underground expanse that greeted my eyes, as they adjusted to the low light of torches. "You should have said, 'a hundred men, on horseback,' I teased Gabriel, for underestimating the immensity of this cave. When Gabriel didn't reply, I looked for him.

I was surprised to see the big monk sitting on the floor of the cave with his head between his bent knees. His shoulders were bouncing, and Gavan and Asa were leaning over him. Gavan looked up to meet my eyes and shrugged his shoulders to imply he was unsure of why Gabriel was crying. The cave was silent except for Gabriel's quaking voice and Bosco's whimpering above us. I looked to Asa for an explanation and got the same confused shrug that Gavan had given me. Even Geoffrey and Nycolas' face was a bit surprised and bewildered as Geoffrey gently laid his hand on Gabriel's heaving shoulder. I had witnessed this big monk confront armed and determined soldiers, with no sign of fear, but something, upon entering this cave, had him crying like a frightened child. We all waited patiently for Gabriel to compose himself.

Nycolas looked at each person present and then at the nearly flat wall that spanned one side of the cave. The wall was at least twelve feet high and fifty to seventy feet into the darkness, where the torch's light couldn't reach. Nycolas looked down at his dear friend, Gabriel, and placed a hand on his shoulder, to calm him.

Nycolas asked, "Be it something written on this wall?" Gabriel didn't speak. He simply nodded his head in agreement and buried his face between his knees again. I got the impression that it was quite embarrassing for Gabriel to show this much emotion. It certainly made the rest of us uncomfortable. I found it much easier to look around the interior of this cavern than continue to watch a man I loved and admired suffer through this moment.

Luke, wanting to be supportive of Gabriel, knelt beside him and said, "It's quite alright to cry, Gabriel, you know how often I cry."

Gabriel, wanting to rid the tension, smiled at Luke, as he said, "It be alright when *you* cry, Luke, you have a *pink aura.*" That did it! The cave roared with laughter.

Within seconds, Gabriel raised his head. "Forgive me, for upsetting any of thee." His eyes were locked onto Gavan. "I be explaining what I be reading to cause it."

Gavan spoke, in Gabriel's defense, "Ye not be having to explain anything to us, Gabriel."

"All of thee be needing to know what I just read, Gavan," Gabriel replied.

As we moved in closer to Gabriel, he took several deep breaths, and then he began, "I be not seeing clearly when I first descended but, after lighting all the torches, I returned to the bottom of the ladder. Here," Gabriel pointed, his hand still shaking, slightly, "at the top left corner of this wall, I be sounding out the first few characters. They read, 'Greetings Brother Gabriel and friends, I be waiting many centuries to share this information with all of ye. Thank ye, Brother Nycolas, for summoning them and providing them with comfort and food." Gabriel's voice was quaking again, and he turned toward Nycolas to share a supportive embrace. The white bearded man leaned forward and wrapped his arms about Gabriel in silence.

Bosco's puppy-like whining had almost stopped, otherwise, the cave would have been completely silent. I heard every word Gabriel had read but my brain was scrambling to put everything into any kind of sequence... and failed. This wasn't the intellectual bantering that Luke and I had shared before we climbed into this cave; this was hand-carved writing on a stone wall from centuries in our history by an author not yet born for many centuries to come.

Gavan asked Gabriel, "Ye be needing something to drink. I brought some water!"

Asa injected, "Here. Try some of *my* water, it be more flavorful and it be helpful." Asa produced his flask and the little red trickles at the side of Gabriel's mouth let us know what kind of 'water' Asa offered.

"Thanks be to ye, Asa," Gabriel replied.

I spoke up and asked, "I hope you brought enough 'water' for all of us, Asa, I have a feeling we may all need it soon."

Gabriel, warmed and comforted by both wine and friends, said, "We be needing to proceed, and take the time, later, to be searching for logic. Right now, we need to record the message just the way it was written one thousand, five hundred, and sixty-odd years ago."

I was reminded of the adage, 'Don't bite off more than you can chew,' and our present experience was much more than a single bite. We were being filled with a universe of knowledge and there was no way my mind could chew on this. I couldn't call it fear but it certainly was reverent trepidation that filled all of us as Gabriel looked at the tiny etched lines and translated it into English. To make it easier for his audience, Gabriel interpreted sentences and phrases.

Gabriel continued, "Amergus be writing that the most important information he be sharing with us is The Passing — how it happens and what be making it happen.

There be a repeated reference here that doth not make sense to me. Amergus be writing about a cave several times but he didn't call it a cave. He referred to the cave as a 'black hole.'"

The instant Gabriel said, 'black hole,' Luke uttered a gasp and looked at me.

I exclaimed, "We are very *familiar* with what a 'black hole' is, Gabriel, but I do *not* know if we can *explain* it to you, exactly. To make it easy to understand, it's a star that can't be seen, in the night sky, because it's black."

Gabriel replied, "I think I be understanding what ye be saying, Raffe, but there be descriptions or movements that Amergus called 'or-bit' and 'gr-a-vit-tee.' These words be meaning anything to ye and Luke?"

"Yes," replied Luke, with obvious enthusiasm. "Can you make whole sentences using these words, 'orbit' and 'gravity?' It may be helpful to us to know how these words are used."

"The word 'orbit,'" Gabriel began, "be in the phrase, 'the path of the black hole inter-sects the 'orbit' of earth each... three-hundred-twenty-six years. I be familiar with this number of years," said Gabriel, "but what be an 'orbit?'"

I didn't want to spend our day interpreting new concepts to these friends and asked Gabriel, "Would it be acceptable to you, if we make a list of these new words and then explain them to everyone around our dinner table? It will save a lot of time and give us a chance to make drawings or charts to help explain."

"Excellent," commented Nycolas, "I wouldst rather spend hours around a table than minutes in this dank hole. You mentioned 'making drawings,' Raffe, and no one is better with that skill than Geoffrey. Anything he sees, he can replicate with lines. Give me a moment to ask him about these markings." Nycolas faced Geoffrey and began

182

making the same hand signals we saw Geoffrey making during last evening's dinner. After a couple of minutes, Geoffrey responded with the same kind of gestures. Nycolas reported, "Geoffrey can make a copy of everything on that wall. We have a couple new items at the monastery that will work perfectly for this purpose."

Gabriel commented, "There be no possible way to translate a small portion of these Runes in one day. We be going to need more torches, a lot more, and many more days in this cave. If ye and Luke will write down what I translate into English while Geoffrey makes copies of these Rune symbols for later use, we be spending time in the evenings discussing the results."

Gabriel asked Oliver to pass down the large roll of paper sheets that he had carried from the monastery. Paper was referred to as a 'new item' by Nycolas because they had only recently acquired some from Chinese traders. I was pleasantly surprised to see several graphite pencils with thin sheaths of soft wood around the graphite core. They were very crude but looked like they would work perfectly.

This idea was acceptable to everyone and Gabriel looked back to the long and amazingly smooth wall. I noted that the wall was smoothed by the Druids to accommodate the large number of Runes that Amergus intended to inscribe on it. So much stone had been chipped and ground away, from the wall, that the floor was leveled with the dust and chips. I noted that the Runes were covering every inch of the wall and might also go below the level of the gravel floor. This wasn't worth mentioning right away but I did make a mental note to tell Gabriel.

I heard Gabriel speak my name and realized that I was thinking about the potential of more Runes and forgetting the translations Gabriel was giving me. "Forgive me, Brother Gabriel, my mind was drifting. What did you just say?"

"Another phrase using the words, 'black hole.' Ye be ready to write?" I nodded and he continued.

"When the 'black hole' folded in... on itself, it obtained empty, or new-trail... mass... gravity." When I stopped writing, Gabriel asked, "That be making sense to thee?"

Luke jumped in, "Collapsed!"

That was exactly what I was about to say for 'folded in,' and wrote it down. The second expression of 'neutral mass gravity' was new to me and when I looked to Luke for help, he shrugged his shoulders.

"I can understand what it might mean," offered Luke, "but I have never heard of a black hole 'collapsing,' maybe that's what happens when a black star can't absorb any more matter."

Of course, this short exchange with Luke sounded like Greek to the others. I could imagine it taking a very long time to explain all of this in 1690 terms.

All of the time in which Gabriel, Luke and I discussed the meaning of the English translation, Geoffrey sat with his large sheet of paper against a particularly smooth portion of a wall and made a copy of the Runes before him. A few times, Gabriel looked at his work and commented on how accurate his work was.

I whispered to Luke, "I believe we have a real Xerox here. He smiled simply because no one but the two of us would understand.

Andrew took this moment to suggest that he, and anyone else who wished to join him, could return to the monastery. He would get more torches and return with some food and water. The suggestion seemed to be very welcome to Asa, Gavan and Nycolas. They climbed the ladder to begin the short walk back. Oliver said he would stay with Luke and Bosco, and remained at the cave opening.

I noticed that every few minutes, Luke looked at the opening above us and Oliver was always attentively looking down. It occurred to me that they were communicating.

184

I asked Luke, "Are you keeping Oliver informed of what Gabriel is translating?"

Luke blushed a little and said, "Yes. Oliver is teaching me to communicate mind-to-mind and he already understands cosmetology from my own college courses."

Other than being a little surprised at the sharing of so much knowledge, I was a little jealous of Luke's advanced experience with mind to mind communication. I commented, "This ability of yours is going to be very helpful when we attempt to explain 'orbits,' 'black holes,' 'collapsing black holes,' and 'neutral gravity mass'... whatever that is."

Just then, Gabriel spoke up, "Found another of yer strange words. What be 'smoky or dark matter?'"

"Can you translate how the words 'dark matter', as they are used?" I asked.

Gabriel studied the massive wall for a few seconds.

"I be translating word by word and ye be telling me what I said." Gabriel once again studied the wall and slowly read, "When the black hole has drank, maybe soaked up, all of the material it can hold, it will fold in, or collapse, into itself resulting in both negative and positive gr-a-vi-ty and follow a path of dark matter. This will allow the black hole to pass very close to earth without gra-vi-tee."

Gabriel looked at us when he finished translating and the matching expressions on our faces caused him to be alarmed. "What be wrong? I be saying something to be making yer faces look so disturbed?"

I was sure Luke could have answered but I didn't wait, since she immediately looked up to Oliver to share what we just heard. "Some of the things you just read, Gabriel, are as new to us as they are to you. We are familiar with a black hole, but we have never heard of a black hole collapsing when it could no longer absorb the matter around it. We certainly haven't heard of neutral gravity and paths based on dark matter. We clearly understand all of the *words* you are using, but these words are being used in *ways* we don't completely understand. Obviously, we have a lot to learn from Amergus of 120AD. That certainly wrecks the title of The Dark Ages."

Gabriel, intently listening to every word we said, asked, "Did the 'Dark Matter' come from the 'Dark Ages?'"

I instantly regretted my own words and the potential for confusion I introduced to my friend. "They are not the same thing, Gabriel, I shouldn't make this any more confusing than it already is."

Andrew had returned with a large bundle of torches, a flask of fresh water and bread for each of us. He shouted down to us that Nycolas was having a grand feast prepared for this evening and instructed him to bring us back in time to clean up before the meal. I looked to Gabriel to see if he had heard Andrew's message and at Geoffrey, to see if he was looking at Andrew. Gabriel was intently reading the Runes and his face grew more intent and disturbed the longer he read and Geoffrey was completely focused on his work.

"What is it, Gabriel, what are you reading that disturbs you?" I pleaded.

"   If ye would allow me some time to think about this, I be sharing everything with ye. I just be not understanding or believing what Amergus be telling us."

Naturally, Gabriel could not have said anything that would generate more curiosity than his last statement. I turned to Luke and asked him if he was about ready to return to the Monastery. He replied that he was very ready, and he really didn't want to walk back after sunset, even with Bosco.

Gabriel exclaimed, "Sun Set. Ye be calling it 'sunset,' doth ye?"

Luke replied, "If you are referring to that big bright sun going below the horizon, in the west, yes I do."

Gabriel's face became calm as he turned back to the wall and began to read. "Time, like sunrise and sunset, be not what ye be taught. 'Sunrise' and 'sunset' be taught, spoken and believed, for so many generations, that we be having not the words to describe the truth. In fact, there be never a 'sunrise' or 'sunset' since the beginning of our earth's... existence." Gabriel's face looks something like a frightened child hearing a truth that conflicted with his entire world.

Gabriel asked, "What be Amergus saying? The *sun never sets or rises?*"

I commented, "This is most certainly one of those explanations that will require a discussion around our table and some illustrations for better communication." I asked Gabriel, "How about we return to the Monastery, enjoy a wonderful meal and begin our explanations on full stomachs?"

It was nice to climb out of that cave and walk back to the monastery with anticipations of an excellent dinner. Luke never spoke a single word during our walk to the monastery. Bosco seemed to be keenly aware of his favorite human's mood and walked so close to him, that Luke rested his arm on the great dog's back. Gabriel was so focused on the discoveries he had encountered in that cave, that he was silent in thought as well. I had no expectation of Geoffrey carrying a conversation, so I walked close to Oliver and when he looked towards me, I nodded my head towards Luke and used my face to ask him, 'Why is Luke so sad?' Oliver was already aware of Luke's silence and shrugged his shoulders to imply that he didn't know.

Even as the cave grew ever more distant behind us and the western sky turned a rose red and faded into twilight, announcing the end of day, my mind was still down in that ancient pit, trying to understand what we learned. The things we learned today were only small windows through which we caught only small portions of far greater knowledge than Luke and I ever expected.

Thinking of Luke again, I wondered if the messages left for us by Amergus, were the reason for his melancholy mood. Luke had always been emotional and often withdrawn, but I hoped this was just a temporary mood swing and some food and friends will cheer him up.

It was a dinner as wonderful as Nycolas had promised. Bosco had his own plate prepared for him. I was still troubled every time my eyes met Gabriel's, I could see that, in his mind, he was still standing before that amazing wall of Runes.

Oliver was able to draw some conversation from Luke and even an occasional smile. This brought some relief to my concerns about his emotional withdrawal. By the time our dessert was consumed, everyone around the table complained that they had eaten too much.

The atmosphere quieted as Nycolas inquired of Gabriel, "What ye be finding on that wall that might affect all of us?" It was obvious that Geoffrey was very interested in reading Gabriel's lips as he changed his table location to be directly across from Gabriel.

Gabriel fixed his eyes on the dining room wall behind Geoffrey for several seconds, before responding, "What affected me most be that Amergus be saying the sun never rises or sets. How this be possible?" Gabriel looked to Luke and me, as if he wanted us to answer.

I knew the answer, and a glance at Luke implied that he also knew, but how can we *explain* it?

"Do *you* want to try an answer?" I asked Luke.

Luke looked at me with passive eyes and mumbled, "No. I don't feel like talking."

I nodded and replied, "But, please jump in or *correct* me if I make any mistakes." Luke just stared at his folded hands and made no reply.

Knowing that I would need some kind of visual support, I decided to use our plates and goblets to represent the planets orbiting within our solar system. No matter how clever I *thought* this idea might have been, I soon felt the pangs of my idiocy when Nycolas interrupted me.

"What be a 'planet'? Nycolas asked politely, "Be having anything to do with 'or-bits' and 'gr-a-vi-ty'?"

Luke was trying to stifle a giggle because he recognized my effort to teach a concept of our solar system, with dishes on a table, was like fighting the tide with a soup spoon. It was comforting to know that these friends wanted to learn terms, concepts and principles, but...

I sat back in my chair and asked my friends to wait as I sought for a way to explain all this. We all sat in silence and I couldn't think. Luke used the silence to excuse himself from the table and walked into the Library. From my position at the table, I saw Luke sit on the floor inside a soft beam of moon light which streamed through the high window on the South wall. As expected, Bosco snuggled against Luke's leg and laid his big head in his lap. It made a very serine picture of a man and his dog, but also very sad.

Asa sat as quiet and patient as everyone else, but I noticed that he twirled a signet ring on his finger, which normally hung about his neck.

Luke broke the silence with a suggestion he spoke toward his own feet, "Use something they are *familiar* with to describe something *new*."

"What would you suggest?" I asked.

"How about the Bible?" was Luke's reply before he returned his focus on Bosco. I was impressed with everyone's patience because I sat motionless for several minutes, before an idea occurred to me.

"In the beginning, God created the heavens and the earth..." I began, "The sun we see in the sky every day is part of the 'heavens' and we are here on earth. The earth 'orbits' around the sun."

Silence was accentuated with friendly blinking eyes.

"Asa," I asked, "may I use your ring and lanyard for an illustration?" Asa handed his ring and long lanyard to Gavan, who looked at it, before passing it on to me.

I took a breath and began, "It is time for us to use the wonderful imaginations that I know you all have. Think of the tip of my finger, as the sun." I was impressed with Geoffrey's total focus. He was riveted on my mouth, but still fully aware of what my hands were doing.

With my index finger pointed towards the center of the group, I waited a moment and observed that each friend was paying attention and showed no signs of a problem. I held up Asa's signet ring, now on the lanyard, and said, "Now imagine Asa's ring to be our earth. The earth is shaped like a *ball*, but just imagine it." The puzzled look on several faces told me that I needed to be clearer before proceeding.

"I see some questioning faces." I observed, with a sigh.

Gavan spoke, "I was taught that the earth is flat and square." Several heads nodded in agreement, but not Geoffrey, he appeared to fully agree with my imagery.

"The simple answer, Gavan," I replied, "is that the earth is not flat but shaped like a ball, a sphere." Geoffrey nodded. I was relieved that no one challenged my words, this time. Wanting to make a single point, I began to spin Asa's ring, at the end of the lanyard, about my extended finger, as I explained, "the *earth* travels around the *sun*... much like Asa's *ring* travels around my *finger*." Geoffrey's eyes sparkled with delight. "The reason the *ring* doesn't fly across the room, is because it is held by a length of leather lacing. *Gravity*... like the wind, can't be seen, but we can see how the wind affects the trees and dust. *Gravity* pulls, or keeps, the earth spinning around the sun, and that *path* is called an '*orbit.*'"

If there were any crickets in the room, this would have been the perfect time to chirp. I was expecting to see some skepticism in my friend's faces, but it was wonderment and the light of comprehension that I saw in their eyes. Every set of eyes, except Luke's, were watching Asa's ring continuing to arch around my finger. Geoffrey's eyes were wide and his mouth hung slightly open with amazement.

Nycolas asked, "Can this lanyard, or gravity, break?"

With some thought, I answered, "*Yesterday*, before Gabriel read some things written by Amergus, I would have said, '*no,*' but like all of us, I am a student who wants to learn more. Amergus put some amazing facts before me and it will take me some time to learn."

I handed Asa's ring and lanyard back, and he put the ring on his finger and spun it. Pointing at his own finger, and looking at me, he said, "Sun," and then pointing at the spinning ring, he said, "Earth." I nodded with delight at how quickly the concept was accepted. Geoffrey was, obviously, a gifted engineer with the evidence of his skills all around us. He absorbed the solar shapes and principles like a vacuum.

Luke softly spoke two words with every intention of not wanting to be involved, "sunrise, sunset."

Afraid that any further illustrations may destroy the progress made today, I said, "We can describe that tomorrow or the next day, if that's acceptable to you, Luke."

Luke continued looking down, and said, "I don't care. It will be you doing the teaching, not me." Luke sounded disinterested and a look from Oliver implied that he was as surprised as me, with Luke's melancholy attitude.

Nycolas broke the silent gloom with his cheerful voice and said, "I be learning quite enough for one day, and be hoping my mind be letting me sleep, this night. Thank you, Luke and Raffe, for an enlightening evening. I be retiring early, for tomorrow I be needing to make a trip into town, while ye re-visit Amergus' cave. I be anxious to hear about tomorrow's revelations."

All agreed, and we dispersed for our beds. Oliver sat in a library chair next to Luke and Bosco without speaking. My brain was tired, and my body was just as fatigued. Sleep came quickly.

I woke well before sunrise and looked about. In the poorly lit room, I could see that Luke's bed was empty, so was Oliver's, and Bosco wasn't on the floor between their beds. I could hear whispered voices coming from the reading room and recognized the voices as Luke and Oliver. I would have stayed in bed to give them privacy, but I heard Luke mention my name a couple times and took this as sufficient justification to join their conversation.

As I entered the room, Oliver looked up and said, "I sure be glad ye joined us, Raffe. Luke be claiming that he not be belonging here, as ye be."

That explained the use of my name and I felt more comfortable joining them. Luke looked as despondent as he had the previous evening. I asked, "Luke, what makes you think you don't belong here? We have discovered some amazing ancient Runes and you are as needed as I am, to explain what we are finding." It occurred to me, that Luke was using the technique of staring into his lap, as an insulation from Oliver's ability to communicate mind to mind, and it worked just as well, with me. I had no idea why Luke was feeling so alienated in the midst of loving and supportive friends.

Luke spoke softly, "I don't belong here. You don't need me, or my education, since you can figure out things without me. None of you understand what it has been like to live in a male body. Even though you are aware and want to be helpful, you just can't understand."

I sat across from Luke and studied her body language for several seconds before softly commenting, "You probably already know this, Luke, but you are not the first Transferred Consciousness who went from a woman's body into a man's. If it is of any comfort, Amergus was a young woman in 2994 and a male Druid in 60AD." Oliver and I sat in patient silence. Both of us held some hopes that Luke would respond positively to our words, but we were both disappointed.

Luke commented, "That was Amergus' life, and this is mine. I hate my life. And, the more love I feel from all of you, especially you, Oliver, the more I hate myself and want this life to end."

Oliver placed his hand on Luke's arm, as he said, "Ye be knowing this matters not to me. I be loving the person I be knowing ye be, and so do all of yer friends."

Luke remained focused on his lap, as he replied, "I know all of you intellectually understand my issue of identity, and I am convinced that you love me, Oliver. The rest of this world does *not* understand, and they don't *want* to understand. I feel alone, and I hate my existence."

"Give us more time," Oliver pleaded. "There be so *much* being discovered in that cave, that there *might* even be answers for ye."

I couldn't imagine what kind of discoveries in Amergus' cave could be helpful for Luke's comfort and identity, but the plea for patience from Oliver was helpful.

"Okay," replied Luke, skeptically, "let's see what kind of miraculous information a Druid Priest from 60 AD has for us, before taking any actions."

Luke's reference to 'taking actions' was disturbing, since it implied, he might already have something in his mind, that he didn't want to share. I didn't ask any more questions and, since I could hear Gabriel, Gavan and Asa stirring, I let the conversation subside.

The smell of brewing *coffee* came from the kitchen and Oliver was the first to praise the aroma and head into the kitchen for a couple mugs for himself and Luke. In Oliver's absence, Luke looked up and even though I couldn't read any of his thoughts, I could clearly see deep and punishing pain in his eyes. Oliver returned with two steaming mugs of coffee, place one before Luke and offered me the second.

"No, thank you," I replied, "I put a couple things in my coffee, if they have sugar and cream. I'll be right back." In the kitchen, I found Geoffrey and two other monks, much older than Geoffrey, were busy baking bread and preparing a breakfast for us. I asked if Brother Nycolas had already left for town and was told that he left an hour earlier and hoped to be back by midafternoon. If there weren't so much to be discovered in Amergus' cave, I would have enjoyed traveling into town with Nycolas. I found honey and thick fresh cream for my coffee. This day was getting off to a very good start.

As I sat basking in the aromas of fresh coffee, yeast bread baking, and some kind of spiced meat cooking, Geoffrey approached the table and sat across from me. His eyes were bright with the inner glow of an amazingly gifted thinker. He made a gesture for me to remain motionless as he retrieved a long round leather cylinder that looked much like a quiver, except it held many sheets of rolled paper. He slowly pulled out a single sheet taking great care not to rip or wrinkle it. He laid this sheet on the smooth surface of the large table and retrieved one of the graphite markers. Spreading this paper out, he began to draw.

At first, his lines were random, and no recognizable object could be identified. Geoffrey kept looking up. At first, I thought he was looking at me, but this wasn't the case, he was looking just to the side of my head at Luke, who was sitting on the floor with Bosco. My expectation was that he saw the same beautifully lit and softly framed image of a man enjoying the company of a dedicated dog. I wondered if he knew that Luke had been sitting in the same place for hours, and even more amazing, Bosco remained at his side.

Realizing that Geoffrey was using me as a screen, I sat still and watched his creation materialize. If Geoffrey was a good artist, I sure couldn't detect anything among the black lines on his paper that would hint of a man or a dog. Then I began to recognize what Geoffrey was drawing; it was a human face. It filled the paper and I could see that the figure had long flowing hair and with a few more lines, it looked like the face of a woman. He had my attention now.

Who was she? She was beautiful with brilliant eyes and an amazingly supple mouth. I was spellbound by her captivating beauty. As Geoffrey was making the last few touches to give the drawing greater depth and character, Oliver walked through the dining room to return the coffee mugs and froze as he passed behind Geoffrey. His eyes were locked on the face Geoffrey had drawn. He put both mugs on the table and whispered one word, "Maria." Stunned, I asked him to repeat his word.

Oliver put his hand on Geoffrey's shoulder and when Geoffrey turned his head, Oliver said, "That's Maria from 2016." Geoffrey nodded his head and pointed at Luke.

Luke heard his '2016 name' and walked into the dining room. His gasp was audible as he fixed his eyes on the mirror like image of his most recognizable face, his *own face* as Maria. I could easily see that Luke was shocked and stunned as tears began to drip from his eyes. Luke looked up at Geoffrey and Oliver, almost speechless, but not quite. Oliver used this moment to share something with Luke, "Luke, this be how I have always seen thee. From our first meeting in the forest to this moment, this be the face I be seeing and loving."

I thought to myself, if this Oliver isn't the most romantic love-sick man on earth, I can't imagine who is.

Just then Asa, Gabriel and Gavan entered the dining room and collected around to table. When Gabriel heard Oliver identify the beautiful woman as Maria, all three men were stunned.

Intending to be an encouragement, Asa said, "Bloody me! Ye be a most handsome las." and padded his hand on Luke's back.

194

To the shock of everyone present, Luke burst from the room wailing bitter tears. Asa immediately asked, "What did me say? I thought I be being nice."

Oliver said to the group, "I'll explain later," as he followed Luke into the library.

Luke was sitting in a padded chair right next to the windows when Oliver sat in the chair beside his.

"Why do ye cry so?" Oliver asked.

It took quite a while for Luke to stop crying and wipe his eyes and nose with his sleeve, to reply. "I understand that you love me, Oliver, but that beautiful face Geoffrey drew is the woman I wanted to offer to you, not this skinny, balding man with hairy legs."

Oliver had to smile at the image Luke described, but he knew that it wasn't meant as a joke. "I will always be seeing ye as ye really be, Maria. You will always be my secret beauty."

Luke was tenderly moved, but resolute in his rejection of how he looked in 1690.

They sat together in silence.

The breakfast table was alive with energetic conversations about the cave, the monastery, Anglesey Isle, the impressive drawing of Maria and the plans of Asa and Gavan to explore the area around the monastery while Gabriel, Geoffrey, Oliver, Luke and I continued our explorations of Amergus' cave.

Andrew announced, "I be having a wonderful time here, but be needing to return to Bangor and care for my family and business."

Gavan asked Andrew, "Ye be telling Nycolas that ye be leaving? Ye may be gone before he returns."

Andrew smiled at Gavan and said, "Aye, indeed. I be explaining everything to him while the rest of ye be chatting about the table last evening."

Gavan shook his head and muttered, "Hmmpph, sure be wishing to spake from mind to mind."

Asa looked at his life-long friend and with a bit of mischief in his voice, asked, "Be ye sure ye be wanting others to hear the thoughts that run *rampant* in yer brain?" Both men laughed a very uncomfortable laugh.

Gavan replied, "No, Asa. I be guessing *not*." They were obviously sharing an inside joke.

To get away from that subject, Asa asked Andrew, "Oliver be going with ye?"

"No," Andrew replied, "he be wanting to stay and return when the rest of ye be leaving here. He be a good helper and friend, and he be relaying me everything about yer discoveries in a few seconds, when ye return." Andrew smiled. "Forgive me, Raffe, I be forgetting to give ye something, from Nycolas." He reached down and picked up a roll of paper and a oversized leather wallet of sorts. "More supplies," Andrew said, and handed them to me.

My eyes of delight said it all, "Thank you and Brother Nycolas."

Andrew nodded and offered, "Afore I be leaving, I be wanting to guide all of you to a beautiful overview that be only a few hundred paces from the opening of the cave."

Breakfast was as delicious as expected and we were soon packing for the day's adventure. I opened the quiver Geoffrey used earlier, placed the roll of paper sheets along the walls, slid the leather sleeve inside the papers, to protect the contents, and placed the wallet of writing tools down to the bottom. "Now, I am ready!" I said, proudly.

Day Two at the cave. We all set out for Amergus' cave together. When we reached the opening of the cave, Andrew smiled and said, "Drop all of yer packs and follow me for a short walk." He led us through the trees for less than a hundred paces and, almost like magic, the trees stopped.

We were standing on top of a gigantic rock outcropping that was about 20 feet from forest to ledge and ran along the rim of a deep gorge. The view was breathtaking! We could see up and down the wide gorge for several miles, in either direction. The gorge was several hundred yards wide. We had to carefully approach the edge, and still could only see the far side of the gorge's bolder strewn bottom, hundreds of feet below. Just as Andrew has said, the view was amazing; and terrifying to people, like me, who didn't enjoy getting too close to cliffs. Even Bosco showed a healthy respect for that ledge and kept a margin of 10 feet between himself and the precipice. I stayed with Bosco, because, to me, he showed the most wisdom. Oliver and Andrew appeared to be very comfortable with walking so close to the edge that their toes extended beyond the rock edge. I had to look away. When I did, I saw that Geoffrey was even further from the edge than me and his face was uncomfortable.

We returned to the cave, Geoffrey clearly in the lead to get away from that open ledge, and bid Andrew a farewell. Gabriel, Geoffrey and I descended into the cave and lit the torches. Luke stayed at the opening with Oliver and Bosco, and Gavan, Asa and Andrew returned to the monastery. Bosco stood at Luke's side and Asa, looking back as they made their way towards the monastery, commented, "We all be certain of who that dog belongs to. They ne'er be leaving sight of each other. Kind of sweet to be seeing since they, obviously, be needing each other."

Geoffrey resumed his soundless work of duplicating the inscriptions. Gabriel looked very pleased when he viewed over Geoffrey's shoulder and noticed that Geoffrey was already familiar enough with the Runes to write the characters as easily as he wrote in English.

The cave was well lit, now, and I had my note keeping materials ready. Gabriel looked at me and asked an open question, "What mind shattering information ye be thinking we be finding today, Raffe?"

I couldn't resist being a bit evasive. "I'll answer that question over dinner this evening." Gabriel nodded and turned towards the wall, searching for the last place from which he read.

"Ahhh," remarked Gabriel, "here be where we finished, yesterday." Gabriel read out loud, "Time, just like sunrise and sunset, be not what ye have been taught. Sunrise and sunset be taught, spoken and believed for so many generations that we hath not words to describe the truth. There *ne'er* be a sunrise nor sunset, since the beginning of our earth's existence." Gabriel looked at me and asked, "Doth this make sense to ye?"

"Yes," I replied, "and it will to *ye also*, once I can teach you some of the discoveries made over the centuries. Just like people with the knowledge of humanity living in the year 2994 will know much more than Luke and I learned in schools. The worst thing anyone can do is believe that they know all there is to know about anything."

A big smile grew across Gabriel's face as he absorbed the concept of my words. "I be hungry to learn more," Gabriel confessed, "ever since a child and heard a language I understood not, and wondered *how* newborn pups be knowing *where and how* to be getting their first warm meal." I smiled and nodded in agreement.

I had a thought and tried it with Gabriel, "Do you know why we refer to the last time we were in this cave as 'yesterday'?"

Gabriel thought about my question and replied, "Because it be the last time the sun be passing over our heads."

"Your *observation* is *true*, Gabriel, but it wasn't the passing of the *sun* from east to west. It was the *rotation* of the *earth* from west to east."

I waited in silence to see if Gabriel could imagine the earth turning, but he answered, "I be not believing that my mind be able to form an image of what ye just spoke," Gabriel replied.

A narrow beam of sunlight was coming through the small cave opening and I picked up an almost round rock and asked Gabriel to follow me to the shaft of light. Holding the rock at shoulder height, I slowly rotated the rock away from us and told Gabriel, "This is like what is happening to our earth." I pointed out a small black spot on the rock and said, "Imagine this small spot to be the land on which we stand. Then imagine yourself a tiny ant standing on this rock, right where that spot is. As I rotate this rock, what would that tiny ant see the sun doing?" I slowly rotated the rock in the beam of light for several rotations and was about to rotate it again, when Gabriel grabbed my arm.

"The ant be seeing the sun... passing overhead... from east to west," he whispered às the concept solidified in his mind. *"We* be what moves, and the *sun* stays *still*." Neither of us took notice of Geoffrey's attentive stare at our lips and the rotating rock.

"Yes, basically," I replied, not wanting to make this any more confusing. "The earth makes one *rotation* in 24 hours and we call this single rotation, '*one day*.'"

"Why ye not be telling us before, Raffe? Ye be with us for months."

"What I just shared with you," I said, "is the kind of knowledge that challenges *old knowledge* and it must be a 'teaching moment' for it to be absorbed."

Just then, we both heard a gasp from Geoffrey as he leaped to his feet. He nodded his head to indicate, he understood. His eyes were wide with amazement, but he couldn't tell us what he was thinking.

Gabriel mumbled, "Teaching moment." I be liking that phrase. Yes!" Gabriel took the rock from my hand and held it, as I had, and rotated it again and again. "Doth everyone know the earth be rotating in 2016?" Gabriel asked.

"Everyone learns about the earth's rotation in schools, but not everyone can attend a school." I replied. Geoffrey's non-verbal excitement told us that he understood this lesson very well.

Gabriel touched my heart when he said, "Schools must be the most amazing place on earth."

"I certainly can't argue with your opinion, Brother Gabriel, maybe we can talk about starting a school when we return home."

"A wonderful idea," Gabriel responded. "I be looking forward to discussing it with Nycolas, Asa and Gavan."

Geoffrey made a hand gesture towards his chest with a pleading look in his eyes. It was obvious to Gabriel and me that this brilliant young man wanted to learn everything possible. I looked at Geoffrey and mouthed the words, "You will be an excellent student, Geoffrey." He beamed with delight.

I said, "We still have a great amount of knowledge to gather here," as I looked into the darkness which concealed the majority of the unread Runes.

Our day passed quickly as Gabriel read and I did my best to write his words accurately in English. Geoffrey worked tirelessly and had to be reminded to pause for water and food. Luke called down to remind us that it was time to return to the monastery. On the walk back, I asked Luke how his day had been since he, Oliver and Bosco spent their day providing us with water, food and moral support.

"It was a good day, Raffe," Luke replied, "every chance we got, we walked to the rim of the canyon and enjoyed the spectacular view. It reminded me of the Grand Canyon where we took several vacations. To be honest, Raffe, it made me more homesick and lost than I was before."

"I'm so sorry to hear this, Luke," I commented. "Gabriel and I talked about starting a school when we return."

Luke's face grew even more sad as he said, "We will never be returning, Raffe, we're stuck in this awful place, for the rest of our lives."

I didn't want to give Luke an opportunity to argue so I quietly walked beside him and tried to imagine him as the beautiful woman Geoffrey drew this morning. It just didn't work in my mind, yet, so I walked silently.

The promise of a special feast by Nycolas was spread before us as we entered the dining room. Many candles were lit and the room was brilliant with light and colors. If Nycolas were living in 2016, I would recommend that he open a restaurant. He knows what to buy and he knew how to manage an efficient kitchen. Dinner was, once again, wonderful and each of us told him so. It was obvious that he delighted in the pleasures of good food. His plump belly was an unmistakable tribute.

The conversations around the table were energetic and filled with each person contributing and supplementing every topic. Asa and Gavan reported that everywhere they went, the island was heavily forested and farm lands had to be cleared through hard work. It was Geoffrey who brought in the drawing he had made that morning and showed it to Nycolas.

After a glance at the portrait, Nycolas turned towards Luke and said, "What a wonderful likeness. I be telling ye that Geoffrey be an amazingly lad? This is a good opportunity for me to share some of the presents I bought today."

With a simple call to the kitchen, a young monk produced a leather quiver similar to Geoffrey's. This quiver was quite distinctive in that its lacing was made with brilliantly colored linen which made a beautiful design. It was made for a lady's art supplies. Nicholas turned to open the top of the quiver towards his dining guests to reveal many sheets of paper and drawing tools deep inside. "I hope these simple items will bring you some happiness, Luke," were the words that flowed from the cheeriest of loving faces. Nycolas was Santa Clause in my eyes.

Luke was very touched and pleased with Nycolas' thoughtfulness and he appeared to richly enjoy the warm hug Luke gave him.

During the pause between the main meal and dessert, Nycolas casually asked Luke, "Ye raise Bosco from a pup in 2016?"

Luke explained that the original Bosco was a golden retriever, a neighbor's dog that spent his days at her home. At the mention of her original life, Luke's demeanor, once again, became somewhat withdrawn but he went on to explain how, "Bosco had found the group of us and once we fed him, he has never left us, except the day Oliver put an arrow in his leg."

Oliver blushed as red as wine and might have left the table if Luke hadn't assured him that no one held any ill feelings, including Bosco. At the sound of his name, Bosco leaped to his feet and laid his big head in Luke's shoulder. Oliver reached over and stroked the big dog's head.

Oliver, once again, said, "I be so sorry big boy." Bosco saw the opportunity and licked Oliver's cheek.

"Dogs sure be teaching us humans a lot about forgiveness," Asa observed. He also noticed that Nycolas had been watching

Bosco's affectionate character and, noticing this, asked him, "What prompted ye to ask about Bosco?"

"Well," Nycolas responded slowly, "While shopping for Luke's drawing supplies today, I saw a notice for a reward for the return of a Danish War dog. The dog was described as being black all over and weighing in excess of three grown men. The announcement warned that this dog, named 'Brutus' was very dangerous and trained to kill at the slightest provocation."

Luke didn't speak, he just leaned over and wrapped his arms around Bosco and buried his face under the massive dog's chin. Bosco didn't understand, but he was certainly enjoying the attention and affection. Nycolas, took Luke's reaction as confirmation that Bosco *was* the Brutus which had been trained as a killing machine, a war dog.

Luke looked up with tear-filled eyes and shared with us, the story all of us knew, and our suspicions that Bosco, like Raffe and Luke, was a transferred consciousness, and Bosco was a loving golden retriever he knew in Pueblo, Colorado in 2016.

Nycolas patiently listened before saying, "This be the first time I be hearing of an animal being a transfer, but there be quite a number of first-time events in the last few days. There be no doubt, in my mind, that Bosco be *not* the dog described. At least the personality of Bosco doesn't fit. and we be needing to be watchful for any bounty hunters who be trying to claim the reward."

"What reward?" Luke asked.

"A reward of 50 pounds be written on the public notice. That be a lot of money, for a dog," replied Nycolas.

Luke could not have heard any news more depressing. He made no effort to conceal his feelings and wept bitterly as he mumbled to Bosco, "I won't let anyone take you as long as I live, Bosco. I would rather die before I'll let you return to that cruel training and brutal life." Bosco was keenly aware of Luke's emotions. He laid his big head over Luke's shoulder and licked away every tear.

Luke repeated his appreciation for Nycolas' gifts and requested to be excused from the table. Oliver offered to go with him, but Luke asked him to stay because he wanted to be alone with Bosco.

After Luke and Bosco had left the room, Asa observed, "It be a wonderful sight to be seeing a massive dog take such tender care of Luke. When Bosco be licking away Luke's tears, I almost be producing a few of me own."

Nycolas, not wanting the whole evening to be sad, asked Gabriel, "What ye be learning today?" Gabriel looked at me and smiled.

"I be happy to tell ye," Gabriel said, "but it be having to wait until the eastern horizon drops in the morning."

Puzzled faces exchanged glances, but Gabriel and I knew that he wanted to explain the passing of a day. He produced the same rock I had used, as an illustration of a rotating earth, and placed it in the center of the table. "It be making more sense on the morrow; it be a 'teaching moment' for all ye, so ye be trusting me, until then."

Geoffrey was smiling from ear to ear as he considered the day's discovery, as well as the cleverness of Gabriel, to inspire curiosity.

I was enjoying the image of Gabriel as a teacher as well. He knew how to generate a desire to learn, by teasing his brother and friends with a mystery. With that, Gabriel pushed back from the table and the rest of us followed his lead. As we filed from the dining room through the library to our bedrooms, we could see Luke sitting on the floor again with Bosco's big head in his lap. They were so completely absorbed in each other that no one spoke.

The next morning, we all entered the dining room early. Curiosity, including my own, nudged us.

Gabriel, as he promised, picked up the rock and walked to where the morning sun was streaming into the dining room. He held his 'earth rock' at arm's length and repeated the exact lesson I gave him. When he finished, he turned to see several completely blank faces, except for Geoffrey, who was smiling with expectation of seeing his new friends light up with an amazing discovery.

"Give it a little time, Gabriel." I coached. "You may need to repeat the procedure a couple times."

Gavan said, "Do that again, Gabriel. Let me see your spinning rock in the sunlight." Gavan watched intently as Gabriel slowly rotated the rock.

A bowl of apples sat in the center of the table. A small bundle of fire starter twigs was lying next to the fireplace and I selected one that was about nine inches long and thinner than my little finger. I pushed the twig through the core of the apple and handed it to Gabriel, saying, "Try this, Gabriel, hold the ends of the stick so your hands won't cast so much shadow on the earth, um apple."

Gabriel immediately saw the advantage and replaced the not-so-round rock with the bright red and round apple. Within a couple rotations, I could see the lights of comprehension brighten in the watcher's eyes. I had one more additional illustration. I poked a toothpick-sized twig into the equator region of the apple as an example of how the light, from the sun, might be perceived by that tiny twig, on the apple's surface.

With each slow rotation, Gabriel emphasized, "Imagine thyself as this tiny twig looking up at the light of the sun." One by one, each man grasped the concept that the earth was rotating before the sun. I knew there was a lot more to teach these men, but I felt very good about their willingness to learn.

I said, "When I have the time, I will build a simple model that will explain more." Luke didn't appear to be at all excited about this moment of breakthrough.

Luke drowsily commented, "I suppose you think you can build a scale model of our solar system." His pessimism was obvious and even though our friends had no mental concept of a solar system, they could clearly hear the negative tone in Luke's words. All four men looked at Luke, who continued to look into his own lap, to avoid any eye contact.

Oliver asked Luke, "Ye be feeling well? Ye be sounding very sad."

Luke didn't respond with words or actions, he just looked down and stroked Bosco's fur. It was obvious that the issues affecting Luke were resulting in a serious depression. Luke was present for breakfast, but he only drank coffee and sat quietly. Bosco even ate little. As Luke's melancholy and self-isolation increased, Bosco stayed at his side, and even curled up around Luke's feet under the table. Several attempts were made to ask Luke about his mood, but these were met with a polite but firm rejection.

Nycolas could see the reaction to Luke in Geoffrey's face and asked him how his day in the cave had gone. Very anxious for a chance to share his day, Geoffrey's fingers began to move and Nycolas put words to his motions. "This day was an amazing day of discoveries as big as the whole world," Nycolas translated. "Before we ate our breakfast, I be looking at Luke when, in my mind, I see a beautiful woman's face, so I be drawing that lady's face. Oliver be saying the name of the face be 'Maria.' Who be this 'Maria'?"

It was then that we realized that during our conversation about Luke, no one was facing Geoffrey and he was unaware of the drawing of a woman's face belonging to the man he was looking at. The amazement on Geoffrey's face was almost entertaining as Nycolas took the time to communicate with Geoffrey. I found myself wishing I could learn their hand-language well enough to learn from this young genius. Geoffrey nodded and smiled at all of us and returned to the kitchen.

Nycolas looked at me and I heard his gentle voice, in my mind. "Ye be a man with a very hungry mind, Raffe. I would very much enjoy teaching you how to make ye words with hand-signs. Geoffrey told me that you are an exceptional teacher and I invite you to practice your teaching skills here on Anglesey Island. Please give this some thought as you work with Gabriel and Geoffrey in the cave."

This invitation haunted my mind as the days passed.

The only thing that seemed to show any change over the next week was my respect for Amergus. His challenges were much greater than Luke's and mine, but he not only survived, he saved hundreds, maybe thousands of lives. I also became more appreciative of Gabriel's dedication and Gavan and Asa's willingness to daily explore the surrounding forests and villages for any sign of bounty hunters asking questions about big black dogs.

It was near the end of our first week that Gabriel used the after-diner conference time to announce that he may soon need to return to his monastery to attend to the many needs there. This really wasn't as much of a surprise as it was an announcement of the inevitable. Our initial goal was based on other cave Runes which contained a tiny fraction of the work done here.

I asked Gabriel if he had established a schedule to end our work here and he replied, "Our work here has but only begun, Raffe. As ye can see for ye self, neither of us be walking deep enough into the cave to be seeing the end of the Runes."

"What do you wish to do?", I asked.

"Allow me some days to consider an answer for thee, Raffe," Gavan said with a very solemn voice, "We began this quest with little knowledge of the task before us. Geoffrey had learned most of the meanings of the Rune alphabet very quickly, but he be unable to speak those meanings. Would you learn to speak with his signs so you could continue this work when I must return?"

I was both pleased and a bit overwhelmed by Gabriel's trust in me. I immediately said, "Yes, Gabriel, I would be honored."

I glanced to Nycolas' beaming smile and received his message, "Me told you so."

Our days were so full, and our every need provided for, by Nycolas, that it didn't seem possible that Luke's underlying depression would grow while everything around him became easier and more comfortable.

While in daily contact with Geoffrey, he patiently taught me the hand-signs that he and Nycolas developed over the years. Many words were basic finger illustrations of objects or actions. Gabriel was also patient with us, knowing how important it was for me to learn. To make it fun, Geoffrey and I often shared jokes which caused us to laugh and Gabriel to frown at us since he was left out. We almost always felt a little sorry for 'talking' behind his back, but he laughed along with us and encouraged our interaction.

Just when we were beginning to suspect the Rune's had no more big revelations, this day happened.

As our workday was drawing to a close, nearly two weeks after Gabriel and I began the monumental translation, Gabriel read, "Ye may be wondering how a Consciousness be transferred. Our belief be the following: since the collapsed Black Hole is gravity-neutral, the Passing hath no effect on matter of any kind, but our consciousness be not matter. History be recording many 'out-of-body' experiences, we know that the consciousness and a body can be separated. Since the discovery of Dark Matter, it be accepted that Dark Matter doth not affect physical matter, but it be having the same effect on non-matter that gravity hath on matter. The Passing be the collection and depositing of thousands of consciousness during each Passing."

After writing down every word, I was glad that Gabriel stopped reading. His face, just like mine, was stunned with the words we just heard.

Gabriel commented, "I be needing not to know as much as ye do, Raffe, about a spinning earth and solar systems to understand what Amergus be saying here. From what I just read, that Black Hole can collect all the memories a person be accumulating, and deposit them into another person from any anniversary of any Passing: past, present or future."

Geoffrey was acutely aware of the important nature of Gabriel and my conversation as he nudged me and signed, "What is so exciting?"

I mouthed the reply, "We found an important Rune which explains how the consciousness of transfers is transferred." I sure was glad Geoffrey could read lips because there were more than a few words in that sentence I couldn't think of how to make a hand-sign.

To Gabriel, I said, "I agree with every word you just said, Gabriel. But the only way a Passing can exchange a consciousness from 2994 back to 60 AD, is if it had already made a Passing in 2994." Gabriel clearly understood what I had just said, but it was obvious that neither of us could comprehend the facts before us.

I paraphrased the words of Amergus and said, "We don't really know what time is, because we have been taught wrongly. I hope Amergus had more to say on the subject of time, itself."

Gabriel slowly shook his head and confessed, "I be having more than enough new information added to my mind for one day. How about we get back to the monastery and see how our friends react to what we have discovered today."

I looked at Geoffrey to relay Gabriel's words, but he had already read his lips and nodded in agreement.

My wordless response of beginning to douse the torches, told Gabriel that I was in complete agreement. I didn't mention it to Gabriel, but I was as dumbfounded as Gabriel with the disturbing description of time, and I wanted some time to organize whatever I could, before hearing more.

I looked at Geoffrey and asked, "What do you think of time?"

Geoffrey instantly responded with hand signs, "I draw pictures for you to show my thoughts on the Passing and time."

I turned to Gabriel and shared Geoffrey's response. His face was filled with anticipatory delight at seeing such images.

Gabriel, Geoffrey and I climbed up the ladder and looked around for Oliver and Luke. It wasn't at all disturbing that they may have gone searching for wild berries or herbs rather than sit around the cave opening for hours. Knowing how much Oliver and Luke enjoyed the amazing overlook at the rim of the canyon, we began walking in that direction. About half there, I thought I would call ahead rather than frighten them.

I shouted their names, and suddenly, two strange men jumped up and ran off through the trees. They had concealed themselves behind Luke and Oliver. Neither of us had any desire to chase them, but they did look a little familiar.

I asked Gabriel, "Did you recognize either of them?"

Gabriel was frowning and, with squinted eyes, slowly replied, "Yes. I clearly be recognizing the taller of the two, the one with his nose twisted to one side, and so should *ye*."

It took me a couple seconds, but I did recall seeing that face when he was lying on his back under the weight of Bosco. "Those be the same two highwaymen who attacked us on our journey here," I observed.

Gabriel frowned again, and noted, "It be appearing that the lesson and mercy we showed them be of no affect. We may be needing to allow Asa and Gavan to deal with them, if they be staying close by."

"It puzzles me that Bosco did not know these thieves be watching." Gabriel questioned.

"You know how gentle Bosco is, Gabriel," I replied, "he didn't do anything but lay at Luke's feet, the *first* time he met these thieves." I asked Geoffrey if either of the men were familiar to him. He replied that he had never seen them before now.

My next call to Oliver and Luke was returned and, as expected, they were quietly talking while enjoying the vista of that great canyon.

As we approached, Gabriel asked, "Did ye two know that ye was being watched?" The shock and fear on both of their faces told us that they hadn't.

Luke replied, "Bosco never gave any indication of someone being close."

Gabriel replied, "As loving and gentle a beast as he be, Bosco may be aware of them but not be reacting since he be recognizing their smell. They be the same two highwaymen who be attempting to rob us. Bosco held the larger of the two men down and I be sure Bosco got a good sampling of his odor."

"Sometimes, I am a little concerned that Bosco is so gentle," observed Luke, "but, I wouldn't change a single hair on his body." With that, Bosco got another hug and an affectionate back rub from Luke.

"I be strongly suggesting," said Gabriel, "that we all travel in groups of two or more until we be knowing what those two thugs be doing around here. We be needing to spake to the others over dinner tonight."

I faced Geoffrey and asked him to inquire of the other monks about the two men we encountered. He responded with the signs that he was already planning to do that since it was common for travelers to ask for food and lodging at Nycolas' monastery.

As we walked back to the monastery, Geoffrey signed to me that he was concerned about Luke. I asked him what he meant, and Geoffrey replied that he was well aware of Luke's loss of appetite and his withdrawal from everyone except Oliver and Bosco. As best as I could, I explained that Luke had told us that he doesn't feel that he belongs here in 1690.

Geoffrey was very understanding when he signed to me, "I often be feeling as if I not be belonging anywhere when my parents sent me to be living in Brother Nycolas' monastery, but Nycolas be an exceptionally wise and loving man. Maybe he be able to be helping Luke, like he helped me."

"Maybe," I signed, as we entered the monastery and separated, to clean up and rest, before dinner.

As we all collected around the dining table for dinner, Gabriel shared our encounter with the same two thugs. The information was every bit as disturbing as we expected it would be.

Asa gave a nod to Gavan.

Asa offered, "Ye not be needing to worry about them if Gavan and I be having a man-to-man chat with them." Gavan held a small crooked smile as he nodded back to Asa.

Luke, still looking into his lap, mumbled one word, "Bosco."

Nycolas heard what he said and asked, "Ye be thinking they be after the bounty placed on Bosco's recovery?"

"Yes." Luke replied. "They had enough time and close proximity to identify Bosco. It's reasonable that they followed us and saw the notices for Bosco's return."

Nycolas thought for a moment before continuing, "How sure be we that these two men be the same thieves who assaulted ye on yer journey here?"

Gabriel immediately replied, "I be absolutely certain. I looked into that thief's face when Bosco be holding him down.

The taller of the two, be most certainly that thief. The bashed nose Gavan be giving him, never healed right, and he be looking terribly funny with both nostrils on one side of his face. We warned him to be giving up his life of crime. The second thug might be his friend who be running off too quick to capture."

Nycolas continued, "I really not be caring if Bosco was once a war dog. He be a loving and devoted friend to all of us, especially Luke, and we not be letting any harm come to him." Nycolas spoke to all of us, but his focus was to comfort Luke's pessimism, and maybe help Luke overcome his gloom. The appreciative smile on Luke's face was comforting to all of us. Luke felt like he was going to get a sound night of sleep, for a change.

With the subject of the encounter with the thugs shared, Gabriel waited until dinner was finished to bring up the subject of his discovery in Amergus' cave. To help him share this day's find, Gabriel read the English translation which Raffe made.

"Our belief be the following: since the collapsed Black Hole be gravity-neutral, the Passing hath no effect on matter of any kind, but our consciousness be not matter. History be recording many 'out-of-body' experiences, we know that the consciousness and a body can be separated. Since the discovery of Dark Matter, it be accepted that Dark Matter doth not affect physical matter, but it be having the same effect on non-matter that gravity hath on matter. The Passing is the collection and depositing of thousands of consciousness during each Passing."

I could almost hear the grinding of their minds as our friends made every effort to comprehend the words Gabriel just read. I was certain that I couldn't understand a lot of it.

Geoffrey caught my attention and signed to me that he wanted to create a drawing to explain a Passing.

I looked at Nycolas in response to Geoffrey's suggestion and his face was as curious and surprised as mine.

"I believe all of us would find such a drawing to be most interesting, Geoffrey." I said.

Geoffrey began picking up his quiver of paper and graphite markers as he motioned with his free hand, "I want to start my drawing right away, so it be ready for all of ye to view tomorrow morning." Nycolas translated.

Having listened to Gabriel's reading, Asa was anxious to get a few issues clarified. "What be this 'gravity neutral' ye just read to us, Gabriel."

"The best way I know to describe it, Asa," Gabriel began, "is something that has absolutely no weight. When ye spun your ring about your finger, you felt the weight of thy ring pulling on the lanyard. That pulling was the weight of the ring. If your ring be 'gravity neutral,' it would be of no weight and ye could not twirl it."

Asa said, "I think I be letting me mind work on that for a while, as I ask ye, what be that 'Dark matter'?

"I believe this be a question better answered by Raffe or Luke," Gabriel replied, as he looked first at Luke, who didn't return his gaze, and then to me.

I told myself, 'Honesty is always the best choice' as I began to speak. "As ye know, Amergus be transferred in the year 2994 back to the year 60 AD and she took with her the knowledge of 2994. Luke and I were transferred from the year 2016 to 1690. Both of us are familiar with the words 'Dark Matter' and 'Black Hole,' but these are quite new discoveries in 2016. All of us are learning to understand more of the words Amergus has used and it will only be through the continued discoveries in that cave, that we will understand more. What seems to be the message from Amergus is that, within that collapsed black hole, all time, is right now. All of the years we know as 'Passings' are taking place at the same time in that 'gravity neutral' 'black hole.'

Gavan spoke, "I not be seeing how this be happening, but I do believe I understand what be happening and maybe some of the why it happens."

Nycolas spoke, "I believe I we be having more questions after my mind has had some time to dwell on ye words, Raffe."

That observation brought about several bobbing heads in agreement.

"Perhaps the drawing Geoffrey be creating for us will give us some clarity and cause us to be having some questions for ye, on the morrow." Nycolas suggested.

As we left the dining room, I noticed Geoffrey working on his drawing and began to walk towards him. Without looking up, he signed to me, that he didn't want to be disturbed while working on this drawing. It was too important to him, to be disturbed. I simply turned away and left him to his work. Like the many nights before this one, sleep was well earned and well spent.

Chapter 11
The Awful Farewell

I was getting very accustomed to waking up between smooth sheets in a soft bed with the smell of coffee, bread and spiced meats to inspire my first thoughts. It no longer disturbed me to hear Nycolas' words about me staying here to 'share adventures' in this well organized and comfortable monastery.

I could hear the voices of Gabriel, Gavan and Asa coming from the dining room and the tone of their words implied they were wide awake, and each had a lot to say. I made my way to and from the latrine with half open eyes as I walked toward the sound of those familiar voices.

As I entered the dining room, Geoffrey greeted me with a much-desired mug of coffee. I cupped my fingers around the mug to put some warmth in my blood and brought the mug to my mouth for that first delightful sip. Nycolas was sitting at the end of the table wearing his usual almost-smiling face with twinkling bright eyes. His face was beaming with delight and I quickly saw the reason. On the wall, immediately above and behind Nycolas, were three large drawings.

I instantly recognized the central drawing as the image Geoffrey was working on as I passed on my way to bed. The other images, which flanked this picture were similar in subject but quite different in their messages... like a camera had taken a before, during, and after shots of the same event. I hadn't had time to give any critical focus to any of the drawings before Nycolas began to speak.

Nycolas made a hand gesture to the drawings, "Be these bringing up any recent memories, Raffe?" Geoffrey was standing close to my right side and I could see with my peripheral vision, that he was looking at me in anticipation of my answer.

I turned my head slightly toward Geoffrey, as I answered Nycolas, "Yes, p feel as if someone made three beautiful and almost disturbing pictures from my own memory." I could see the smile of delight form on Geoffrey's face as the same smile brightened Nycolas.

I turned to Geoffrey and said, "These are amazingly beautiful. How did you know exactly what to draw?"

Geoffrey immediately began to make signs with his hands, and Nycolas, knowing only three of us could understand, began to interpret, "These images are not from my mind, Raffe, they are the images I have been seeing for many weeks. They were very faint at first, but as our friendship grew, so did the clearness of these pictures. The last picture was shared by you and Gavan and because I had two friends with the same image, it came to me very clear and strong."

Gavan had walked up behind me as Geoffrey was sharing and the instant Nycolas finished interpreting, he asked me, "Be ye feeling the same towards the right picture as I be?"

I turned to face Gavan before speaking and found his tender eyes to be as full of tears as my own. "Yes, Gavan," I replied, "the image on the right was what we saw as we walked to your home, that first night."

"That it be, Lad," commented Gavan, "and it be making tears in me eyes for the fear and confusion ye suffered that night."

I took a moment to study Gavan's big face. He, like Gabriel, had the potential of being formidable with their bulky frames and powerful limbs, but they both, by will and character, were the warmest and safest friends imaginable. "Wish I knew you then, as well as I know you now, Gavan." I spoke softly.

Geoffrey was about to burst with delight at the affect his drawings were having on all of us. He excitedly signed the question, "What think ye of the first two images?"

With my finger pointing at the left and center images, I asked Geoffrey, "These two came from my memory only?"

Geoffrey nodded and waited like a statue for my opinion. His eyes were almost lights of their own and even though I had seen evidence of it, these pictures proved that Geoffrey was not only brilliant, he had somehow, developed the ability to absorb critical images from the minds of his friends. What surprised me was that this ability didn't bother me because Geoffrey was totally honest and sincere without judgement.

I pointed at the left image and said, "This is the night sky that Jake and I saw while camping in the mountains." Pointing at the center image, I commented, "This is the last thing I saw before everything went black and I woke up in Asa and Gavan's pissing corner."

I could hear Asa and Gavan chuckle behind me. I didn't turn to enjoy their faces because I wanted Geoffrey to be able to read my lips. "Geoffrey," I began, "your skill with a graphite stick is wonderful. You have created so much detail that I can almost see movement within each image of the Black Hole approaching, Passing and departing from the earth." I walked closer to the pictures and placed my hand on Nycolas' shoulder as I studied each image from only a few inches away. My eyes discovered an almost imperceptible detail that was present in each drawing. As I focused on this detail, my fingers wrapped slightly tighter around Nycolas' shoulder and he immediately place his soft hand over mine. In amazement, I slowly turned to look at Geoffrey. He knew exactly what I had discovered, and he was about to burst if he couldn't share my discovery. I mouthed the words, "Please tell them, Geoffrey?"

Geoffrey's hands began to move, making words for Nycolas to translate, as his eyes were fixed on me. "What ye see in the center image be the collection and deposit of consciousnesses affected by the close proximity of the neutral-mass black hole to earth. In the right image, the black hole approaches and no consciousness be affected, and on the left, the black hole departs, taking no consciousness with it. This happens every 326 years, as ye already know."

Nycolas looked up at me, and with a twinkle in his eyes, asked, "Now, what ye think?"

Before I could reply, a sleepy faced Luke, with Oliver and Bosco at his side, entered the dining room. All eyes were on them to see their first impression of Geoffrey's drawings. Oliver's eyes grew large and his mouth opened slightly as he took in the drawings. Luke's reaction was quite different.

It was clear that Luke immediately recognized the subject of Geoffrey's work. He began to show some interest as he focused his eyes on the rounded surface of the earth at the bottom of each rendition. I could detect Luke's wonderment at how Geoffrey could have come up with a view of earth from space. The creation of a moving black hole was obvious puzzling, when he thought about a young man from 1690 having such a view. Then, suddenly, he lost interest, diverted his eyes from the drawings and everyone in the room. He turned and walked out of the room without speaking, Bosco was close at his side.

Asa spoke, "Me thinks Luke sees what we see, but his heart be not caring anymore."

Not allowing Luke's depression to dampen the atmosphere, Nycolas spoke up, "How about we enjoy the breakfast prepared for us and share our day's plans."

With this welcome invitation we found our chairs and sat down as Geoffrey went into the kitchen. Immediately, hot pancakes were brought, and bowls of honey placed before each of us.

I asked, "Should we wait for Luke?"

Oliver suggested that we start eating because it may be a while, if Luke feels like eating any breakfast at all.

I had finished my pancakes and began to sip the last of my coffee when the expected question was asked. "If that be the earth at the bottom of each drawing, how did Geoffrey get so high to see this view?" Asa asked.

Scrambling in my mind for an acceptable answer, I asked Asa, "Have you ever had a dream in which you were a bird?"

"Certainly." replied Asa.

"Your dreams of flying high above the trees and hills is something like Geoffrey's view in his drawings. He just flew much higher than any real bird can fly and used the images in Gavan, Luke and my memories to create these drawings." I knew that my illustration was very simple compared to Geoffrey's view from space, but I hoped it would allow Asa to expand his own imagination.

After another excellent breakfast, we made the resolution to think about Geoffrey's drawings and explore our questions after dinner.

We made the short trip to Amergus' cave, each of us carrying a bundle of torches. Standing above the entrance, Gabriel repeated, to no one in particular, as he thought outloud, the comments he and I had read pertaining to time."

"Why be time so important?" asked Oliver. "We not be doing anything to change what be happening since time began."

"I'll answer you, Oliver, with something Gabriel and I be found in Amergus' Runes," I replied. 'Time, as we be taught, may not be having a beginning or end as we be thinking of a day having a beginning when the sun appears in the east and an end when the sun be going below the horizon in the west.'

Oliver looked at me for a few seconds, before admitting, "I be confused."

My response of, "So am I, most of the time," didn't help our conversation, or anyone present feel enlightened, so I continued, "Maybe Gabriel and I should gather more information before we try to sound like we know so much about 'time' ourselves. We have a lot more information to be discovered and Luke and I are learning, just like all of you." Having said these words, I looked around and asked Oliver, "Where is Luke?" Oliver's face turned a bit sad as he replied, "He hath returned to his bed. He told me that he will join us about mid-day with food and water."

As Gabriel began to descend the ladder, Gavan said, "Asa and I be going to do some scouting round this area. Hopefully, we be finding those cowardly lurkers. If we do, we be scaring them out of their grubby stockings and sandals with fear that be not as easy to overcome as thy threats to send war hounds after them."

I looked at Gavan's broad shoulders and thick arms with a bit of pity for the scrawny would-be thieves. Gavan was a powerful man, who never gave the impression of being self-protective. The first hint of a threat, however, towards anyone he considered a *friend*, morphed Gavan into a raging hulk of punishing vengeance. It was on this morning, that his most menacing personality was very evident.

Asa repeated their intentions and spoke over his shoulder as he and Gavan departed, "We be telling all of ye about our day over dinner."

Geoffrey descended the ladder and I followed. Oliver made himself comfortable next to the cave's opening so he could assist us throughout the day. I smiled and nodded to Oliver, in a gesture I hoped would encourage his faithfulness toward Luke, and disappeared into the cave.

Gabriel, Geoffrey and I followed what had become our daily routine of placing and lighting torches. I was preparing to record Gabriel's translation of the Runes, while Geoffrey, some distance away, organized his materials to meticulously copy the Rune symbols. I couldn't help noticing how fast he seemed to be copying.

"Would it be any help, Gabriel," I suggested, "if you taught me to read Runes? I've recognized quite a few of the lines and characters and I would like to be more helpful."

Gabriel looked at me and smiled, "I be having hope that ye would ask this for several weeks. I be liking, very much, to be having ye as an apprentice. We be starting this evening after dinner. Our days be better spent recording these Runes. Ye know, with Geoffrey copying the Rune symbols, we be having an excellent reference of symbols for ye to study."

"I look forward to beginning this apprenticeship with you. I expect this evening's conversations will be centered around Geoffrey's drawings." I then changed the subject. "I certainly would not care to exchange shoes with either of those thieves, if Asa and Gavan catch up to them,"

Gabriel turned his face from the wall and spoke calmly, "With the tracking skills and experience of Asa, I be expecting their after-dinner report to be very exciting to us and unfortunate for those thieves."

Gabriel found where we had finished last and studied the small grooved lines and chipped divots. Before reading anything new, he asked, "What if time had no beginning or end? Be meaning that all of time be the present, right now, at any one point between infinities?" Both of us stood in silence for a minute before Gabriel continued. "The Bible says that God be without beginning or end and that we be 'in Him.' I never be believing that this text be referring to our physical bodies, but to our non-flesh beings, sometimes called souls or consciousness."

"WOW!" I commented. "That kind of thinking deserves some serious consideration, Gabriel, what you just said is very deep."

Just as I expected he would, Gabriel asked me, "What doth ye mean, 'deep?'"

"A better word would be 'profound' or 'thought provoking,'" I explained. "Your ability to think in non-traditional ways is a gift which will help you understand things well beyond the knowledge of 1690."

"Let us be seeing what Amergus be saying with his 2994 knowledge, and maybe both of us will find some answers," he offered.

I felt very comfortable with Gabriel because he didn't expect me to have all of the answers.

Gabriel studied the Runes, found where we had finished yesterday and began to slowly translate, "It be not time which passes, but the *markers* we be using to catalogue time which comes and goes. Time be the event, the individual entity, and the recording of events between infinity past and infinity future. The Black Hole be interacting with every event because it be not confined by a material world or any single event. As the Black Hole encounters a material object, or earth, it be bringing with it, the presence of every material-controlled event and gravity-controlled movement." Gabriel waited until I stopped writing to ask, "Doth that be making sense to ye?"

I wanted to be completely honest with Gabriel and confessed that I would have to spend some time thinking about Amergus' words. I had no desire to doubt what Amergus, or any educated adult in 2994 had to say, but I was struggling to comprehend the wisdom and knowledge before us.

We had learned to approximate the time of day by the location of the shaft of light coming through the small cave opening. I called up to Oliver, and he immediately put his face in the cave opening. "Would you drop down something to eat and some water?" I requested.

Oliver said, "Bosco ate our bread, but I be running back to the monastery to fetch more." He didn't wait for a reply because he felt a bit guilty that he hadn't watched their lunch more carefully. In the silence that immediately followed Oliver's departure, the thought occurred to me... 'Bosco?' Oliver said Bosco ate our lunch. That means Luke must be at the cave entrance. I cupped my hands to my mouth and called 'Luke!' but got no reply. The instant Gabriel heard my call, he also surmised that Luke should be there if Bosco was present.

Thinking nothing more of the situation, we returned to our translating to wait for Oliver's return. About thirty minutes had passed, when Oliver returned and quickly climbed down the ladder, with a bundle of bread and a flask of water. He apologized for not watching our lunch and looked towards the large wall filled with Runes. "This be amazing," Oliver commented. "I be certain ye be learning much. How about ye, Luke, be ye learning some new things?"

I looked at Oliver and said, "He's not down here. We thought we heard you talking to Bosco before you went for food and assumed Luke was with you."

Oliver immediately turned about and began walking towards the ladder, as he said, "He be not anywhere in sight all morning. No Luke or Bosco be up there now. I be going to search for them. As much as he be enjoying the view of the canyon, I expect he be there." With those few words, Oliver climbed out of the cave and we sat down with Geoffrey to enjoy a much deserved break and lunch.

We surmised that as soon as Oliver had left to get a lunch for Gabriel, Geoffrey and me, Luke decided to enjoy the grand vista over the canyon with Bosco.

Luke was at the canyon's edge, but he hadn't stopped by the cave entrance on his way, only Bosco made the short visit to the cave opening to enjoy the unguarded bread before joining Luke at the overview.

Luke was sitting with his elbows resting on his knees and Bosco came up behind him, licking his chops as he sat quietly at Luke's side. Luke may have noticed that Bosco had turned his head a few times to look into the dense trees and thought it was most likely a squirrel or rabbit that captured the attention of Bosco's keen ears. Each time Bosco looked around, he returned his gaze to share the serenity of the vista before them. It's easy to think of Luke saying, "It sure is peaceful and beautiful here, isn't it, Bosco?" Bosco didn't respond with his typical lick to Luke's cheek.

Luke turned to see Bosco calmly staring forward... *with a rope around his neck.* Luke immediately reached up to remove the rope when a second loop of rope was tossed over Bosco's head. The ropes were both drawn too tight for Luke to simply flip them off Bosco's head. He began to loosen the second rope when pain shot through his hands as a short club was used to strike Luke's wrist. Luke jumped to his feet and turned to confront the same two thugs who had been stalking them for days. Luke's mind was in anguish trying to find a way to get those ropes off Bosco and avoid the thug's clubs. He reached again to loosen a rope and was again stopped by a painful crack to his wrists from both thugs. Bosco remained motionless. He knew these men from their first encounter along the road and, being the loving and trusting dog he was, he simply sat quietly as Luke made several failed and painful attempts to free his dog.

"You can't take my dog!" Luke shouted, hoping to be heard by his friends, but no one heard him.

"What are you going to do?" taunted one of the thugs. "Get your head bashed for a dog that's too stupid to defend itself?" If looks could kill, Luke's eyes would have already bashed the brains out of both men, but he knew that they would beat him senseless and lead his gentle giant dog away to be trained as a war dog or killed when their training failed. Luke had been thinking about the awful fate that awaited Bosco if he were taken away. Both of Luke's hands were throbbing and bloody from the repeated attempts to untether Bosco.

The thugs could have hurried off as soon as they had their ropes over the gentle dog, but they thought it would be fun to torment Luke, since he was present at the shaming of the taller thief, several weeks before. "Where be all of yer tough friends *now*?" he taunted Luke through his yellow teeth and thin snarling lips.

When Bosco remained calm and still, the smaller thief suggested, "Maybe we be beating him so badly that he not be telling his friends about us. We can be walking out of here fifty pounds *richer, plus* any money he may be having on his carcass."

Luke stood up and allowed his face to become as calm and resolute as his mind. His voice was steady, and his eyes took on the strength of his convictions, when he said, "I will give you *one more chance* to release Bosco and *run away,* like the cowards you *are.*"

The taller thief recognized the sincerity in Luke's words and voice, but he was not deterred. He slowly wrapped his end of the rope holding Bosco around his wrist, a few more times, to emphasize his own determination. The second, shorter thief followed with the same deliberate twisting of Bosco's rope until it covered most of his forearm. "What are ye going to do *now? Cry?*" taunted the shorter thief.

Luke turned his back towards the thieves and walked to the edge of the canyon ledge, before turning back to face his tormentors.

"That's good," snorted the short thug, "He wants us to jump off the edge." He tried to make a fake laugh to accompany his words, but no sound came out.

Luke knelt on one knee, as if to pray, and looked into Bosco's tender eyes.

"Praying not be helping ye," the tall thief taunted, as a shadow of fear crept over his face.

Luke kept his eyes focused on Bosco, and the great dog slowly rose to his feet, with anticipation of obedience to any words spoken by Luke. His massive muscles quivered with the excitement of obedience as both men stopped looking at Luke, and peered down at the quaking mass between them. They had no time to react.

Luke stretched both of his arms toward Bosco and said, "Come Bosco! *Come to me!*"

Both men were nearly jerked off their feet as Bosco, unfettered by their weight, lunged forward to obey Luke's commend. The taller thief immediately recognized the danger and began to unwind the rope from his wrist. The short thief soon recognized their peril, and attempted the same escape, from his self-made bondage with death. Both men were propelled forward by Bosco's determination to be with Luke.

Luke's eye-lock with Bosco was unbroken as the great dog, with two flailing and terrified thieves stumbled to keep their feet under them, approached his favorite human. When Bosco was close enough for Luke to gently touch his muzzle, Luke leaned into the abyss with one more, "Come Bosco." spoken softly.

Bosco never took notice of the precipice as he launched himself toward Luke. They fell with their eyes fixed on each other, totally Ignoring the screaming and futile flailing of the thieves who couldn't free themselves until it was much too late...

Oliver was just stepping from the trees when he saw Luke, followed by Bosco, and then the two screaming thugs topple into the canyon. He was stunned beyond belief and for a second, froze, unable to believe what he was witnessing. He stepped to the edge of the canyon and looked at the rocks and bodies below him.

Oliver's eyes met Luke's and he heard Luke's voice, in his mind, saying, "Thank you for loving me", before Luke's life slipped away. Bosco had landed on Luke's legs, and wasn't moving at first, but Oliver noticed that Bosco's muzzle was next to Luke's hand, as the dog's big tongue reached out to give Luke one more loving lick, and he too, was still.

Oliver's knees buckled and he slumped to the ground, unable to think or act. All he could do was to allow the tears to flow.

Gabriel and I were about to get back to the task of translating when I remembered the partially exposed line of Runes that I found near the base of the wall and asked Gabriel if we could take a moment to expose them.

Gabriel said that he didn't know there were any runes below floor level, but he would expect them to be significant if they were intentionally hidden. I used the shaft of a burned out torch to scrape away the top two inches of gravel and revealed a single line of runes. Geoffrey was very interested in these Runes because he wasn't aware of them previously. I stepped back and held a torch near the wall to use the side lighting to expose the small chiseled lines.

Geoffrey immediately began to make a copy of the newly exposed Runes. Gabriel read the Runes and stepped back without saying what he read out loud. His eyes were instantly filled with tears, fear and sadness and he went to the beginning of the line and slowly translated the words distinctly.

"I be crying bitter tears every time I read your account of Luke and Bosco's death." He looked up at me with the same bewilderment that I felt in my face. Geoffrey was reading Gabriel's lips and stepped backward as if he had been pushed by pain. No one spoke during the seconds before we heard Oliver's voice frantically shouting. His words were too jumbled to understand until he began to repeat the same phrase.

"They jumped. They be dead. They jumped. They be dead," Oliver repeated.

By the time Oliver stopped repeating this phrase, his voice was soft and quaking. Gabriel, Geoffrey and I had exited the cave and found Oliver sitting on the ground with his face buried in his hands.

Not being able to connect what he just read with Oliver's words, Gabriel asked, "What ye be meaning, 'they jumped' and who is dead?"

Oliver sobbed into his hands, "Luke and Bosco, they jumped into the canyon."

Gabriel gave me a quick glance as I heard Geoffrey gasp behind me and place his hand on my back. Instantly Gabriel was running for the overlook that Andrew had shown us with Geoffrey at his side. I turned toward Oliver and he was up and starting to follow Gabriel. In just a few steps, the four of us were standing at the edge of the canyon. With his arm around Oliver's shoulders, Gabriel noticed that there were four bodies lying on the boulders. It was obvious that the two unknown bodies belonged to the bounty hunters. He asked Oliver to share what he saw, and the horribly sad incident was related to us with Oliver's quaking and choked voice. It was fortunate that Gabriel and I were standing on either side of Oliver, because he began to collapse. Geoffrey was first to notice Oliver's drooping body and responded instantly. We all took hold of him to guide him away from the edge.

Oliver wept openly as he told us, "I loved Luke. I be knowing he was a woman before the transfer, I saw his beautiful face and I loved him, her, because he be kind, smart and accepted my love." Gabriel wrapped his arms around Oliver's and drew his head to his chest. Oliver welcomed the strength Gabriel offered and rested against him. "We not be leaving them down there," Oliver said softly, "they be deserving a proper burial."

"We'll take care of that," I told Oliver. "Relax as much as you can, and let your friends take care of Luke and Bosco." Geoffrey didn't attempt to communicate, but he did lay his hand on Oliver's shoulder for support.

The three of us escorted Oliver back to the monastery. Along the path, Oliver was the only voice heard in the hush of the forest. It seemed to me that even nature was stunned by this loss.

"I ne'er witnessed or be hearing of a dog being as devoted as Bosco," Oliver softly said, as if he was expected to say something and this was his only thought. "That dog be following Luke without any hesitation. He appeared to know and understand that this would be their last moment together."

"Who were the two strangers we saw down there?" I asked Oliver.

Oliver took his time to answer. "I be not certain since I only be seeing them as they be yanked over the ledge by ropes that be around Bosco's neck. One looked like the highwayman ye warned to ne'er steal again, Gabriel, and the other was about the size of the short thief who ran away."

"Do you think they were attempting to take Bosco for the reward?" I asked Oliver. I had my own strong suspicions, but I was hoping our conversation might be a sufficient distraction to help Oliver get back to the safe surroundings of the monastery.

"That be making sense, but we may ne'er be knowing for certain," Oliver replied, gaining some composure. "Both of them be trying to unwrap the rope from their arm but Bosco be having them over the edge before they be freeing themselves." Oliver continued, "Why would Luke jump? Why he be wanting to die? Why did he call Bosco as he be falling?"

Gabriel looked down at Oliver, before attempting to reply to his questions. "Luke be despondent and withdrawn for weeks, Oliver. If the two of ye communicated yer feelings, I be expecting ye be having awareness of this. Luke be having emotional issues that the rest of us really be not understanding."

"Ye be right, Gabriel, but I ne'er be thinking he be taking this way to escape."

I suggested, "Maybe we should get back to the monastery and make arrangements to recover their bodies before dark." Oliver didn't speak but he nodded his head and stood up between Gabriel and me. Geoffrey signed, "I'll run ahead and make the arrangements." Without waiting for any response, Geoffrey ran for the monastery. The walk back to the monastery seemed so much longer than ever before.

When we entered the monastery, Nycolas was already informed by Geoffrey. I started to ask Nycolas about sending a recovery team and he told me that a few of the novices had already been sent to recover Luke and Bosco. It was obvious Brother Nycolas, being a kind and tender-hearted man that he was deeply affected, he could hardly speak. Oliver tried to lay down, but instantly sat up and then stood up and began pacing with his hands holding his own head.

Nycolas, with a tip of his head, invited Gabriel and me to follow him to the dining room as Geoffrey stayed with Oliver.

Once we were out of listening range, Nycolas assured us that his novices would recover the bodies and prepare them for burial. He suggested that we should relax in the reading room until they return because he wanted to spend some time with Oliver.

I felt as if a great void had opened and everything I knew to be associated with time, was lost somewhere within that void.

We walked to the reading room, where fresh coffee was brought to us. Gabriel showed amazing composure and I marveled at his ability. I was a little surprised to see Nycolas direct Oliver to a chair and request a cup of tea for him.

The silence was deeper and thicker than it had been in weeks. The first thing I noticed, was the profound absence of Bosco's panting, licking and scratching because he was so painfully on my mind. I almost spoke Luke's name as I had a strong impulse to ask him a question about the Runes which Gabriel and I had discovered only seconds before their death. Catching my thoughts before I uttered Loke's name left me feeling terribly hollow and anxious... anxious to know what Luke's opinion would have been... and that left me feeling sad and foolish.

Asa and Gavan returned shortly after Nycolas and several novices had left on their recovery mission. We could hear them laughing and teasing each other, as they always did when in their own company. Asa shouted, expecting only Nycolas to be there to hear him, "We not be finding those thugs, but we sure be having a great day of fun and adventure!"

Oliver looked toward the approaching men and flatly said, "They be dead. The thugs be dead." At first, I thought Oliver's words were referring to Luke, Bosco and the thieves, but then I realized that he was only speaking of the dead thieves and made no reference to Luke and Bosco.

Gabriel stood and walked to meet Asa and Gavan in the dining room. We could hear Gabriel's subdued voice as he shared with them about the death of Luke and Bosco and how they died.

Gavan gasped, "Dear *God! Why?*" I don't think Gavan really expected an answer to his exclamation. Both men walked to either side of Oliver, knelt and embraced him in sobbing silence. The genuine love was obviously comforting to Oliver and he returned their embrace.

It was almost dark when we heard the men and cart returning. The horror of seeing these dear friend's bodies so broken from the fall almost caused me to refuse viewing them. I was not, in any way, accustomed to viewing bodies and the bodies of dearly loved friends was unbearable to think about.

It was for Oliver's sake, when he asked me to steady him, that I found my own courage, "I not be feeling I can stand up or walk, right now, Raffe." I assisted Oliver, and Asa quickly stood on the other side of him. I never said anything to Oliver, but I knew that I needed the excuse of helping him, to confront my *own* weakness.

Looking down into the cart which held their bodies, I heard myself thinking that it was helpful that Luke had impacted on his back since his face looked so peaceful. The sad expressions that he had worn for weeks, was gone. I looked to Bosco and he looked like he always did when he slept next to Luke. There was a small smear of blood across the back of Luke's right hand that appeared to be different than his other wounds.

I was looking at this smear when Oliver, noticing my attention, said, "That's where Bosco managed to give Luke one more lick, after they fell." It seemed so odd that the sight of a small smear of blood could so deeply affect me until I appreciated the great effort it took for Bosco to offer one more act of love.

It was only then that I noticed that only Luke's and Bosco's bodies had been recovered. "Did you find the bodies of the thieves?" I asked Nycolas.

"Yes," was his initial reply. "I be guessing ye be wanting to know why we left them where they landed." Nycolas continued, "They lived a life of violence and crime, and their present location be seeming to be a most appropriate destination." Geoffrey and I nodded in agreement.

Geoffrey signed, "We be bathing them and wrapping their bodies for tomorrow's burial, Raffe. This work be part of our calling."

I asked, "Is there anything I can do to help?"

"Yes." Geoffrey signed, "Please be keeping a close watch of Oliver and be letting. him know that he be loved by us."

"I can do that." I replied.

It rained that night and it was very welcome to soften the soil in the monastery's cemetery. By daylight, only a fine mist was falling from dark gray clouds. The morning songs of the monks echoed through the dark green trees, and their harmonies were a most appropriate accompaniment for this solemn and last of all events in a human life.

The care taken by the novices was evidence of their genuine love for Luke and Bosco. Bosco had become a frequent visitor in the kitchen and his gentle spirit was both appreciated and rewarded. Luke was carefully laid on his back. No coffin was made since it was the local tradition that quick decomposition was best. Then, with the help of more novices, the great body of Bosco was placed beside Luke. Knowing it would be what both wanted, Boscos big head was once again, and forever, laid on Luke's chest. There were more water drops running down cheeks than were falling from the trees.

I felt as if my heart would burst if I didn't look away, but a movement caught my eye, and I looked to see Geoffrey saying something with his hands as he looked upon his friends.

Nycolas also noticed Geoffrey and began to interpret his signs. "I be but a small child when I suffered my first rejection. My parents be giving me away because I be an embarrassment to them. Here, I be finding the same love ye found. My heart be healed by the love that lives in this place. The two of ye already be knowing what real love be, for ye be bonding before ye came here. I be wanting both of you to know that I understand why ye made this choice. Ye, Luke be knowing that you could never return to 2016. Bosco's future be hopeless as a loving pet, and he chose death with ye, Luke, over any life without ye. I promise to ne'er be forgetting ye and ne'er stop loving ye."

Geoffrey was not aware of Nycolas translating his sign because he was looking down at his dear friends. Nycolas said to Geoffrey, "Thank ye for those beautiful and loving words. You said what every heart here be feeling."

The novices waited until Oliver had returned to the monastery before sealing the two friends in their forever embrace, with earth.

Our meals were very quiet for the next week and we forced ourselves to function at the translation task which had so deeply affected all of us. Geoffrey's drawings of the Passing were discussed for several evenings and, as before, the deepening of our understanding matured into comfortable questions and brilliant speculations, but no absolute answers.

It was our brave member, Asa, who ventured the question around the evening meal when the pain of Luke and Bosco's death became a little easier to mention, "Anyone be having an explanation for the uncanny timing of ye discovery of the Runes which forecast the death of our dear friend, Luke, and his dog, Bosco?"

If I were still back in 2016, I think I might have said, 'If I had a nickel for every time that kind of question entered my mind, I'd be a millionaire,' but I knew that kind of comment was centuries in the future, so I remained silent.

Maybe that's why Nycolas' comment was so shocking to me. Nycolas spoke to the room, "I be wondering how many nickels be needed to be making a millionaire?" To the others, his words were abstract and held no meaning. To me, however, he had just told me that his mind, and mine, were connected, somehow and I really liked the idea.

Asa responded with a puzzled expression, "What be ye asking us, Nycolas? Be this one of yer mysteries that ye and Gabriel be sharing?"

Gabriel replied to Asa, "This be not any secret between Nycolas and me, since I not be having a clue to know what a 'nic-kel' and 'mill-ion-aire' might be.

Gavan smiled as he caught Nycolas and me looking at each other. "Me be thinking I know... who knows...what Nycolas be saying, don't I, Raffe?"

"Yes, Gavan," I admitted, "I was just thinking of a common expression from 2016 and Nycolas responded with two of the key words. The expression wasn't as important as hearing him speak the words which were in my mind." Nycolas just smiled warmly.

Asa spoke up and said, "All of that be very nice, but it not be answering me question about the Runes be written in 60 AD being discovered, at the same moment, as the prediction happened."

After several minutes of very uncomfortable silence, Asa looked to Geoffrey and asked, "Any suggestions or theories?" I was impressed with Asa's recognition of Geoffrey's brilliance. It would not surprise me if, in intellect, they could be very similar.

Geoffrey signed and I translated, "I not be having a clear and satisfactory answer for ye, Asa, but Raffe and I be translating some comments about time that be very difficult to understand. I be getting the impression from Amergus' writings, that the accumulation of knowledge, pertaining to the movements of the stars in the night sky, have a strong influence, on the events here on earth."

"Here on earth?" asked Asa, "ye be making it sound as if there might be another 'place.'"

I knew this translation for Geoffrey was going to open a very big topic, but I said it anyway. "There are many *other* '*places,*' Asa, more than any of us could count in a lifetime." I was always humored by Asa's dead pan face, but I knew his excellent mind was working when his impressive mustache began to wiggle.

"Would ye say that again?' Asa asked sincerely.

"I can only share what we have learned as of 2016, Asa," I began, "If you think of the whole earth as a '*place,*' then there be many *more places*, called *planets*, in space." I anticipated my last word, space, wasn't going to do anything except amplify the confusion, and it did.

Asa's justified reply was, "How big be this 'space,' if it be holding more than one earth?"

I looked at my own hands, pretending to be thinking, while my mind was scrambling for a way to share what I know, with my friends. In desperation, I finally said, "I can't give you the answer that you deserve, Asa, but I *want* to, and I *will*, when we are in a place where such knowledge can be shared."

Nycolas spoke up, "In the school which Raffe and I shall be using to teach the knowledge of 2016 to young and willing minds, living today." This was the second time Nycolas spoke about a shared future and I very much liked the idea.

Oliver indicated that he had a question and asked, "How much longer do ye and Gabriel be needing to complete yer translations? I be not anxious to leave, I be curious to be knowing how long we be expecting to enjoy this beautiful area and accommodations."

Gabriel answered, "If we be continuing at the same pace, we should be finished in a week or so." Turning to Geoffrey, Gabriel asked, "How long will you need to copy all of the Runes?"

Geoffrey thought for a moment, then replied, "I have made copies of almost all that you have translated, but should you need to return, I can continue with my work and send the documents concealed in quivers... quivers carried by an archer like Oliver, who we both love and trust."

"Excellent idea." said Gabriel, "this will give you time to complete your work and it will give Oliver opportunity to visit here as well as at our monastery."

"We be going to miss these living quarters and yer warm hospitality, Nycolas," Gavan offered. "It be a joy to be sharing time and food with ye."

The next two weeks, we were quite busy. Gabriel and I spent six days per week in Amergus' cave. There were more references to time being only a man-made system for organizing our lives, and recording of specific events in the never ending sequence of human progress.

A couple days before our scheduled departure, Nycolas looked at me over the dinner table. It was getting much easier to send and receive communications with him and the more I saw of this man and the amazingly comfortable monastery Geoffrey designed, the more I entertained Nycolas' suggestions that I should stay here and become a teacher. The flaw in this idea was that there were no students, and for me, to be a teacher, I needed students. I shared all of this with Nycolas while chewing a mouthful of roasted carrots and the image of me 'talking with my mouthful' made me smile, thinking of how many times I had been told, "never talk with your mouth full."

That's when Nycolas said out loud, "Never say never." My smile was his reward.

The others looked at Nycolas and me with blank expressions because they believed Nycolas' prophecies about me becoming a teacher, more than I did.

When I asked, "What kind of school?" Nycolas acted a little surprised that I didn't already know.

Nycolas patiently replied, "Ye be knowing that ye and Luke be not the *only* transferred consciousness during this Passing, right? There be many hundreds, and possibly thousands, who, unlike ye and Luke, entered this year from far distant past years, and equally distant future years. Some may be accepted and some, like Luke, be outcasts with vast knowledge and technical skills. If we can find and rescue as many as possible, teach those with foreign tongues, to spake English, and find a home for them... this area will eventually be filled with the most intelligent and productive citizens."

Nycolas' words were amazingly far sighted and wise. I had no idea about the many logistics and preparations needed to start up such a school, but I knew that Nycolas has all of the organizational skills needed. "If you can provide the students, Nycolas," I responded, "I'll be here to teach them."

Nycolas just smiled a bright and beaming smile, and repeated his words, "... sooner than ye expect."

Gabriel and I finished translating the Runes and packaged all of our records in a big bundle. Gabriel said that he almost hated that our time for this mission was completed because he enjoyed being around Nycolas and he very much enjoyed having a library to read in, whenever the opportunity presented itself. "If the prediction from Nycolas is correct, ye be finding yer self in the very best of company with him, since he be not only brilliant, he be having a joyful soul, and ye be loving yer time with him."

I didn't disagree with Gabriel on any point, but I could not foresee the details, especially students, being available on this remote island and dense forest.

The morning of our departure was, indeed, a sad parting. Nycolas warmly embraced each of us and kissed us on the cheek. Some of the novices who had so faithfully prepared our meals and kept us in clean clothes and bed linens, made a tearful farewell, including Geoffrey, but with a big smile and a thumbs UP! Geoffrey signed, "See you soon." and smiled with his whole face.

When it was my turn to say a final good bye to Nycolas, he wrapped his arms around me and drew me very tight. He kissed my right cheek, my left cheek, and then he kissed me on my mouth. His thick white beard and mustache tickled more than I expected, but it felt delightful because I believed he loved having us at his monastery.

Once again, Nycolas predicted, "I be seeing thee very soon," and kissed my mouth again.

Asa said, "I'll take one of those kisses with me, Nycolas." Without hesitation, he kissed each of us again, on the mouth. It was like a seal of fidelity between us.

The return trip, as far as the west bank of the Menai Strait, was uneventful. It was a special delight when Geoffrey said he would travel with us as far as the Menai Strait.

It was only then that we discovered the communications between Asa and Geoffrey. It was subtle as first. Asa turned his back to the rest of us when he signed to Geoffrey, but his secret was lost when Geoffrey signed back. Asa explained, when he noticed us watching, "Hey, ye be having yer mind to mind... we be having signals! Asa looked at Geoffrey and gave a thumbs up. Geoffrey returned the signal with a broad smile, Asa laughed, "He be reading yer lips, too; so, choose yer words carefully."

As if we didn't already know.

We met several travelers but seldom received any more attention than a passing glance. Without Bosco, the six of us looked like any traveling group. Oliver had asked to pull the cart. He said it kept his mind busy concentrating on his work, rather than thinking of the recent past. We made camp at the west edge of the Menai Straight at the same location where we had crossed. The rope which spanned the strait was still strung between the same two trees, but our boat was on the east side, deep into the trees and we couldn't see Andrew, or anyone else on the far bank.

I asked Oliver, "Do you have a way of notifying Andrew that we are here and need to cross?"

Oliver replied, "It not be taking more than a short wait, if the right people pass by." Oliver looked carefully at each person who walked near the Eastern bank of the strait and finally said, "There be our connection." Oliver kept his eyes on the woman carrying a large bundle on her back and waved his hands to draw her attention. The instant she looked our way, she stopped walking and looked at Oliver before resuming on her way.

"Andrew should be there soon," Oliver announced. "That was Marta, she knows Andrew and his family. She said she will get my message to him right away."

Gavan, marveling at Oliver's mind-to-mind wordless communication, commented, "Ye actually exchanged all of this information in a such a quick look?"

"I be telling her a lot more, Gavan, I told her who we be, where we be coming from and some of the findings, of Gabriel and Raffe, that I be understanding. She be an aunt to Andrew's wife. We be having shared a lot more, but she be in a hurry."

Gavan just shook his head in amazement.

Gabriel said, "We should be making camp and be prepared to spend the night here, on the West Bank, because we be having to wait for the tides to be up afore Andrew be crossing to us, and then wait for another high tide, to return.

Andrew appeared on the far bank and he and Oliver spent a few minutes communicating. There was no need for words to tell us that Oliver was relating the tragic death of Luke and Bosco as tears streamed down his face. We patiently waited for Andrew and Oliver to finish their exchange before inquiring.

Oliver turned to me with a broad smile as he said, "That must be a very special kiss Nycolas be giving ye, Raffe, because

236

ye may be returning to start yer school 'sooner than ye expect,' to quote Nycolas."

I had one word for Oliver, "What?"

Oliver suggested that we all sit down to hear what has happened on the Bangor side of the strait. "It be appearing that fortune guided yer steps and timing," Oliver began. "Troops of soldiers be searching for the dog we knew as Bosco and these troops be having several war dogs with them, intending to kill Bosco if they could find him. The king's war dogs be following Bosco's scent, to the east of Menai Strait. As sad as we be about Bosco's death, we be grateful that he died quickly and with the man he loved and be so devoted to. For a dog, that be the best possible way to die."

"Thank ye for sharing this, Oliver," Asa said. "All of us can feel a little better knowing that Bosco's death be not quite the tragedy we be feeling."

"That's not the half of what Andrew told me," replied Oliver.

"Go on," pleaded Gabriel.

"Part of the soldier's mission be to be finding and kill Bosco," Oliver said, "but they be also told to locate and kill every transferred consciousness they be finding, and to use bribes and treachery as be needed to accomplish this." Oliver's continence fell as he continued, "Andrew spake of the bodies of dozens of transfers be found hanging in trees right outside the villages, where they be discovered."

We were all silent as the pain of such an atrocity washed over us. The others didn't have the mental images of Nazi Germany that my mind held, and I envisioned those transfers being as brutally tortured and hanged as the German Jews were.

"Did the soldiers kill *all* of the transfers?" I asked Oliver.

"No," he replied. "I be asking Andrew that same question. Those transfers who spake not English be easier to find, if locals not be risking their lives to protect them. Some be escorted to hidden locations near Bangor. Andrew and his friends be prepared to ferry them to the west bank."

Asa asked, "What be our purpose when these refugees get to our side of the strait?"

"Start a school!" I replied, as surprised to hear my own words, as my friends. "This must be what Nycolas was expecting. Now we need to decide who stays here and who goes back to Gabriel's monastery. Gabriel needs to return with the translated runes, and I have to stay on this side, for safety and to begin my career as a teacher."

Oliver replied, "I'll go with Gabriel to pull the cart and help as many transfers as I can in memory of Luke and Bosco."

Gabriel looked to Asa and Gavan and asked, "What about each of ye? What do ye want to do?"

Asa spoke first, "I believe I be more helpful at Gabriel's monastery and help Oliver with the rescue of more transfers. Maybe this scarf that identifies me as a member of the royal family be helpful in saving some lives."

Gavan became the center of our attention, as he weighed his options. Gavan put his thoughts into words. "I be loving and caring for ye, Raffe, long afore ye became a transfer, and I actually be loving ye more dearly, since. Like Asa, I be able to travel on both sides of this strait and that may be helpful in the risky future, each of us be facing. I be liking to stay with ye, Raffe, if for no other reason than my heart be not surviving our separation."

"Then It's settled!" observed Oliver, "I be telling Andrew and he be prepared for the crossings. Andrew spake of all our crossings be at night. We not be simply crossing at the next high tide."

"I have more than enough confidence in Andrew to trust him to cross at the best time." Gabriel said.

Oliver added, "Andrew be disassembling the two boats with staves connecting them to be less suspicious to marauding soldiers, but it not be taking long to re-assemble the pieces, when needed."

The next two days were spent sharing plans and trying not to show the raw emotions associated with the prospect of being separated.

"I never dreamed I would have lived through so many adventures," I commented.

Gavan asked with a tease, "Like the night I be recovering ye from that nasty piss alley?"

"I be *telling* ye to leave him *there*, Gavan," Asa quipped, "If ye be remembering that night, as I be, we agreed that Raffe, the *first* one, was *dead*, and the piss alley be a *suitable resting place* for him."

Gavan blushed at the cutting humor that Asa always seemed to have, in abundance.

"True enough, Asa," Gavan retorted, "but we both be coming to love and respect *this* Raffe, *our* Raffe."

Oliver listened with delight to Gavan and Asa showing their affection with friendly bantering before asking, "Gavan, why *did* ye return to that smelly alley?"

Gavan gave me a rakish smile, and confessed, "I be having to *piss*."

Geoffrey laughed louder than anyone else.

As the second day drew to a close, Oliver and Andrew communicated across the strait. Oliver announced, "Tonight, be the night Andrew be crossing to the west side. He be bringing several transfers with him, *if* he be getting them out of hiding safely."

It was exciting and a bit frightening to anticipate meeting others who had been taken from centuries past and future to 1690. The potential of future technology and experienced history collected on Andrew's ferry was very difficult for my mind to comprehend.

The hours passed painfully slow, but they did pass. The sun was gone and no moon was visible when Oliver announced, "As soon as the tide be slack, they be leaving the east shore."

All of us were like children on Christmas morning... much too excited to carry on a normal conversation. The far bank was a black mass of tall trees which turned into a mirror image as the incoming tide slowed to a calm. In a few minutes, the black form of Andrew's boat with three men pulling the craft with great urgency began to separate from the east shore skyline. The boat's silhouette became sharper as they reached the mid-way point and we could see the three men standing and pulling on the rope. Just as it had happened during our crossing, the calm surface began its slow motion, to the North, and the once placid surface began to heave and roll as the speed of the water increased.

Long before any of our eyes could identify any of the men pulling on the rope, Oliver cried out, "It be *Andrew*!" The ferry boat was close enough to shore to see what looked like long bundles covering the poles which made up the deck spanning the two boats. There was a shore line of sand by the time their boat came to rest. Andrew spoke to the bundles at his feet and they rose like black specters emerging from the ground.

"How many people did Andrew bring?" I gasped.

"I carry seven," Andrew replied. "Naturally, they all transferred the same night as ye and Luke, but these people be found over the whole of *Wales*. They be having some good and some terrible stories to be telling."

Gavan stood behind me, and placed his big hands on my shoulders. He leaned close enough to my ear that I could feel his bushy whiskers, as he whispered, "It be looking like ye be having yer first class, *professor*."

"Nycolas was right," I signed to Geoffrey. "I wonder how many other things that dear man knew about my future with him?"

Geoffrey signed back to me, "I wish I knew, because he has always been able to predict events in my life before they happen."

I also wondered what Amergus would say if I used the expression, "Only time will tell."

The End ?

Made in the USA
Columbia, SC
22 November 2019